A<small>UTHOR</small>

The story within these pages is completely fictional but the concepts of BDSM are real. If you do choose to participate in the BDSM lifestyle, please research it carefully and take all precautions to protect yourself. Fiction is based on real life but real life is *not* based on fiction. Remember—Safe, Sane and Consensual!

Any information regarding persons or places has been used with creative literary license so there may be discrepancies between fiction and reality. The Navy SEALs missions and personal qualities within have been created to enhance the story and, again, may be exaggerated and not coincide with reality.

The author has full respect for the members of the United States military and the varied members of law enforcement and thanks them for their continuing service in making this country as safe and free as possible.

Who's Who and the History of Trident Security & The Covenant

***While not every character is in every book, these are the ones with the most mentions throughout the series. This guide will help keep readers straight about who's who.

Trident Security (TS) is a private investigative and military agency, co-owned by Ian and Devon Sawyer. With governmental and civilian contracts, the company got its start when the brothers and a few of their teammates from SEAL Team Four retired to the private sector. The original six-man team is referred to as the Sexy Six-Pack, as they were dubbed by Kristen Sawyer, née Anders, or the Alpha Team. Trident had since expanded and former members of the military and law enforcement have been added to the staff. The company is located on a guarded compound, which was a former import/export company cover for a drug trafficking operation in Tampa, Florida. Three warehouses on the property were converted into large apartments, the TS offices, gym, and bunk rooms. There is also an obstacle course, a Main Street shooting gallery, a helicopter pad, and more features necessary for training and missions.

In addition to the security business, there is a fourth warehouse that now houses an elite BDSM club, co-owned by Devon, Ian, and their cousin, Mitch Sawyer, who is the manager. A lot of time and money has gone into making The Covenant the most sought after membership in the Tampa/St. Petersburg area and beyond. Members are thoroughly vetted before being granted access to the elegant club.

There are currently over fifty Doms who have been appointed Dungeon Masters (DMs), and they rotate two or three shifts each throughout the month. At least four DMs are on duty at all times at various posts in the pit, playrooms, and the new garden, with an additional one roaming around. Their job is to ensure the safety of all the submissives in the club. They step in if a sub uses their safeword and the Dom in the scene doesn't hear or heed it, and make sure the equipment used in scenes isn't harming the subs.

The Covenant's security team takes care of everything else that isn't scene-related, and provides safety for all members and are essentially the bouncers. With the recent addition of the garden, and more private, themed rooms, the owners have expanded their self-imposed limit of 350 members. The fire marshal had approved them for 500 when the warehouse-turned-kink club first opened, but the cousins had intentionally kept that number down to maintain an elite status. Now with more room, they are increasing the membership to 500, still under the new maximum occupancy of 720.

Between Trident Security and The Covenant there's plenty of romance, suspense, and steamy encounters. Come meet the Sexy Six-Pack, their friends, family, and teammates.

The Sexy Six-Pack (Alpha Team) and Their Significant Others

- Ian "Boss-man" Sawyer: Devon and Nick's brother; retired Navy SEAL; co-owner of Trident Security and The Covenant; husband/Dom of Angelina (Angel).
- Devon "Devil Dog" Sawyer: Ian and Nick's brother; retired Navy SEAL; co-owner of Trident Security and The Covenant; husband/Dom of Kristen; father of John Devon "JD."
- Ben "Boomer" Michaelson: retired Navy SEAL; explosives and ordnance specialist; husband/Dom of Katerina; son of Rick and Eileen.
- Jake "Reverend" Donovan: retired Navy SEAL; temporarily assigned to run the West Coast team; sniper; husband/Dom of Nick; brother of Mike; Whip Master at The Covenant.
- Brody "Egghead" Evans: retired Navy SEAL; computer specialist; husband/Dom of Fancy.
- Marco "Polo" DeAngelis: retired Navy SEAL; communications specialist and back up helicopter pilot; husband/Dom of Harper; father to Mara.
- Nick "Junior" Sawyer: Ian and Devon's brother; current Navy SEAL; husband/submissive of Jake.
- Kristen "Ninja-girl" Sawyer: author of romance/suspense novels; wife/submissive of Devon; mother of "JD."
- Angelina "Angie/Angel" Sawyer: graphic artist; wife/submissive of Ian.
- Katerina "Kat" Michaelson: dog trainer for law enforcement and private agencies; wife/submissive of Boomer.
- Millicent "Harper" DeAngelis: lawyer; wife/submissive of Marco; mother of Mara.
- Francine "Fancy" Maguire: baker; wife/submissive of Brody.

Extended Family, Friends, and
Associates of the Sexy Six-Pack

- Mitch Sawyer: Cousin of Ian, Devon, and Nick; co-owner/manager of The Covenant, Dom to Tyler and Tori.
- T. Carter: US spy and assassin; works for covert agency Deimos; Dom of Jordyn.
- Jordyn Alvarez: US spy and assassin; member of covert agency Deimos; submissive of Carter.
- Tyler Ellis: Stockbroker; lifestyle switch—Dom of Tori; submissive of Mitch.
- Tori Freyja: K9 trainer for veterans in need of assistance/service dogs; submissive of Mitch and Tyler.
- Parker Christiansen: owner of New Horizons Construction; husband/Dom of Shelby; adoptive father of Franco and Victor.
- Shelby Christiansen: stay-at-home mom; two-time cancer survivor; wife/submissive of Parker; adoptive mother of Franco and Victor.
- Curt Bannerman: retired Navy SEAL; owner of Halo Customs, a motorcycle repair and detail shop; husband of Dana; stepfather of Ryan, Taylor, Justin, and Amanda. Lives in Iowa.
- Dana Prichard-Bannerman: teacher; widow of retired SEAL Eric Prichard; wife of Curt; mother of Ryan, Taylor, Justin, and Amanda. Lives in Iowa.
- Jenn "Baby-girl" Mullins: college student; goddaughter of Ian; "niece" of Devon, Brody, Jake, Boomer, and Marco; father was a Navy SEAL; parents murdered.
- Mike Donovan: owner of the Irish pub, Donovan's; brother of Jake; submissive to Charlotte.

- Charlotte "Mistress China" Roth: Parole officer; Domme and Whip Master at The Covenant; Domme of Mike.
- Travis "Tiny" Daultry: former professional football player; head of security at The Covenant and Trident compound; occasional bodyguard for TS.
- Doug "Bullseye" Henderson: retired Marine; head of the Personal Protection Division of TS.
- Rick and Eileen Michaelson: Boomer's parents; guardians of Alyssa. Rick is a retired Navy SEAL.
- Charles "Chuck" and Marie Sawyer: Ian, Devon, and Nick's parents. Charles is a self-made real estate billionaire. Marie is a plastic surgeon involved with Operation Smile.
- Will Anders: Assistant Curator of the Tampa Museum of Art Kristen Anders's cousin.
- Dr. Roxanne London: pediatrician; Domme/wife (Mistress Roxy) of Kayla; Whip Master at Covenant.
- Kayla London: social worker; submissive/wife of Roxanne.
- Grayson and Remington Mann: twins; owners of Black Diamond Records; Doms/fiancés of Abigail; members of The Covenant.
- Abigail Turner: personal assistant at Black Diamond Records; submissive/fiancée of Gray and Remi.
- Chase Dixon: retired Marine Raider; owner of Blackhawk Security; associate of TS.
- Reggie Helm: lawyer for TS and The Covenant; Dom/husband of Colleen.
- Alyssa Wagner: teenager saved by Jake from an abusive father; lives with Rick and Eileen Michaelson.

- Dr. Trudy Dunbar: Psychologist.
- Carl Talbot: college professor; Dom and Whip Master at The Covenant.
- Jase Atwood: Contract agent/mercenary; Lives on the island of St. Lucia; Dom of Brie.
- Brie Hanson: Owner of Daddy-O's in St. Lucia; submissive of Jase.
- Tahira: Princess of Timasur, a small North African nation.

The Omega Team and Their Significant Others

- Cain "Shades" Foster: retired Secret Service agent.
- Tristan "Duracell" McCabe: retired Army Special Forces
- Logan "Cowboy" Reese: retired Marine Special Forces; former prisoner of war. Boyfriend/Dom of Dakota.
- Valentino "Romeo" Mancini: retired Army Special Forces; former FBI Hostage Rescue Team (HRT) member.
- Darius "Batman" Knight: retired Navy SEAL.
- Kip "Skipper" Morrison: retired Army; former LAPD SWAT sniper.
- Lindsey "Costello" Abbott: retired Marine; sniper.
- Dakota Swift: Tampa PD undercover police officer; submissive girlfriend to Logan.

Trident Support Staff

- Colleen McKinley-Helm: office manager of TS; wife/submissive of Reggie.

- Tempest "Babs" Van Buren: retired Air Force helicopter pilot; TS mechanic.
- Russell Adams: retired Navy; assistant TS mechanic.
- Nathan Cook: former computer specialist with the National Security Agency (NSA).

Members of Law Enforcement

- Larry Keon: Assistant Director of the FBI.
- Frank Stonewall: Special Agent in Charge of the Tampa FBI.
- Calvin Watts: Leader of the FBI HRT in Tampa.
- Colt Parrish: Major Case Specialist, Behavioral Analysis Unit.

The K9s of Trident

- Beau: An orphaned Lab/Pit mix, rescued by Ian. Now a trained K9 who has more than earned his spot on the Alpha Team.
- Spanky: A rescued Bullmastiff with a heart of gold, owned by Parker and Shelby.
- Jagger: A rescued Rottweiler trained as an assistance/service animal for Russell.
- FUBAR: A Belgian Malinois who failed aggressive guard dog training. Adopted by Babs.
- BDSM: Bravo, Delta, Sierra, and Mike, two Belgian Malinoises and two German shepherds, the guard dogs at the Trident compound: Ian named them using the military communication's alphabet.

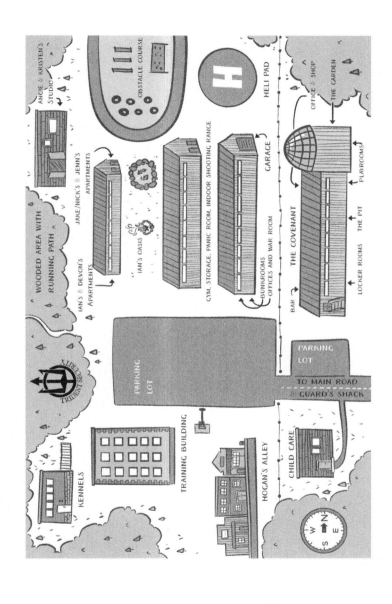

PROLOGUE

"What the hell do you mean Princess Tahira's been kidnapped?" Ian Sawyer barked into the phone. Sitting at her desk in front of him, Colleen Helm's eyes grew wide. Then, proving she'd become an efficient office manager since starting at Trident Security almost three years ago, she used a texting program on her computer to send a message demanding all available operatives report to the firm's compound.

"Exactly what I said," responded Mousaf Amar, head of security for the royal family of Timasur, a small country in Northern Africa. "The princess left the cruise ship and went ashore at Montego Bay, Jamaica, with her two cousins and two members of her security detail. They rented an SUV to take them to a waterfall about an hour away from the port, and that was about six hours ago. I just received word my men were found shot to death next to their rental in the park's lot. Princess Tahira, Lahana, and Nala are missing.

"It seems they were getting ready to leave the park about two hours ago when they were attacked. The guards' weapons and IDs were taken, but the police were able to identify them through fingerprints and the rental agreement. They contacted us as soon as they realized what they were dealing with. According to their investigation so far, no gunshots were heard, and there are no witnesses."

"Suppressors—that means they were hit by professionals; more than one if they were able to get the drop on your men." The royal security teams were highly skilled men, and Ian had seen them in action on more than one occasion during training exercises.

He strode purposely into the war-room where Nathan Cook, one of Trident's two resident tech geeks, was sitting in front of his massive console. The man looked up with his eyebrows raised, and Ian used a finger to silently tell him to hang on a sec. "So, we have no idea who took them or where they might be."

"No, we don't. There has been no ransom demand and no one claiming responsibility. If Her Royal Highness or her cousins could contact us, they would have. I need your help, my friend. I'm on my way from Timasur, but you can get a team there faster."

"What's the name of the falls they were at?"

"Dunn's River Falls and Park."

Ian repeated the name to Nathan. "Get me eyes there, pronto. I doubt there are any decent security cameras around, but check anyway. Patch into the traffic cams and any at the airports and marinas. Find out if any satellites have images from four to five hours ago over that park. Princess Tahira is missing, probably kidnapped. Run her picture through the imaging software. Find her—now!"

Leaving the former NSA employee to do what he did best, Ian headed to the conference room, with the phone still to his ear. "I'll get boots on the ground as soon as possible. Do you have a contact with the police?"

"Inspector Jamal Lewis is the man in charge. Lahana's

brother, Farid, and his friend were supposed to be chaper-oning the women during the trip, but they didn't want to go to the falls and were to meet up with them afterward for a late lunch. They haven't heard from the women either."

Filing that bit of information in his head for later, Ian jotted down the name of the inspector on a scrap piece of paper. "I'll contact you as soon as I have any information. What time do you expect to land?"

"In approximately ten hours at Sangstar International. I have five men with me."

"I'll have cars waiting for you. We'll get her back, Amar." Disconnecting the call, Ian shouted to be heard out in the reception area. "Colleen, call CC and tell him to get his ass to the airport—taking off in less than an hour, heading to Montego Bay, Jamaica!"

"On it!"

Knowing the company's pilot would have their private jet ready to go as soon as possible, Ian sat back in his chair and ran a hand down his face. All available personnel would be arriving shortly, but it would be a mix of both teams. Brody Evans, Trident's other computer geek and one of seven retired Navy SEALs who were now co-owners of the company, was returning from his honeymoon too late that evening to come with them. Two more co-owners, Marco DeAngelis and Ben Michaelson, were on a joint-task force assignment with operatives from Deimos, a US-government, black-ops agency most people didn't even know existed. Darius Knight, Lindsey Abbott, and Valentino Mancini, from the Omega Team, were down in Argentina on an undercover op. So that left Nick Donovan, the youngest Sawyer brother, his husband, Jake Donovan, Tristan McCabe, Cain Foster, and Kip Morrison available to fly down to Jamaica with Ian. His other brother, Devon, and Logan Reese would have to stay behind and hold down the fort in Tampa.

Ian hoped to God they'd be able to figure out who'd kidnapped the princess and the others. While he'd been helping to protect the royal family for several years, it wasn't until he and his wife Angie had gotten engaged and accepted an invitation from King Rajeemh and Queen Azhar to visit them in Timasur's capital city of Diado, that he'd gotten to know Tahira better. She'd matured over the past two years, and although she still liked to drive her bodyguards nuts with shopping sprees and flirting with the ones who were single, she no longer acted like a spoiled child. She'd even gotten involved in charity work. Last year, the princess and her brother, Prince Raj, had attended Ian and Angie's wedding. Their parents had been unable to join them due to Her Royal Majesty recovering from an illness.

Picking up the phone, Ian hit the speed dial to the small studio that'd recently been built on the west side of the TS compound. Angie, an artist, and Devon's wife, Kristen, an author, had moved their workstations into it, getting them out of their respective apartments for a few hours each day. The other buildings housed the Trident offices, a gym and indoor shooting range, and The Covenant, a BDSM club owned by Ian, Devon, and their cousin Mitch.

As he waited for the call to be picked up, he let out a heavy sigh. His pregnant wife was going to flip when he told her about Tahira, but since he'd just gotten back in her good graces, Ian wasn't going to keep it a secret from her. She'd divorce him if he did. "I'm getting too old for this shit."

CHAPTER ONE

Five hours earlier…

Sitting between Nala and Lahana, in the backseat of the
SUV her bodyguards had rented, Tahira tried to relax
and enjoy the excursion. That meant pushing her impending
marriage from her mind, even just for a little while. She had
forty days left . . . forty days to choose a husband or her
father would take the choice from her.

Up until her mother had been critically ill with renal
failure last year, Tahira had always been told it would be her
decision who she chose to marry. That went against the
generations of family members who'd all had their marriages
arranged for them at a very young age—usually by their fifth
birthday. The weddings had then taken place within weeks of
the men turning eighteen, while most of the women were
still a year or two younger. The way her mother had
explained it to Tahira, her parents had barely known each
other on their wedding day and neither had liked their
chosen spouse at first. Over time, though, that all had
changed, and by their first anniversary, they'd fallen in love.

They'd also vowed not to force their future children into unwanted marriages, forgoing a century and a half of royal tradition. But then, six weeks ago, following her brother's wedding, Tahira's father had reneged on the decision he'd made years ago. He wanted her married while he and her mother were still alive to see it happen.

Tahira was convinced her soulmate was out there somewhere. She even sensed she'd met him already, but neither of them had yet realized they were destined for each other. Her maternal grandmother had what some referred to as "the sight," the ability to see a person's aura when others couldn't, and apparently, it had been passed down to Tahira. The problem was her grandmother had died a few days before Tahira's fourth birthday, so there hadn't been anyone close to her that could help develop her gift as she'd grown older. What she did learn about it had been by wading through countless websites and blogs over the years, trying to figure out what was false information versus what was truth. While she didn't understand all of what she saw in other people's auras, she'd learned how to interpret many of the varying energy fields surrounding them. Every person was different, with some of their colors changing with their mood or experiences. Myriad shades of the primary and secondary hues of the rainbow meant different things. The color red surrounding a person could mean strength, anger, tenacity, passion, and sensuality, among other things, while pink represented love, deep friendship, compassion, and an appreciation of beauty. It had been a combination of pink, red, and a few subtler colors that'd helped her realize one of her Trident Security bodyguards, Brody Evans, had met his future wife about a year ago. While he'd known he was attracted to Fancy, he hadn't yet figured out she was "the one" his heart had been made for when Tahira had read his aura. That had since changed, and the couple was now married and expecting their first child. Tahira was thrilled for them.

Occasionally, she came across people whose auras she couldn't read. Ian Sawyer was one of them, and so was Mousaf Amar, the head of the royal guard. There were also times when she misinterpreted a person's colors. When Tahira had reached the age of eighteen, and had gained more freedom, she'd researched many healers who'd mastered the talent of reading auras. When she'd found one who was willing to be her mentor, she'd often invited him to visit the palace to tutor her. Knowing Tahira had inherited her mother's gift, Queen Azhar had encouraged her to learn what she could, despite the beliefs of some people who thought it was nothing but nonsense.

"What about this one? Iggi Kwei—he's a good-looking doctor." Nineteen-year-old Nala showed her cousins the profile photo of one of the potential Timasurian husbands that had been posted in a private Facebook group.

Tahira glanced at the photo. While the doctor was a handsome man, she wasn't drawn to him in any way. Most marriages were arranged in their country, with dowries being offered in exchange for the bride's hand. In some instances, couples never met prior to their engagement parties. Tahira had seen several of her friends married off to men who were not ideal mates. More than one of them were in abusive marriages, but none would admit it. To do so would be an insult to their husband and both their families.

Tahira had hoped that by being allowed to choose her own spouse, it would encourage other parents to allow their children to do the same. While her brother, Raj, had chosen his wife, it would be viewed in a completely different manner if Tahira chose her husband. Raj had also been in love with his bride and proposed before his father had decided to reverse the edict his children had grown up with. Their impending engagement and wedding had just been earlier than the couple had expected—their nuptials had been a huge affair with citizens of the small country, and beyond, lining the streets to get a glimpse of the happy couple. Now that they were husband and wife, King Rajeemh had turned his attention to making sure his only daughter was wed soon.

Being the second born, Tahira never expected to ascend to the throne. Her father was in his midfifties, and Raj was twenty-eight, two-and-a-half years older than his only sibling. Both men were very healthy and didn't participate in any risky activities that might cut short their lives. While there was a remote chance something could happen to both of them before Raj and his wife, Princess Kainda, produced an heir, it was highly unlikely, and for that, Tahira was grateful. She was loyal to her country but did not want to rule it. Politics and international relations were not her aspirations. She was content to be involved in charity work to help improve the social situation of Timasurians who had not been born to privilege. Part of the work she loved to do was visit the children's hospitals. She loved seeing the little ones' faces light up in delight when they realized Her Royal Highness was there to see them. Tahira could spend hours interacting with them and often hated to see the day end when she had to say goodbye.

She shrugged and looked out the window at the passing countryside. "I would rather enjoy my day instead of picking a husband I am not in love with."

Beside her, twenty-four-year-old Lahana rolled her eyes. "I don't know why you're being so resistant, cousin. Most women your age have already been married for years and have children in school. You will learn to love your husband —just like your mother, my mother, and Nala's mother did with their husbands."

Gritting her teeth, she fought to keep her tone respectful.

"I do not want to *learn* how to love my husband. I want to marry because I already *do* love him."

"Ugh, that's so American. And their divorce rate is what? Fifty percent?"

Tahira frowned. "That is because people have gotten married for the wrong reasons or they only thought they were in love. If it was not so difficult for our courts to approve divorces, I am sure there would be a lot more of them."

"I doubt—"

Holding up a hand, Tahira stopped her cousin from going any further with her argument—one they'd had multiple times before. "Seriously, Lahana. I do not want to talk about it anymore. I just want to have fun on our excursion. We have five days left on the cruise, and then I will figure out what to do about finding my future husband. Can we not just go and enjoy ourselves? Please?"

A smile spread across Lahana's face. "You're right. Let's go have some fun. We'll flirt with a few guys who don't stand a chance with us, bask in the sun, and play under the waterfalls." Her gaze shifted to the bodyguard who was driving. "Are we almost there, Kojo?"

"Yes, Miss Lahana. According to the GPS, we'll be there in three minutes."

As their journey continued, Tahira stared out the windshield, while her cousins tapped away on their cell phones. She wished she could dismiss the subject of marriage from her mind as quickly as she'd successfully removed it from the conversation, but it was nearly impossible. At least Farid and his friend had allowed the women to go to the park without chaperoning them. Tahira was tired of her cousin trying to play matchmaker between her and Diallo. The businessman was nice, but something about him turned her off. She couldn't put her finger on what really bothered her about him, but his penchant for giving others the impression they were together on the cruise was annoying her. She was glad to be free of him for a few hours.

Farid could be a pain in the ass too, but she had no problem putting him in his place as she'd done while growing up with him. The man liked to throw around his status as a member of the royal family, even though he was too far down in the line of succession to ever take the throne. He was too much of a playboy to even want to be king— running the country would put a damper on the extravagant lifestyle he'd become accustomed to.

Moments after they'd arrived at the crowded parking lot of the Dunn's River Falls and Park, Tahira was happy to see there were plenty of sights to catch her attention and get her out of the funk she'd found herself in once more. The falls were a popular tourist attraction, and they had to park at the far end of the lot, in between two empty tour buses. Once Kojo and his partner, Alake, had done a visual sweep of their surroundings, ensuring the women's safety, they stayed close to the princess without being intrusive. They'd both been part of her team of royal guards for over three years now and knew their jobs well. They were handsome men, but Tahira never flirted with them for two reasons. One—they were both married to lovely women, and Alake was the father of three precocious boys. Two—she only did that with body-guards who were temporarily assigned to her outside of Timasur, like the men of Trident Security when she visited the royal family's estate in Clearwater, Florida. She also reserved her flirting for when she was out of the public eye. After studying their auras, she knew which men she could tease and not worry about them reacting to it in a negative way. They were strong, protective men, who would never use their strength to take advantage of a woman.

There had been times during visits to the royal residences

in New York City and Los Angeles when Tahira had sensed some of the men on her detail were not as trustworthy as they tried to portray, and she'd avoided flirting with them. But the Trident Security operatives were her favorite, and it had been bittersweet over the past few years as each one of the original six-man team had met their soulmates and, therefore, had to be removed from her "flirt" list.

Whether some of them realized it or not, she cared for them as friends and was happy they'd found their true loves but saddened she couldn't tease them anymore. However, there were new employees who'd recently been hired that Ian Sawyer had introduced her to. Tristan and Cain were the leaders of the Omega Team, as it was called. Their subordinates included Darius, Kip, Valentino, Logan, and Lindsey. Logan was living with his soulmate, so he was off-limits, and Lindsey was a female operative who Tahira adored. Apparently, her head of security, Amar, liked Lindsey very much as well. They'd managed to keep their attraction hidden from others, but Tahira had seen through their charade and was happy for them.

Smiling, Lahana grabbed her cousins' hands as they walked across the parking lot to the entrance. "Let's go! I can't wait to see the falls. They looked gorgeous online."

Tahira had to admit she was looking forward to seeing them too. It felt wonderful to act like just another tourist and not a member of the royal family. Being so far from home, it was doubtful anyone would recognize her and fumble over themselves trying to please her. While she'd gotten a kick out of that when she was younger, it'd gotten annoying as she'd reached adulthood. She knew many people were overly nice to her merely because she was a princess and not because they liked her as a person. Everyone always seemed to have an ulterior motive for wanting to be her friend—well, not everyone, but most people fell into that category. It was one of the many reasons she enjoyed the company of Ian and Angelina Sawyer and their friends and family. While they had always been respectful of her title, she felt as if they treated her like everyone else they knew. And that's the way she liked it. She wasn't better than them or beneath them. Yes, Ian used to think of her as a spoiled child—all her Trident Security men had—but that was back when she was younger, less mature, and used to flirt with him, before he'd met his wife. Since they'd visited Timasur and stayed in the palace at her parents' request two years ago, Ian had gotten to know the real Tahira—the one she tended to keep hidden from the rest of the world due to self-preservation. Now, he acted like a big brother to her, and she loved it. In fact, she couldn't wait until Angelina gave birth in a few weeks. Tahira had already picked out a few gifts for the baby—she was just waiting to find out, like the rest of them, if it was a boy or a girl. No matter the gender, the child would be gorgeous, as Ian and Angelina made a stunning couple.

The thought of her friends' baby had Tahira thinking of the children she would hopefully have someday. A flash of a young boy with her dark hair and soft brown skin appeared in her head. It was an image she'd had before, but this time, she noticed something different. The boy's eyes weren't hazel like hers—they were green. A deep, rich, emerald green. They reminded her of the jeweled necklace and earrings she'd received from her parents on her eighteenth birthday. Was her mind playing tricks on her? The boy's eyes looked so familiar, yet she couldn't recall who they belonged to.

"C'mon, cousin!" Nala said on a laugh, tugging on Tahira's hand and breaking her out of the mental spell she'd been under. "Let's go have some fun!"

CHAPTER TWO

Tahira struggled to awaken. Her eyelids were so heavy, she couldn't lift them. Her head pounded, and her tongue felt dry and swollen.

Where am I? Am I sleeping? Mother? Father? Is anyone there?

She wasn't sure if the questions were in her mind or if she'd spoken them out loud, but either way, she didn't receive an answer. A shuffling noise, and then what sounded like a sniffle, penetrated her thoughts. Still unable to open her eyes to see, Tahira concentrated on her other four senses and took stock of what she could figure out.

The surface she was lying on was hard, with a scratchy, musty-smelling blanket or other material underneath her. She shivered as cold, damp air seeped into her flesh and goose bumps spread across her skin. The acrid odor of urine and feces filled her nostrils, and she fought the urge to gag. Soft murmurs and sobs caught her attention, but she couldn't make out what was being said.

Tahira's leg twitched, and she startled when a hand landed on her arm and shook it. Nala's voice was barely above a whisper. "Tahira? Wake up! Please!"

Finally forcing her eyes open, Tahira blinked several times until the dimly lit room came into focus. Not that it was exactly a room, per se. Stone walls and iron bars weren't exactly a common decor in any room she'd ever been in. She tried to sit up, but her head hurt too much, and a wave of nausea washed over her, so she laid back down. "Wh-where are we?"

"I don't know, but wherever we are, it's c-cold. Lahana is still unconscious. I-I think we were drugged. Do you remember what happened?"

She thought hard, her last memories coming back in flashes. They'd spent about three hours at the falls, having a wonderful time. They'd chatted with other tourists, flirted with a few guys, and simply enjoyed the beauty of the tropical paradise. With about five hours left before they had to be back onboard their ship, the women had decided to head back to Montego Bay to go shopping for souvenirs. After that, they'd meet Farid and Diallo at Jimmy Buffett's Margaritaville for food and drinks. Tahira loved the American singer, with his laid-back style of music, and had visited many of his restaurants in other cities and countries. The one in Montego Bay reportedly had a 120-foot water slide that deposited participants into the sparkling, blue Caribbean Sea, and Tahira had been looking forward to trying it out.

"We . . . we were leaving the park and walking back to our vehicle." Her brow furrowed. "Didn't a man approach us and ask . . ." Before Tahira could finish the thought, most of what'd happened flooded her mind. *"Mon dieu!"* While English was the national language of Timasur, French was a close second. Tahira had learned both during her education and occasionally the latter slipped into her speech, especially when she was upset—and upset was an understatement for what she was experiencing now.

"What?" Nala whispered, her eyes going wide in fear.

Under the impression that her cousin knew what she was about to say but was afraid to say it herself because that would make it real, Tahira lowered her voice. "There were several men, and Kojo and Alake were—were shot!"

Horror took root in her stomach as her hand went to her neck where she found a tender area. She remembered a sting followed by a burning sensation before everything went dark. They must have been drugged, and her bodyguards had to be dead. Tears filled her eyes. The two men who'd protected her for several years had both been shot in the head. Tahira couldn't remember hearing the guns fire, but she'd seen them in the hands of the men who'd attacked them and then blood, bone, and brains splattering the side of the SUV before her bodyguards fell to the ground. Her heart broke for their families.

As her eyes became accustomed to the dim light enveloping them, Tahira gingerly tried to sit up again and looked around. All she had on was her bikini and sarong, neither of which provided her with any warmth. Her sandals were gone—not that they would've helped in the cold. Despite the musty stench of the blanket she'd been lying on, she pulled it up and around her back and shoulders as she took in their surroundings.

Lahana was lying on another blanket on the other side of Nala. They were in a jail or something similar, trapped behind iron bars. There were several other cells, each holding two, three, or four young women—Tahira counted sixteen total—all of whom appeared shell-shocked, with vacant gazes or red, swollen eyes.

What's going on? Where are we?

There was warmer air being forced through a small vent above her head, instead of air conditioning, so wherever they were, they'd left the summer heat of Jamaica. There weren't any windows either, so it was impossible to tell if it was night or day. Depending on what drug had been used and the dosage, they could've been out for just a few hours or much longer—she had no idea which.

Tahira slowly got to her feet and was about to ask the other women if they knew where they were when a loud clanging noise echoed throughout the area. At the end of the walkway separating the two rows of cells, a heavy wooden and iron door opened. Chills went up and down Tahira's spine as several Latino-looking men strode in, and she didn't think it had anything to do with the temperature. It didn't escape her notice how the other women backed away from the doors to their cells and cowered against the stone walls.

One man stopped in front of the cell Tahira and her cousins were in, while the other five or six men spread out around him. Two others had stayed back by the door. She couldn't see them clearly—they were in the shadows—but it didn't matter since the man at her cell door silently demanded her attention. He was about an inch taller than her own five-six and weighed about two-hundred-and-thirty pounds. His brown eyes held no warmth under his trim dark hair. A mustache and goatee covered the lower half of his face but didn't hide the pockmarks on his skin. He was dressed in a sweater, dress slacks, and expensive-looking shoes. The other men were dressed similarly, but Tahira knew without a doubt the man in front of her was in charge. His dark aura gave it away.

"Well, hello, sleeping beauties. I see you're awake," he stated in English with a thick Latino accent. He glanced down at Lahana, still lying on the floor, and frowned. "Well, at least two of you are."

Pulling the blanket tighter around her shoulders, for both warmth and to conceal her bare skin from the men's leering gazes, Tahira stood tall and lifted her chin. "Who are you and why do you have us caged like animals?"

The man didn't answer her right away, which grated on her nerves, but she refused to let him see how afraid she was. Putting an unlit cigar he'd been holding into his mouth, he removed a lighter from his pocket and lit it. As he exhaled, rings of smoke filled the air. "My name doesn't matter—you won't be here long enough for it to make a difference."

Tahira had no idea what that meant, but it sounded like their next destination would be worse than their current situation. God help them.

CHAPTER THREE

Argentina, near Buenos Aires . . .

Darius "Batman" Knight's day and mission had just gone to hell on a Harley. Yeah, the cliché was "hell in a hand basket," but in his opinion, that had gone out of date a long time ago and his version was better—not that it really mattered. What *did* matter was his undercover identity was a few seconds from being blown unless he could do something about it.

He stayed in the shadows in the underground prison on Emmanuel Diaz's vast property in the hills just north of Buenos Aires, Argentina, hoping the woman he recognized in a nearby cell wouldn't see him. If she did, it was highly unlikely she could disguise the fact she knew him.

Shit! How the hell did Princess Tahira end up here?

She should be safe in her homeland of Timasur, or at one of her family's many vacation homes around the world, including their estate in Clearwater Beach, Florida. No matter where she'd been, she would've been guarded. He remembered his real employer, Ian "Boss-man" Sawyer, saying, in the briefing in which Darius had received this assignment six weeks ago, that Tahira and her cousins had changed their vacation plans and had decided to take a luxury-liner cruise. Had that been scheduled for this week or last week? He couldn't remember, not that it made any difference now.

Tahira looked ready to spit nails, her eyes flaring with anger, and her arms crossed over her chest. "I demand you let my cousins and me go! Do you have any idea who I am?"

A drug czar, who also participated in arms dealing and sex slavery, Diaz and three of his minions leered at the beautiful twenty-five-year-old who was wearing a pale pink bikini with a pink and black sarong wrapped around her waist. Her feet were bare. From what Darius had learned on the way down to the mansion's dungeon, Tahira and her two cousins—he didn't know their names, having never met them before—had been snatched and flown to Argentina in a private jet and had arrived at midnight—just about an hour ago. Five members of the royal guard were supposed to accompany the princess during her travels, with at least two staying with her at all times, but clearly, they hadn't been able to thwart the kidnapping. Whichever ones had been with her, they'd either been killed or, at least, disabled. Mousaf Amar, the head of the royal guard, had trained with several special-ops teams around the world and passed those practices onto the men he supervised.

Standing outside the cell that contained Tahira and her cousins—there were five other cells filled with other women who huddled together in terror-filled silence—Diaz responded, "Of course I do, *Your Highness.*"

Double shit! Darius managed to hide his surprise. At first, he'd thought the three cousins had been randomly selected by the bastards who kidnapped young women throughout Central and South America and the Caribbean in order to sell them to Diaz who would then sell them into slavery. The kind of slavery that meant being repeatedly drugged, raped, and tortured for the remainder of their lives. But Diaz had known immediately who the princess was. Had she been targeted? The head of the cartel had to know there would be a massive manhunt for Her Royal Highness. Why snatch a high-profile woman? It would be all over the internet within minutes of the media discovering Tahira had been kidnapped. Why take that risk?

When Diaz had emphasized her royal address in a condescending manner, Tahira's obvious rage spiked. Her face reddened, eyes flared, and jaw clenched. Darius had to hand it to her—despite the situation she was in, she wasn't cowering in the corner of the cell like her two cousins were. Unfortunately, that attitude might get her hurt— more so than what fate she'd face if Darius didn't get ahold of his teammates who were backing him up on this mission. He wondered if Trident Security, the black-ops company he worked for under six of his retired former teammates from SEAL Team Four, had any idea Tahira had been kidnapped. They probably did by now—Ian and Devon Sawyer had a contract with the royal family and joined forces with their team of bodyguards to protect them any time they visited Florida. Amar would have contacted the black-ops team as soon as he'd heard the princess was missing.

The acknowledgement of Tahira's title seemed to catch her off guard, but she recovered quickly. "So, you want my father to pay a ransom to release us? I assure you he will not. Instead he will send a team of the best men he has to rescue us and leave this place in ruins."

Chuckling, Diaz sneered. "Well, I can assure you, I never planned on asking your father for money. You're worth far more than that to me. Men will bid millions in money *and* information for a princess. Tell me, *Your Highness*, are you still a virgin? That will double the starting price."

Tahira's bronze complexion paled, and Darius's gut clenched, knowing she'd just figured out what was in store for her if things went according to the cartel's plans. He wished he could let her know he'd do everything in his power to make sure she and her cousins got out of this mess unscathed, but he couldn't let her see him—not yet. She would recognize him immediately, despite the longer hair, beard, and mustache he'd grown out at the start of the mission, and give away his cover. He'd been on her security detail a few times, during her visits to Tampa, since joining his former teammates at Trident over a year ago. For now, he had to remain in the shadows. The sex-slavery auction was next week. Sometime between now and then he had to figure out a way to get Tahira out of there. He'd save as many of the women as he could, but the princess was now his top priority, instinctively knowing that would be Boss-man's order, if and when Darius was able to pass an update to his backup who would forward the intel.

The radio on his hip, and those in possession of most of the other men around him, squelched before the voice of a guard stationed at the estate's entrance came over the air, speaking in Spanish. It was one of the languages Darius could speak fluently and was one of the reasons he'd been chosen to go undercover on this mission. The other reason was he'd been on the op when Emmanuel's brother, Ernesto, had been killed by members of SEAL Team Four.

A truck carrying weapons and ammo they'd been expecting had arrived. Diaz's right-hand man, Felix Secada acknowledged the alert and then snapped his fingers. "Hamilton, Torres, go meet the truck and make sure the full load is there before they leave. If it's not, kill them. Take Lopez and Acosta with you."

Darius, aka Glenn Hamilton from Miami, was relieved Secada had issued the order, so he could get the hell out of the cell area before Tahira recognized him. Seeing her turn her head, following Secada's gaze in his direction, he stepped further back into the shadows and spun toward the stairs. He hated leaving her down there, but aside from being locked up, she should be safe until the night of the auction. With Torres on his heels, Darius took the stairs two at a time until he reached the first floor, wishing to God he could've erased the look of fear from Tahira's pretty face. Somehow, someway, he'd get her, her cousins, and the other women out of there. Now, he just had to figure out how to do it without blowing his cover. *Triple shit.*

CHAPTER FOUR

J ust after 12:00 p.m., Valentino "Romeo" Mancini sat with his teammate, Lindsey "Costello" Abbott, in the shade outside a little cantina they'd been coming to three or four times a week for the past couple of months. The two Trident Security employees were working undercover as environmentalists/missionaries helping to create a new well system for a small village and a nearby orphanage run by several nuns. They'd been staying at the orphanage, which was about a half hour from the Buenos Aires city line, with the permission of Sister Patrice. One of her former charges was now an operative for a US black-ops agency, and she fully trusted no harm would come to her children for aiding the private security team. With over twenty real missionaries working on the well and other necessities for the locals, two more people in the mix wouldn't raise any eyebrows. Val and Lindsey had even helped the do-gooders whenever their undercover work allowed. Today, they were taking a break from picking up supplies for the orphanage, which would cover up the fact they'd be retrieving intel from Darius.

The first week in Argentina, they'd figured out some of the low and middle-level men of the Diaz cartel came to town a few times a week to eat and drink at the cantina and blow off steam with some of the local working girls. Once Darius had worked his way into the cartel using an alias that Deimos had spent years cultivating for just this kind of mission, it hadn't taken him long to "bond" with some of the men. Now, when either Darius or Romeo needed to pass on information to each other, they hid it in a loose wall board in one of the bathroom stalls. It was a primitive system, but it worked for them. They couldn't risk Darius going into the Diaz compound with a hidden phone or any other communication device that could be found and blow his cover. He did have one way to contact them in case of an emergency, but it was only to be used when shit went upside-down and back-ass sideways—in other words, totally FUBAR.

Three seemingly unrelated items—a watch, an electric razor, and a belt buckle—contained hidden components Darius could put together very quickly, and send out a code yellow, red, or black signal to a satellite, which would then alert his backup team. The first two meant things had gotten fucked up, but he wasn't in immediate danger. A code black, however, meant they had to extract him fast. Less than an hour ago, they'd received a code yellow, sending them scurrying to their communication exchange point.

They'd arrived at the cantina and taken seats at their usual table, covertly eyeing the surrounding area for any signs of trouble. After ordering a bottle of spring water and three *carne picante empanadas*—his favorite meal they served there—Val stood and headed inside the cantina. Costello would be fine on her own for a few minutes.

Since joining the ranks at Trident Security, the retired Marine sniper had more than proven her worth, and he trusted her to cover his six as much as his male teammates.

Slap a fifty-pound ruck on her back and she could stay ahead of the boys while slogging through mud and muck, but clean her up and put her in a dress and the brunette would turn heads no matter where they went.

Striding past the long, scarred, wooden bar and the six drunks that always seemed to be sitting on the same stools every time he walked into the place, he made sure nothing and nobody seemed out of the ordinary. The voluptuous bartender gave him a flirty grin, like she did every time she saw him. It was something he'd gotten used to as a teenager —he'd been blessed with good genes and what his friends called Hollywood looks, and women tended to throw themselves at him. Back when he was younger and cockier, he had no trouble getting his kicks with any woman who turned him on, but as the years went by, and he rolled into his thirties, one- and two-night-stands had gotten boring. He'd dated a couple of women for a few weeks or months over the past few years, but none of those relationships had worked out. There was one woman, though, that he couldn't seem to get out of his head. The problem was she'd turned him down when he'd asked her out. Maybe that was why he couldn't stop thinking about her—she was the only woman he'd really wanted who'd said no. If she'd gone out with him, and to bed with him, would he still be obsessing about her all these months later?

Summer Hayes was an internationally-known country singer, with Grammy, CMA, and other awards lined up on the mantle of one of the three mansions she owned. Despite being famous, though, the petite blonde was a down-home kind of girl. She was friends with the wives and girlfriends of some of the Trident guys, and that's how Val had met her—at one of the barbecues Boss-man's wife had thrown at the compound.

Val and Summer had gotten along great that day, and he'd

been ready to ask her out to dinner the next night, but something had changed after she'd spoken to Devon's wife, Kristen, and their friend Shelby Christiansen. She'd become more reserved and stopped flirting with him. Val just wished he knew what it was, but the other women told him it wasn't their place to fill him in. If Summer wanted to tell him, that was her choice.

Even though he barely knew her, he'd freaked when he'd heard she'd been in a bad car accident yesterday. While it was all over the internet that she'd been airlifted to a trauma center, there had been no official statement released about her condition. When Costello had called the Trident headquarters and gotten an update from Colleen this morning, they'd learned Summer had needed emergency surgery for a compound fracture of her lower leg. Aside from that, everything else had been simple bruises and lacerations that would heal completely over time. She'd been damn lucky considering her SUV had flipped several times.

That wasn't the only news they'd gotten this morning—the other piece of intel was still under wraps as far as the media and public were concerned. Princess Tahira and her cousins had been kidnapped after two of her royal bodyguards had been killed. Boss-man had scrambled a team and flown to Jamaica ahead of Mousaf Amar's arrival, but the last Val and Costello had heard, the three women were still missing and there were very few clues leading to where they'd been taken and by whom.

Entering the bathroom, he was glad to find it empty and bypassed the urinals. The second stall was his destination, and after shutting the plywood door and locking it—not that it gave him much protection—he pulled out his Leatherman and used the blade to loosen the board they'd been hiding intel behind. He immediately spotted a folded piece of paper Darius had left for him.

Unfolding the note, he quickly scanned the message. And, just like that, their mission had become a cluster-fuck. "Aw, hell."

CHAPTER FIVE

I an stood by the airport security check point, waiting for Amar and his men to get through customs—with their Interpol security clearances, one would think it would make things quicker, but that wasn't always the case. The paperwork could be a hassle, depending on which country they were from and which one they were entering.

The Trident team had been on the ground for several hours, and, unfortunately, Ian didn't have much to report to his friend, although his team was still looking for a potential lead. Realizing they might be on the island for a few days, Ian had arranged for two large suites at a local hotel where they could set up a headquarters, in addition to rotating combat naps. He had a feeling they were going to need it.

Using his Pentagon and NSA contacts, he'd gotten the necessary clearance for Jake and Nick to board the cruise ship Tahira and her cousins had been vacationing on. They'd met with the head of security and gained entry to the princess's luxury suite. There were three bedrooms, one for each woman. Farid and Diallo had taken a suite right next door. Jake and Nick would comb through both to see if there was any clue as to how and why the women had been kidnapped.

The local police had found two people who'd seen the women being forced into a van from across the parking lot, however, they hadn't seen the kidnappers kill the two guards. The witnesses had delayed contacting the police because they hadn't wanted to get involved, but then their consciences had gotten the better of them. Ian hadn't needed to confirm the kidnappings had happened, but it was good to have the information. If they had to go public about the missing women, the more evidence they had that a crime had been committed, the better. That was a last resort though. They wanted to avoid an international media frenzy at all costs—it could force the kidnappers to kill their hostages.

While Jake and Nick were busy on the ship—they'd fly back, with Farid and Diallo, via a helicopter, when they were done since the cruise had set sail again—the rest of the team were doing what they could to find even the tiniest of clues. Back in Tampa, Nathan had done a good job locating the van on surveillance and security cameras. After leaving the park, it had been driven to a small private airstrip, where it had been abandoned. Unfortunately, they hadn't found anyone willing to admit they'd seen the kidnappers and the women board any planes and take off or change vehicles and drive away. Nathan had hacked into the security system, but none of the few cameras at the airport had been pointing in the right direction or the kidnappers had known how to avoid them.

"Ian!" Amar called as he and his team hurried toward him, each carrying large duffel bags. It was a safe bet they'd brought a small arsenal of weapons with them, just as the Trident men had. The latter had an easier time of getting them into Jamaica though, after arriving in the company jet at one of the smaller airports that didn't have a customs checkpoint. After a quick shake of hands between the two friends, Amar introduced Ian to his team as they all walked toward the exit leading to the parking lot. "What have you found out?"

During the drive to the police station, Ian filled them in on what little they had to go on so far. It was 5:30 p.m. local time. No ransom demands had been made. They still had no idea why the princess and her cousins had been taken.

Twelve and a half hours later, they were no closer to finding the women. That morning, Ian and Amar had paired up a Trident operative with a member of the royal guard. Foster and his partner were sticking with Investigator Lewis. The man was more than willing to accept their help. He didn't want the headache that went with an international incident any more than they did.

McCabe was with the crime scene investigators, who were processing the van for any evidence that may have been left behind. Morrison was over at the morgue, waiting on the autopsies of the two royal guards. Once the bullets were recovered from the bodies, he'd have the lab techs forward the images to Nathan, who would then run them through the NSA interface he still had access to after Trident had hired him away from the agency.

Without giving away any identities, the police had released a statement about the incident at the falls in time for the morning news, and Ian, Amar, and the guards had spent a few hours helping the detectives follow up on a few leads that had come in—unfortunately, none had panned out. They still didn't know if the women had boarded a plane or if the van at the airstrip had been a red herring and they'd left by boat or hadn't left the island at all. They'd managed to track down and cross off their list four of the eight small planes that had allegedly taken off from the private airport in the two hours following the kidnapping. None of the aircraft, their pilots, or passengers had been involved in the crime. Ian wasn't too hopeful that the remaining planes would pan out either. All it would take was a little bribe money to let one take off without filing a flight plan—an advantage not found at regulated, public airports.

Back in Tampa, Brody had returned from his honeymoon late yesterday afternoon, and he and Nathan had spent the entire night and morning scouring the Dark Web for chatter about the missing royal. They hadn't found anything yet, but they were still at it. People went missing without a trace all the time, but the more well-known they were, the more likely evidence of their location would show up at some point.

Arriving at the police station, where everyone would be checking in, Ian parked the rented minivan. As he and Amar strode toward the building, Ian's phone rang. Retrieving it from his pocket, he eyed the screen. *Romeo.*

Connecting the call, he said, "Mancini, unless it's important, it has to wait. I'm in the middle of—"

"We've got a cluster-fuck, Boss-man."

Ian pulled up short, causing the other man to slow, then stop and stare at him. "Batman?"

"He's fine, but the mission has gone FUBAR, and the objective has changed. You're not gonna believe this, but apparently, Princess Tahira and her two cousins have become guests of Diaz, and it's not by choice."

Disbelief and horror coursed through him, his body stiffening. "What!"

"That was my reaction too. Don't ask me how it happened because I don't know. But it gets worse. The time frame for the sale has been moved up. We have fifty-two hours before the women disappear into the wind."

"Fuck! Hang on." His gaze shot to Amar. "We're headed to Argentina."

The man gaped at him in confusion. "Argentina? Why?"

"Because we have two days before Her Highness and the others are sold as sex slaves."

Amar's olive skin paled. "Oh my God."

AFTER PLAYING THE PART OF A FAITHFUL CARTEL ASSOCIATE and helping unload the shipment of guns and ammo that had arrived last night, Darius had returned to his room in a cottage on the estate property. "Glenn Hamilton" was the playboy son of a wealthy businessman, portrayed by a Deimos operative. His cover had been solidly cultivated over the past several years by the black-ops agency, and the computer geeks there had easily photoshopped Darius's image into dozens of photos and flushed them out onto the internet. In the meantime, Hamilton also had an extensive history on the Dark Web as being a wheeler and dealer in all sorts of dirty markets—drugs, guns, and human trafficking among them. As far as Diaz and his men knew, Darius had become an "acquisition manager" for several very wealthy men with perverted appetites for women, after his father had cut his monthly allowance. He'd contacted Diaz after his former supplier had been killed in a raid. With his airtight background in place, it hadn't taken Diaz long to welcome him into his organization. While Secada had been warier than his boss, Darius had done what he could to ease the man's suspicions. So far, it had worked.

There had been no chance to slip out of the compound unnoticed during the night, so he'd caught up on his sleep, thinking he had plenty of time before the auction to alert his teammates of Tahira's presence. A few hours wouldn't hurt, and he couldn't risk any actions that were out of the ordinary and would raise suspicions. However, when he'd joined

Diaz, Secada, and two cartel lieutenants for breakfast, he'd been advised that the sale date for the women had been moved up a week and all bidding parties would be made aware of the change throughout the day. At Diaz's directive, Darius called his two "clients," two Deimos operatives posing as men in the market for sex slaves and letting them know about the change of plans. Once that was accomplished, Darius's main concern was letting his Trident bosses know about Tahira and her cousins. The auction would take place at the compound with the bidders arriving an hour or two before things got started to look over the "merchandise."

A raid was planned for when the auction started, and all parties were in place. Not only did the FBI, DEA, ATF, NSA, CIA, and Deimos want to destroy the Diaz cartel, they also wanted to take down as many of their clients as possible, no matter what illegal business they were in. The problem, until recently, was the higher ups believed there was a mole in more than one of the US alphabet agencies, which was why the Trident team had quietly been brought in. With Diaz constantly moving between estates in several Central and South American countries, it had been hard to nail the guy down. They'd almost had him about ten months ago, but he'd escaped, using his wife and two kids as shields as they boarded a helicopter amid the gunfire between his men and the Deimos agents and two black-ops teams.

After breakfast, Darius had volunteered to head into town with Guillermo Torres, one of the cartel members he'd befriended, to run a few errands. One of the things they had to do was pick up the clothes Secada had ordered from a local dress shop for the women to wear the night of the auction. As usual, it hadn't taken much to convince Torres to stop for a beer or two at the cantina. The man had the hots for the bartender and would be too busy to notice when Darius spent a few minutes in the restroom, leaving a message for Mancini, then activating the code yellow signal. His two teammates would make sure the troops would arrive early for the raid. It would be hairier than expected with Tahira thrown into the mix. No matter what, there would be a chance the women would be harmed when all hell broke loose. Darius hated the fact, but they needed as much evidence as possible to bring the cartel and its clients down for good.

Tomorrow night, he'd suggest to Torres and one or two others that they head into town for a drink after hours. By that point, the black-ops teams would've covertly made their way into the area. At the cantina, Costello would be waiting for him to hit on her, after she'd gotten into a fight with her "boyfriend." A trip to a local hostel up the street for a little nooky would be the cover for Darius to meet with the team and quickly go over the planned raid. He just hoped like hell the op didn't get any more fucked up, because it had already become a cluster-fuck and the clock was ticking.

CHAPTER SIX

Tahira shivered under the threadbare blanket and tried to ignore the fact she had to urinate. Their "toilet" was a foul-smelling bucket in the corner of the cell. After inspecting every inch of the prison, she finally admitted what the other women had said was true. There wasn't any way to escape. The only time anyone had come down there was to bring them food and water, three different times. From the contents of the meals, she'd figured out that they were breakfast, lunch, and dinner. It was the only evidence of what time of the day it was. At first, she and her cousins had been afraid to eat or drink anything, but the other women had all scarfed everything down, proving that nothing was drugged. Knowing they had to keep up their strength, in case a moment presented itself where they could get away, Tahira had encouraged her cousins to eat. Lahana had refused at first, demanding the guards delivering the food let them go. But the younger woman's arrogant confidence had faded as the day wore on.

They'd been given no further information on what the man in charge had been talking about, so they could only speculate, but it wasn't too difficult to figure out. It was clear to the women that they were going to be sold into sex slavery. Why else would this many women, in their late teens and early twenties, be kidnapped and held as prisoners? Tahira couldn't come up with anything worse than that, although, she was certain she could imagine how bad it would be. There was a good chance some, if not all, of the women would be begging for death in the near future to escape the horror that their lives will have become.

Over the past several hours, Tahira had gotten to know some of the other women—a few were too shy or traumatized to talk to her. The ones who had spoken had all been kidnapped from various places throughout the Caribbean and South and Central America. Most had been vacationing from the US and Canada, while a few had been taken from their hometowns or somewhere nearby. None of them knew where exactly they were being held, but several thought they were somewhere in the lower half of South America due to the lower temperatures and the dialect of Spanish that most of the men holding them spoke.

One of the women in the next cell had introduced herself to Tahira as Melinda Stuart, who'd been abducted from the island of Caicos by an American man she'd met at the resort where she'd worked. Tahira had been shocked when she realized the young woman had been held captive for almost two months, based on the date she stated she'd been taken. But then several others gave their kidnapping dates—all arriving after Melinda. Although she'd been the first of this group of women—the second showing up a day or two later—Melinda believed there had been others before her based on some evidence she'd found in the cell areas. She now believed they'd been sold into sex slavery, and everyone there now were part of the next bunch to be auctioned off. Unfortunately, Tahira agreed with her—especially after what the man in charge had asked her about being a virgin.

Despite her initial shock and horror, Tahira had told him she was sorry to disappoint him, but she wasn't a virgin. She wasn't sure if he believed her lie or not.

Taking a seat on the floor next to Nala, Tahira leaned back against the stone wall and put her arm around the shoulders of the nineteen-year-old. She been crying softly for hours, stopping only when exhaustion had forced her to sleep, and Tahira did what she could to comfort her. A few feet away, Lahana was curled up on her side, with her blanket wrapped around her. She tilted her head back and looked up at Tahira. "What's going to happen to us?"

"I do not know, cousin, but as God is my witness, I will do everything in my power to get us out of here. All of us." Her gaze swept the other cages. "Or I will die trying."

"We're going to be raped and killed," Nala muttered flatly.

"No!" Tahira responded. "We *will* get out of here. We just have to wait until a chance appears and then take it."

The heavy door leading to the outside world opened with a clang and three men strode in—none of them were the man in charge. As always, when any of their captors showed up, most of the women cowered in the back of their cells. One of the men moved slowly along the walkway, studying the women with a cruel eye. A shiver shot through Tahira. She'd seen him with the man in charge when she'd first woken up. He'd given two other men orders about checking a delivery and killing someone if it wasn't right. But she'd been too focused on the man with the cigar to give the other man any consideration. Now that he stopped in front of her cell, she could see his aura was darker than she'd ever seen on anyone before, and it scared the hell out of her.

His gaze met Tahira's, holding it for a moment before shifting to Lahana. "Get up."

Lahana's eyes went wide. "Wh-why?"

The man unlocked the cell door and took a step inside. "Because I said so, bitch. Get. Up."

When Lahana still hesitated, he reached down, grabbed her by her arm, and yanked her to her feet. Her cry of pain combined with Nala's scream of terror. Tahira jumped up, lunged forward, and grasped Lahana's other arm, trying to pull her back to safety. "Leave her alone!"

With a sneer, the man backhanded Tahira, sending her sprawling to the floor again, pain exploding in her cheek and eye. Her head spun, and nausea roiled in her stomach. Through unwelcome tears, she watched helplessly as her cousin was, literally, dragged out of the cell, crying and begging to be let go. After locking the iron door again, he forced Lahana from the prison. The other two men followed. Once the main door was relocked, a heavy silence filled the air as Lahana's cries faded away the further she was taken.

Sobbing, Nala crawled over to Tahira. "Are—are you okay? Where are they taking her?"

Sitting up, Tahira caught Melinda's gaze. The blonde shook her head sadly. "I think his name is Secada—I heard one of the guards call him that—he's second in command to Diaz, who's the asshole with the cigar from last night. Secada has taken a few of them upstairs over the past three weeks. I get the feeling Diaz doesn't know what he's doing, but I'm not sure." She nodded in the direction of several women who'd remained quiet the entire time Tahira and her cousins had been there—the ones who appeared traumatized. Melinda lowered her voice so only Tahira and Nala could hear her. "The lucky ones had enough time for whatever drugs he gave them to kick in before he raped them. The others . . . they remember most of what happened. From what a few of them said, if they don't make him hard, that's when he beats them."

Tahira wasn't so innocent that she didn't understand what Melinda meant. Apparently, the man had some impotency issues and blamed it on the women.

Wrapping her arms around Nala, Tahira prayed for Lahana. It was all she could do, and she'd never felt as terrified in her life as she did at that moment.

CHAPTER SEVEN

Lindsey sipped her glass of beer—her first at the cantina, but as far as everyone could figure out, she'd had plenty more before she and Val had gotten there. Her partner appeared just as plastered, if not more. When he wasn't nuzzling her neck and making her giggle, his droopy gaze had been roaming, landing on several woman in the bar. With his good looks and flirtatious wink, he'd garnered plenty of female attention. Since his upcoming fight needed to be with Lindsey, he was wisely avoiding the women who obviously had a green-eyed significant other with them. Someone in a jealous rage was not what they needed tonight —except Lindsey, of course.

Darius and his cartel cohorts had shown up a little while ago. The plan was for Lindsey and Val to wait about a half hour before getting into an argument. Val would storm out, leaving her behind for Darius to hit on. In her "inebriated" state, it wouldn't look strange for her to leave with him after another fifteen or twenty minutes, getting back at her dog of a "boyfriend."

After checking an incoming text on his cell phone, Val

drunkenly swayed in close to Lindsey and whispered in her ear, "Everything's all set. Whenever you're ready, kick my sorry ass to the curb."

"What!" she shrieked in indignation, shoving him and making him stumble back a few steps. "Who the fuck is Brenda, you cheating son of a bitch?" Grabbing her half-full glass, she tossed the beer at him.

Pretending to be shocked, Val dried his face with his shirt sleeve and slurred, "Babe, w-what the fff-uck?"

"You just called me Brenda, you asshole! Who is she? Another one of your fucking whores?" She threw a basket of tortilla chips at his head, but he managed to duck, and it landed on the floor behind him.

They argued back and forth, with her throwing a few more things at him, while the bartender and patrons looked on in amusement. Lindsey was careful enough to keep things directed at Val and not anyone else. She didn't want to get kicked out of the bar.

After another round of cursing at him, Lindsey sent an off-balance kick to Val's crotch, which he easily blocked. Finally, she huffed and pushed her dark hair, which was now in disarray, away from her face. "That's it! You know what? I'm fucking done with you."

A sneer spread across his face as he swayed on his feet. "That's fine with me. You're nothing but a fucking bitch, you know that? Find your own way back to the US—I'm getting out of this fucking piss-hole." Turning, he stumbled and weaved out the door, disappearing into the night.

With calm and order now restored, the rest of the bar went back to their own conversations while still sending amused looks in her direction. Taking her seat again, Lindsey slapped the bar top and let her inner bitch, which she only let out every once in a while, continue her ranting. "Can I get another beer, here?" When the bartender ignored her,

Lindsey snapped her fingers a few times. "Hey! Hey, you! Cerveza! Do you understand me?"

Darius sidled up to her and sat on the next stool. "You know, a little *por favor* goes a long way 'round here."

She glared and frowned at him. "Who the hell are you?"

"An American who knows how to get another beer without raising my voice."

An unladylike snort erupted from her, and then she indicated with a flash of her hand for him to order for her.

After about fifteen minutes of flirting, Lindsey's character decided to get even with her cheating boyfriend and invited Darius to accompany her to a hostel up the street. They pulled on their heavy jackets, and then Darius threw some pesos on the bar for a tip. On their way out the door, the knowing smirks they got from his cartel comrades said their charade had worked perfectly. Darius waved to one of them. "Hey, Torres. I'll be back in an hour."

Out of the corner of her eye, Lindsey saw Darius leer at her ass and grin. He raised his voice a little louder. "Better make that two hours."

There were cat calls and whistles as they strode out into the cold night air. "Ride her hard, amigo!"

Once they were about a block away from the bar and certain no one was following them, Lindsey shook her head at Darius. "I need a shower. I can't remember the last time I felt so skeevy."

He put his arm across the back of her shoulders and pulled her in close, sharing his body heat. "As always, Costello, you did good. Next time, though, don't go so easy on Romeo. He needs a good ass-kicking every once in a while."

"That he does, but he made me promise to let him block the kick to his gonads."

Lindsey loved the esprit de corps she'd found with the

men of Trident Security, especially the Omega Team. While she'd been close to some of her teammates in the Marines, she'd also dealt with sexual harassment in the Corp as well. There were many men who'd thought she was a little piece of puff, unable to do the same job they did, but she'd proved them wrong, time after time. What had gained the respect of the unit she'd been assigned to for several tours in Iraq and Afghanistan had been that she'd placed first in her sniper school and had saved their asses on numerous occasions as a result. There were several from her team that she'd kept in contact with since opting out and joining Trident.

She'd been surprised when none of her new teammates had given her a hassle over the fact she was a woman. They didn't take it easy on her in training—which was a sign of great respect—and they'd never given any indication they thought less of her as a woman. In addition to being her co-workers, the men of Trident had also become her friends. They laughed and joked with her, hung out with her, and had never hit on her. She felt they were more her brothers than her real brothers had ever been.

Their significant others had welcomed her as well. The women had never given her any indication they felt threatened by Lindsey's status as the only female on the teams, aside from TS's helicopter pilot/mechanic, Tempest "Babs" Van Buren. In fact, they often invited the two women to their girls' nights out, which was always a load of fun.

Darius and Lindsey chatted and laughed as they walked into the hostel via a side entrance, and he followed her up the stairs to where the others were waiting for them in one of the rooms. There were a few more people than she'd expected there to be, and they were all standing around the small bedroom. Members of both the Alpha and Omega teams were there, in addition to several men she'd never seen before.

The first person Darius held his hand out to and greeted was Ian. "Hey, Boss-man. Sorry to be the bearer of bad news."

"Actually, you were the bearer of good news, in a way." He stepped to the side and that's when Lindsey noticed Mousaf Amar. Her heart rate picked up as every cell in her body became aware of the man she hadn't seen in several months, and she almost missed Ian's next words. "The King had already been notified of the princess's kidnapping. We had boots on the ground in Jamaica with Amar when Romeo called us."

The head of Timasur's royal guard gave her a friendly smile before he shook Darius's hand. "How is Her Royal Highness, Knight?"

Lindsey wasn't put off by the tepid acknowledgement of her presence. The two had ended up in each other's arms several months ago, after dancing around each other for quite some time. However, before things could really heat up, Amar had been called away on an urgent matter at the royal family's estate in Clearwater Beach. That had been the last time they'd had a chance to be alone together. Since she didn't think anyone knew of their attraction to each other, she was grateful he was keeping it under wraps, just as she was. However, she wished her body would get the message to keep things hush-hush because it was reacting to simply being in the same room with the man. His deep, smooth voice had her female parts tingling.

Darius took off his coat. "Holding her own, at the moment. She's in an underground prison area, with her two cousins and the other women the cartel plans to auction off. She's not aware of my presence, and I'm trying to keep it that way until it's time to rescue her. I can't have her giving away my cover."

"Understood."

"Other than that, she's a tough cookie. So is the taller of the two cousins—"

"Lahana," Amar supplied. "Nala is the younger one."

Darius nodded. "Yeah, Nala's the one that's been freaking out a bit—which, of course, is completely understandable."

"She is only nineteen and the daughter of Queen Azhar's sister. The cruise was the first trip she's taken without her parents or her brothers. Lahana is twenty-four and the daughter of the king's brother. She has been afforded more freedom since turning twenty-one, however, on trips like the cruise, the women are always accompanied by at least one of their family members. In this case, it was Farid and a friend of his."

Darius, Lindsey, and Val all rolled their eyes. They'd met Farid on more than one occasion, and they all had a dislike for the man who seemed to think anyone who wasn't considered royalty to be beneath him. He treated the staff at the Clearwater Beach mansion like dirt. The only person he would answer to there was Amar or whomever oversaw security at the time, as long as it was someone from the royal guards—the contract agents, i.e. the employees of Trident Security—were peons according to the little twerp. He'd also crudely hit on Lindsey a few times, which made her despise the creep even more. Not wanting to cause problems between Trident and the royal family, she'd kept that to herself, however, she'd made it painfully clear to Farid the last time he'd propositioned her and put his hands on her that his actions were unacceptable. The man had needed to ice his bruised balls after that encounter.

Taking control of the meeting, Ian quickly introduced Darius and Lindsey to several members of the royal guard and three Deimos operatives she'd only met once. Surprisingly, the only two US black-ops spies she, personally, did know weren't there.

"Where are Carter and Jordyn?" Lindsey asked, glancing around the room. The couple was supposed to be in attendance for the upcoming raid.

"They got held up on something else," Ian replied. "Moving the time-frame up had us scrambling. We have several eyes on the compound, with more bodies on the way. Babs is also en route to Bolivia to contract a helo from a merc she used to serve with—I want a fast way to exfil the hostages. So, there will be plenty of boots on the ground by zero hour."

Lindsey hoped so—with all the surprises as of late, there was always a chance things would go FUBAR. As if it wasn't already fucked up enough.

Stepping over to the bed, Darius stared down at several maps that had been spread out. Locating the one depicting the Diaz estate, he put it on top of the others. "All right, let's start breaking this down. I've got two hours max to rock Costello's world and then get back to the bar."

Several men chuckled, and Lindsey grinned as she playfully smacked Darius on the back of his head. "In your dreams, Batman. In your dreams."

CHAPTER EIGHT

The door to the cell area opened, and Secada dragged Lahana in by her upper arm. Tahira jumped to her feet. Her cousin's hair was in disarray, her eyes were red and swollen, and she had a bloody, fat lip. Bruises covered her face, arms, and legs. Her gaze was vacant, as if she'd been drugged. Tahira hoped she wouldn't be able to remember the assault. That would probably be best from the looks of things. Lahana was still wearing her bathing suit, but her sarong and sandals were missing.

As Secada unlocked the door to their cell, Tahira felt a rage she'd never experienced before. "What did you do to her? You bastard!"

The man sneered cruelly at her, while shoving Lahana into the cell before closing the door behind her again. She fell to the floor, and Tahira dropped to her knees beside her, pushing Lahana's hair back from her abused face. Secada shut the cell door again. "Nothing she didn't enjoy."

Before she realized what she was doing, Tahira was on her feet and lunging at the man, her arms extending past the bars. But Secada took a step back, out of her reach. "Hmm.

Your cousin was feisty, but it looks like you'll be even more of a challenge. Maybe tomorrow night, you and I will have some fun."

A combination of fear and rage coursed through Tahira and flared in her eyes. Secada cackled loudly as he turned on his heel and headed for the door. "Oh, yes. I definitely think we'll play before you're sold, *princesa*."

The door clanged shut. Spinning around, Tahira joined Nala who'd crawled over to Lahana. The injured woman was moaning in pain as tears rolled down her cheeks. Her lips and hands trembled as she grabbed Tahira's arm. "H-he h-hurt me, T-Tahira."

With tears welling up in her own eyes, she petted Lahana's long, dark hair with a soothing motion. "I know he did. I am so sorry, my cousin. There is nothing I can do to change what happened. If only I could take away your pain, I would. Just know that I am I here for you. Nala and I will take care of you."

Tahira's head whipped around at the sound of the door opening again. One of the guards strode in with a bucket and some rags and set them down just outside of their cell. He pointed at Tahira, and there wasn't an ounce of sympathy in his eyes or voice when he said, "Clean her up. We'll hide her bruises with makeup and clothes for the auction."

Without another word, he left. Silence filled the air, broken only by the occasional sob or whisper from one of the other women. Tahira reached between the bars, grabbed one of the rags, and wet it. Returning to Lahana, she gently wiped her face, neck, shoulders, and arms. Angry red welts circled her throat.

"Did he strangle you?" Tahira asked.

"Y-yes. While he—he was . . ." Lahana gulped and cried harder, but Tahira could figure out what she'd left unsaid. "I-I almost passed out, and all he did was laugh."

She did her best to clean away the evidence of the assault. She could see Lahana's eyelids getting heavy. "It is over now . . . you will be okay. Just close your eyes."

In the next cell, Melinda sat on the floor next to the row of bars that separated her from the three cousins. "If he gave her the same stuff as the others, she'll sleep for a few hours. If she's lucky, she'll forget what happened when she wakes up— some do, some don't."

Tahira nodded, her heart heavy with sorrow for Lahana. When they were rescued, she would make sure her cousin received the best care, physically and emotionally. And she was certain they would be rescued. Once the royal guard discovered the three women were missing, they'd move heaven and earth to find them. Amar would immediately bring in every special operative he knew to help. Ian Sawyer would be his first call—over the past eighteen months or so, Tahira had become close to the retired Navy SEAL and his wife. She no longer saw him as a guard, but as an older brother or uncle who cared for her well-being.

She cared about his employees, as well. In fact, she looked forward to her visits to the United States when the Trident Security teams would join her bodyguards in watching over her. Yes, she loved to tease many of them—taking them shoe shopping was one of her favorite ways to rile them—but she trusted them completely and thought very highly of them. They were honorable men, and many of them had found their soulmates. She loved to discover when one of them had fallen in love. Sometimes she knew before they did just from studying their auras. Yes, Ian, Amar, and their teams would find them—Tahira just hoped it wouldn't be too late.

"Then I will pray that she does."

SEVERAL MONTHS AGO . . .

Darius took a bite of the sandwich he'd just made and then glanced toward the hallway leading to the foyer as the sound of shuffling feet caught his attention. He'd pulled "Princess duty" tonight after several guards, stationed at the Clearwater Beach mansion with Her Royal Highness, had come down with some stomach virus that had them puking and shitting up a storm. The captain in charge had contacted Trident Security to fill in for the incapacitated guards, and Darius had pulled one of the short straws. So, there he was, at two o'clock in the morning, wondering who else was up besides the two bodyguards from Trident's Personal Protection Division, who were walking the perimeter of the gated estate, and the one monitoring the security cameras in a little cottage in the backyard. No alarms had gone off, and all the windows and doors were locked up tight, so whoever it was belonged there.

A shadow flashed a moment before Princess Tahira sashayed in. She gasped when she spotted him, then relaxed again. "Darius Knight, shame on you for startling me. I did not realize anyone was down here."

He stood in respect of her title, but he couldn't keep the slight sarcasm from his voice. "I'm sorry, Your Royal Highness. Next time I'll leave a sign at the bottom of the stairs to let you know I'm in here taking my dinner break."

Giving him a small smile, she strode over to the commercial-sized refrigerator and opened the door to the freezer, pulling out a pint of Häagen-Dazs ice cream. As she moved about the kitchen, he finally noticed what she was wearing. No sexy lingerie or satin pajamas for the glamorous princess. Nope, she was wearing cotton lounge pants with Hello Kitty all over them. The matching pink T-shirt was a size too big for her. Glancing down, he saw she had a pair of fuzzy, pink slippers on her feet. Her face was devoid of makeup, and her hair was held back from her face by a black, fabric band. She looked cute, and he quickly shook the thought from his head. This was Princess Tahira—the woman who could make his life miserable with the mere mention of two words . . . shoe shopping. Thank God there were no stores open at this hour.

After grabbing a spoon from a drawer, she approached the table and took a seat across from him. "Please sit, Darius Knight. That is if you do not mind me joining your repast."

Sitting, he picked up his sandwich again. "I don't mind at all, Your Highness, as long as you call me either Darius or Knight, not both names together."

"I apologize. It is a habit I have had for a very long time, but I am trying to break it when I am in the United States. Obviously, I am still working on it." She put a spoonful of ice cream in her mouth, savoring it a moment before swallowing. "Do you have a preference? Darius or Knight?"

He shrugged as he chewed a bite of his sandwich. A sip of soda washed it down. "Nope. Whatever you want to call me is fine. You can even use my nickname."

"Batman? No. I would feel silly calling you that . . . besides, I am a Superman fan." He chuckled at that surprising fact. "I think I will call you Darius. It is a strong name, and it suits you. Did you know that it means kingly or wealthy?"

"No, I didn't. It's a family name. My grandfather was Darius and *his* grandfather was too."

"Hmm. Maybe there is a royal bloodline in your family from a long time ago. In fact, Darius the Great was one of three Persian kings to have that name."

He snorted and wiped his mouth with a napkin. "Well, sorry to disappoint you, but if I'm in line for a throne somewhere, there's probably a few thousand people who are ahead of me." They sat in silence for a few minutes, enjoying their food, but Darius found he wanted to hear her talk some more. He had a feeling he was seeing a girl-next-door quality to the princess she rarely showed the public.

"So, where did you get the habit?" When she raised her perfectly-arched eyebrows at him, he clarified, "I mean, calling people by both their given name and surname."

"Ah. It started when I was about ten. As a member of the royal family, I am constantly being introduced to people—sometimes dozens in a single day—and many of them have the same first or last name. I found it easier to remember their names if I repeated both names in my head several times after hearing them for the first time. Some people have photographic memories, I have a memory for names. I see them in my mind like you might see them in a . . . oh, what is that thing called again? It is a bunch of small cards on a wheel."

His brow furrowed, and then a light bulb went off in his head. "A Rolodex?" he asked.

She smiled triumphantly. "Yes! That is it. A Rolodex. It sits on a desk, yes, with names and phone numbers on the cards?"

"Yup. You remember those things? I haven't seen one in ages."

"When I was little, my mother's secretary had one—I liked sitting at her desk and spinning it." Tilting her head, she studied him for a few moments. "You are a very handsome man."

Darius stood, picked up his empty plate, and carried it to the sink. "Well, that didn't take long," he murmured.

"What do you mean?"

"For you to hit on me." He cleaned the plate in the sink, then set it on a rack on the counter to dry. "You do know that Ian threatens all his operatives with unemployment and castration if they mess around with you, right?"

"Mess around? You mean if they try to get me into their

beds. Yes, I do know that. Although, I do believe the warning is that my father will see to the castration. However, I was not *hitting on you*, as you say. I was merely making an observation. It is not often I can let my guard down and act like a normal woman."

Crossing his arms, Darius leaned against the island counter and stared at her. "Normal? In whose world? Everyone's definition of normal is different."

She swirled her spoon in the ice cream container. "Normal like the wives and girlfriends of your Trident men. Please do not get me wrong—I love my country, its people, our history, and our culture. But being a princess is not like what most little girls fantasize about. My every move is watched by the guards and reported on by the news and tabloids. And forget social media—most of the things posted about me on there never happened. While I use certain sites to promote my charity work, I learned long ago not to read anything I am tagged in. People can be so cruel and easily believe the lies that are told on Facebook, Twitter, and Instagram. They have no problem viciously attacking people they have never met.

"My life can be very lonely, even though I am constantly surrounded by people. I must always be smiling in public and never raise my voice or do anything to dishonor my crown or family. I must confess that is why I have enjoyed flirting with some of my American bodyguards. Ian Sawyer . . . I mean, Ian is a man my father and Amar trust implicitly." She smiled. "I also have a sixth sense, if you will, about whom I can trust. It is only those men who I will flirt with, if they do not have a wife or fiancée, because I know they will not try to take advantage of me. They will not dishonor the man they respect. Ian is a good employer, but he is also a good friend to all of you. You would never do anything to betray his trust."

"Wow." Darius was a little stunned. He'd always thought she was a spoiled brat, but now he knew his assessment had been completely off its mark. "Forgive me for making false assumptions, Your Highness."

"You are forgiven, Darius, on one condition. When we are alone like this, out of the public eye, please call me Tahira. I do not hear my name often, without my title, unless I am with family. I have asked Ian and several of his family members to call me by my given name only, and now, I am asking you as well."

He dipped his head once. "If you insist, Tahira, it would be my honor."

Standing, she returned the half-empty container to the freezer and placed her spoon in the sink. "Thank you, Darius. Now, I am going to return to my room and try to fall asleep. I hope you have a pleasant and quiet night."

Watching in silence as she left the room, Darius tried to wrap his head around this new side of her he'd never seen before. She was a completely different woman than she'd been during his past bodyguard details and had definitely matured over the past two years. After a few moments, he grinned. He liked this new version of her—a lot.

CHAPTER NINE

Present...

As he drove Torres and the others, who were drunk off their asses, back to the Diaz compound, Darius ran the minutes of the meeting with the teams through his head again. They'd tried to cover every detail and alternate ending to the planned raid, but with their experience, they knew shit could go sideways in the blink of an eye. As much as they wanted Diaz and his sleazy connections, the women came first. There would be no innocent casualties on Darius's watch—not if he could prevent it.

He'd given Ian the names of some of the women being held hostage. He'd gotten them while hanging out in the compound security office, shooting the bull with the guards on occasion. The cell area had been wired for sound, and the women talked. He had first names on more than half of them, but only a few last names from when they'd introduced themselves to the newer captives. Darius had been surprised when Ian had recognized the name Melinda. Apparently, an acquaintance named "Lady Cara" believed a teenaged woman she knew had been kidnapped from St. Lucia by the human-trafficking ring. When his boss had shown him a photo on his phone of the missing woman, Darius had been able to confirm Melinda was one of the hostages being held at Diaz's estate. She'd been in the makeshift prison for longer than Darius had been under-cover as Glenn Hamilton.

After driving past the security shack at the gate, Darius parked the vehicle next to the bunkhouse the guards lived in. He helped the drunken idiots inside, then turned and headed for the main house under the guise of wanting something to eat from the kitchen. When he entered the large room, with its state-of-the-art appliances that any chef would be jealous of, he found it occupied. Two of Diaz's flunkies were sitting there, stuffing their faces with food left over from dinner.

They both nodded in his direction, and the one named Carlos gestured to one of the empty chairs. "Hola, amigo. Beer's in the fridge. Pull up a seat."

When Darius had first arrived at the compound, he'd intentionally mangled the Spanish language to the point most of Diaz's men spoke to him in English. They'd switch to Spanish when they thought he couldn't understand their rapid speech. Little did they know he understood every word.

"Hey, guys, gracias." Despite the warmth of the room, he left his bulky winter coat on. Grabbing a beer from the fridge, he popped the top and took a swig. "How's your shift going? Quiet?"

"Pretty much," Carlos responded before smirking. "Although it wasn't as good as Secada's night."

Darius leaned against the counter and raised an eyebrow. "What do you mean?"

"While we were walking around the compound in the fucking cold, he was getting some tail."

Something in the other man's tone set Darius's bat senses tingling. "He hooked up with one of the women on staff? Or did he bring someone to the compound?" The latter was against the rules Diaz had laid out for his men.

The other man, Javier, snorted. "Didn't need to. He helped himself to one of the *putas* downstairs."

Oh, fuck. He tried to not let his anger or revulsion show. "Yeah, which one? They're all hot."

"Oh, yeah. I'd fuck any one of them in a heartbeat. Especially that princess."

Carlos laughed. "Right, amigo, like she'd ever give you the time of day."

"Don't need her to. I'd just do what Secada did—drug her up and tie her down."

Darius's gut sank, and he fought the urge to shoot both Carlos and Javier, then go find Secada and tear him limb from limb. He paused a few moments, making sure he had himself under control. The last thing he needed to do was raise any red flags. "Are you saying Secada did the princess? I thought Diaz was going to ask double the money for her because she was a virgin."

"Nah, he didn't do her. It was one of the other two with her—the taller one. From the looks of her when he brought her back downstairs, he had a good time. Beat her up good— she must have fought him like a wildcat. Secada's fucked a few of them, but Señor Diaz doesn't know that." He lowered his voice as if afraid he'd be overheard. "The *cabrón* won't let anyone else have a taste either."

His jaw clenching, Darius poured the rest of his beer down the sink. While it killed him that Lahana or any of the other women being held had been raped by that asshole, he couldn't help but be relieved it hadn't been Tahira. Maybe it was because he'd never met the other women or spoken to them before. But it really didn't matter because when the raid went down, Darius was going to make sure Secada suffered before being arrested or, better yet, killed.

Pushing his chair back, so it made a scraping noise as he stood, Carlos frowned. "*Mierda*—I gotta do my rounds."

It was obvious the man would prefer to finish eating the enchiladas and beans on his plate, so Darius took advantage of that. He thought he would've had to wait until his morning shift to hide the little surprises Ian had provided him with, but with everyone in the forty-room main house sleeping at this time of night, it was the perfect opportunity for him to do what he needed to do.

"I'll do it." He shrugged. "Got nothing better to do—stay and eat."

"You sure? Gracias, amigo."

"No *problemo*. Won't take long."

Striding out into the hallway, Darius began to make his way around the first floor, under the guise of making certain the windows and doors were secure. He pressed a button on his watch and waited a few seconds before entering the formal living room. The black timepiece was something out of a James Bond movie, and Darius freaking loved the thing. It looked like a common multifunction smart watch, but there was nothing like it available to the public. The tech gurus at Deimos had made some changes to a $60 version you could buy anywhere. The button Darius had hit was for a jammer that would interfere with the compound's surveillance cameras. Some of the camera feeds would blink in and out, but the ones Darius was closest to would show nothing but static back in the security office. He'd been randomly fucking with the system for about three weeks now. At first everyone had freaked, but after finding no breaches, they'd finally written it off as a glitch in the system. In fact, the guards no longer alerted Diaz and Secada when it happened. They'd gotten complacent, and that's exactly what Darius had hoped would happen.

Entering the living room, he made sure he was alone, then unzipped the lining of his jacket. He pulled out a small block of C-4 and a detonator. The great thing about the putty-like explosive was that it was easy to carry without worrying about blowing yourself up. Only the shock wave from a detonator or blasting cap would set it off.

After inserting the wires of the detonator into the two-inch-square block, Darius lifted the top of a bench next to a baby grand piano, and gently set the explosive on a pile of sheet music. Ian had the device that would transmit the signal for it to blow when the time was right. They didn't have to worry about Diaz's wife or kids playing the piano before the raid. Last week, the man had shipped his family out to one of his other homes in South America. He hadn't wanted them around for the auction, although Darius got the impression Diaz's wife knew all about her husband's illegal businesses but was too afraid to go against him and turn him in to the authorities. If she ever tried, she probably would've been dead within hours.

From what Darius had been told by the others, most of Diaz's house staff would not be at the compound during the auction either. For that he was grateful, knowing that many of the women and a few of the men were innocent—unlike the guards. The only reason most of the house staff worked there was because they either really needed the money to support their poor families or they owed Diaz some sort of debt.

Once he'd strategically placed explosives in all the down-stairs rooms he had access to, Darius climbed the elaborate, grand staircase in the foyer to the second floor. Diaz's room was down the hallway to Darius's left, with Secada's and two cartel lieutenants' rooms in the opposite direction. Diaz's kids' rooms and several guest rooms were all empty.

There was a seating area at the top of the staircase, with glass doors that led out to a balcony. All the windows in the mansion had been replaced with reinforced, bulletproof glass, while the wooden doors had steel inserts, which made it difficult for anyone to blast their way in. Difficult, but not impossible.

Avoiding the occupied rooms, Darius slipped into the other ones and hid the last of the C-4 under beds or behind dressers—anywhere they, hopefully, wouldn't be found before it was showtime. The main objective of the explosions was to create enough confusion for the special-ops teams to attack. If anyone there for the auction was injured or killed in the blasts, Darius saw that as a bonus. The sick bastards deserved everything that was coming to them.

A little less than forty-eight hours from now, Darius and the hostages in the basement prison would be on their way to the United States. The women would receive treatment at a secure facility and then be returned to their families and homes. Darius prayed they'd be able to put this horror behind them at some point, but he knew it would be difficult for Lahana and any others that Secada had raped. Forty-eight more hours and that bastard would be dead, and Darius vowed he would be the one to slaughter him.

Sixteen hours later . . .

Tahira shivered and wrapped her blanket tighter around her body as she sat on a threadbare mattress on the floor. As dirty as the thing was, she'd been grateful when one of the guards had tossed three of them into the cell. Although heat came through the ceiling vents, she still wasn't appropriately dressed for the cold, damp dungeon. What she wouldn't give for an electric blanket right now—actually, she'd give up her crown for a one-star hotel in the United States or anywhere else than this prison right now.

Based on the meal deliveries, she and her cousins had been there for almost three days. How long would they and the other women be held until they were sold?

Sold.

That word conjured up all sorts of horrors. She may be a virgin, but she was fully aware of the human trafficking that took place around the world. A charity to help fight it was one of the many Tahira supported. She'd heard all about the vile atrocities abducted women had been subjected to, with some of the stories coming directly from those who'd lived through it before being rescued. Unfortunately, the number of those rescued was a stark contrast to the ones who'd been killed or were still being held captive in some unknown part of the world.

She glanced over at Lahana lying in a fetal position on her own mattress. Her cousin had been sleeping on and off and had refused to talk about what had happened to her aside from the fact the bastard had hurt her. Tahira's cheek still hurt from when he'd struck her, so she couldn't imagine the pain her cousin was in—her body was covered in bruises.

Even though she hadn't been assaulted, Nala had also been very quiet since Lahana had been returned to the cell. She was sitting against the stone wall with her arms holding her knees to her chest as she stared at the floor in front of her and rocked back and forth. She'd been traumatized, yet in a different way. The nineteen-year-old was terrified about what was going to happen to them and was emotionally and mentally shutting down. While Tahira had never seen that happen to anyone before, she recalled talking to victims of human trafficking who mentioned they'd done the same thing as a coping mechanism. In a way, Tahira envied Nala, but she knew that if they were rescued, Nala would need professional help to recover from their abduction just as much as Lahana would.

In the near silence of the cell area, footsteps echoed, announcing someone was coming down the stairs. Tahira wasn't the only one who'd heard them—the other women shifted around in their cells, probably trying to make themselves invisible, yet failing to do so. They'd already gotten their dinner a little while ago, as meager as it had been, so the only reason someone would be coming down there at that hour couldn't be good.

Tahira looked around. From what Melinda in the next cell had told her, none of those assaulted had been taken a second time. Secada took a new woman each time. But maybe that wasn't who was coming. Melinda had said after Lahana had returned that they were safe for a few nights. The perverted bastard only chose one of them once or twice a week.

All thoughts about safety fled her mind when Secada strolled through the door with two armed men on his heels. Out of the corner of her eye, Tahira saw Nala tuck her head under her arms as she shivered uncontrollably. She couldn't let the younger woman be taken by the bastard.

Pushing her terror down, Tahira stood and moved so she was between the cell door and Nala, blocking her from Secada's view as the man stopped in front of her.

His leering gaze trailed from her face to her feet and back again. A swirling black aura surrounded the man—pure evil. She shook under his scrutiny but wouldn't back down. She couldn't let his attention turn to Nala.

"Defiant, aren't you? I love to break the defiant ones. To show them I hold all the power. And now that Diaz is out of the way, it's my decision on whether or not I should sell your royal virginity or take it for myself."

Oh, no. She had no idea what he meant about Diaz being out of the way, but right now, it didn't matter. Without conscious thought, she took a step back and to the side, and the man's feral eyes flitted to Nala. Tahira quickly blocked his view of the younger woman again, drawing his attention once again.

"Maybe I should let you wait for your fate and take her instead."

Tahira's eyes flared as her hands clenched. "Over my dead body."

The man snorted. "Oh, Princess, you wouldn't be dead, but you'd wish you were. I can guarantee it."

As he put the key into the lock of the cell door, Tahira took another step back before remembering Nala, then stood her ground. She would not let her cousin, who was in no condition to fight, take her place, but that didn't mean she wouldn't put up a fight.

She waited until the man entered the cell before lunging at him. Her fingernails tried to claw his face, but he knocked them away before Tahira could do any damage. Secada grabbed her upper arm in an agonizing grip and yanked her off balance. She stumbled forward and stubbed her toes against the open cell door, but the pain didn't register in her brain—only fear and rebellion. "Let me go!"

Tahira twisted and pulled her arm, trying to get free, but she was no match for the man's strength. Oh, why had she refused Amar's numerous offers to teach her self-defense while in her teens? With her ever-present bodyguards, she never thought she'd need to fight for her life. But that's what she was doing now. Maybe not her life, but her virginity, her mind, and her soul.

As Secada dragged her like a rag doll toward the door to

the stairs, she heard one of the other men close the cell with a loud clang. Several of the women sobbed, but no one made an attempt to come to her aid. Not that there was anything they could do—just like she'd watched helplessly when Lahana had been taken. But Tahira wasn't going to go quietly. She'd raise hell every step of the way . . . and pray.

CHAPTER TEN

Kicking, thrashing, screaming, and panting, Tahira was roughly led up to the second floor of what she now realized was a mansion. Judging by the decor, and the fact most of the people she'd encountered had heavy Spanish accents, it was most likely a hacienda. And since no one came running at the sound of her cries for help, it must be an empty hacienda—or one filled with people who didn't care. Probably the latter, because she knew there were other men around. The ones who'd followed her and Secada up from the cell area had veered off in another direction on the first floor.

Once they reached the top of the stairs, and she didn't have to worry about falling backwards down them, Tahira went on another attack. However, her punches, scratches, and shoeless kicks did nothing to deter the man as he strode down the hallway with her in tow. Stopping at a door, he opened it and shoved her inside. "Get in there, puta!"

She hadn't expected the sudden thrust and stumbled before her hand found the wall, and she steadied herself. The door shut behind her and the lock was engaged. Her heart pounding, Tahira turned to see Secada stalking toward her. She backed away, moving further into the room. Looking around frantically, she searched for something she could use as a weapon, but aside from a large bed, two nightstands, a dresser, and an armoire, the room was sparse. There wasn't even a lamp she could grab and swing at him. The only light came from bulbs attached to a ceiling fan. The shades were pulled down over two windows, but there was a little light coming through the edges. Rain pelted against the glass as thunder roared. A brief thought flashed in her mind—this was a scene out of a horror movie. At least she wished it was but knew that wish wouldn't come true.

The backs of Tahira's legs hit the corner of the bed—the last thing she wanted to be near. Pivoting, she stepped closer to the armoire, trying to keep as much difference between Secada and herself as she could. He was surrounded by a swirling combination of black, grey, and red—his aura was pure evil. Tahira had never seen such a violent aura before, and the panic and fear she'd been feeling since he'd dragged her from the cell turned into sheer terror. She gulped for air.

Alive . . . the others he assaulted are still alive. Remember that.

The other women had lived through whatever he'd done to them. She would too, but she sure as hell wouldn't make it easy on him. She would still fight the bastard, and no matter what happened, she'd be alive when it was over. She would see her family again. All she had to do was survive until she and the others were rescued.

The man grabbed a plastic bottle of water from the dresser and moved toward her. When she realized she was being backed into a corner, Tahira changed direction and rushed toward Secada, trying to take him off guard and push past him, but he caught her around the waist and pinned her against the wall. She struggled, but he used his larger body to hold her in place. His hot, putrid breath hit her face, making her nauseous. She tried to scratch his face, but he grabbed both her hands in one of his and secured them above her head.

Using his teeth, Secada twisted the cap off the water bottle, spit it out of his mouth, and then spoke for the first time since they'd entered the room. "Drink it."

It took her a moment to remember Melinda saying he drugged the women he attacked. Whatever he used must be dissolved in the water. Pursing her lips shut, she turned her head as he brought the bottle to her mouth, but he let go of her arms and viciously grabbed her chin, digging his fingers into her flesh. He forced her jaw open as she groaned in pain. "I said drink it."

Her hands grasped his wrist, sinking her nails into his flesh, trying to pull him off her, but he was so much stronger than her and unfazed. Unable to keep her jaw closed under the agony and pressure, she tried to move her head back and forth. But the bottle followed her, and water filled her mouth. He tilted her head back, so she couldn't expel the liquid. She had no alternative but to swallow or it would go down into her lungs.

Survive.

Most of the water ended up in her stomach, but some of it ran out the corners of her mouth and down onto her heaving chest, scattering goosebumps across her shoulders and down her arms.

Once the bottle was empty, Secada dragged her by the grip he still had on her jaw and propelled her onto the bed. The dark blue bedspread felt deathly cold against her skin. Tahira jumped to her knees and glanced at the door. It was too far away. He'd be on her before her feet ever hit the floor.

Her nostrils flared, drawing oxygen into her lungs far too quickly. A wave of vertigo hit her, and she wobbled while struggling to remain upright. She was starting to hyperventilate as Secada stood at the foot of the bed and stared at her. She had no idea what he was waiting for, and for a moment, anger pushed aside her fear. Her hands clenched tightly as she yelled at him, "What are you waiting for, you bastard?"

An ugly sneer crossed his face. "Anxious to get started, Princess? I would think you'd want to hold onto your precious virginity as long as you could."

As Tahira glared at him, the man split into two then three. Dizziness overtook her, and her mouth went dry. The water in her stomach churned, and she closed her eyes, trying not to vomit.

If he gave her the same stuff as the others, she'll sleep for a few hours. If she's lucky, she'll forget what happened when she wakes up—some do, some don't.

Melinda's words came back to her. This man was going to rape Tahira no matter what, but if she kept the water down, her body would absorb the drug into her system. There was a chance she wouldn't remember what was about to happen. She didn't want it to happen at all, but it was clear she didn't have a choice, so all she could do was pray she didn't remember anything when it was all over.

When she opened her eyes again, the room spun. Everything appeared to be moving—the furniture, the door, and Secada—in slow motion. Her soon-to-be rapist had taken his clothes off, but he was nothing more than an indistinguishable blob of tanned skin. Multicolored lights flashed before her eyes as the din of the rain and thunder increased in her mind. Her senses were bombarded. Her surroundings appeared more vivid yet shapeless. Sounds were louder than normal. The air crackling around her felt more intense.

She fell onto her back and closed her eyes again, hoping her world would stop spinning and she would slip into unconsciousness. Her body had become defenseless under the influence of the drug. Her breathing slowed. Her limbs were too heavy to lift. Tears rolled down her cheeks to wet her hair that was spread out underneath her head.

Secada moved to the side of the bed and picked up her hand. Tahira tried to pull it away, but her muscles wouldn't listen to her screaming mind.

"Make me hard, bitch!"

Her hand was forced to close around something soft and unfamiliar. Tahira couldn't open her eyes even if she wanted to, which she didn't. She willed her mind to think of one of her favorite places on Earth. She'd been in many beautiful locations, all around the world, but she loved to sit on the beach of the Gulf of Mexico and watch the dolphins play as the sun set behind them. That's where she wanted to be right now—with her soulmate.

A man with dark hair and green eyes sat behind her and wrapped his arms around her, keeping her safe. He nuzzled her ear and whispered, "I have you, Princess. You're mine, and I'll never let anything bad happen to you ever again. Keep thinking of me. You'll get through this if you just keep thinking of me. I love you."

CHAPTER ELEVEN

"**B**atman, you there?"

Unable to verbally acknowledge Costello's question, Darius coughed once. Her voice had come through the comms unit in his ear canal. The thing was so small no one would be able to see it—that also meant it would have to be carefully removed when the mission was over. The microphone that went with it was on Darius's watch, but Carlos was standing next to him on the patio, so he had to use prearranged signals.

"Have you seen Diaz lately?"

Frowning, Darius glanced toward the mansion behind him. He didn't know where she was going with this and let out two more coughs. It didn't mean much that he hadn't seen the head of the cartel all day–there had been several days he hadn't seen the man or had only spotted him once or twice. With about twenty-four hours left before the auction, it was doubtful Diaz had left the compound.

"You okay, amigo?" Carlos asked. "Getting sick or something?"

Staying in character, he snorted. "Yeah, probably. Wish I

was back in Miami or anywhere else that's warm this time of year." While it was winter in the southern hemisphere, the local temperatures had been hovering in the high fifties and low sixties during the day for the past six days, and about ten to fifteen degrees lower at night. According to tonight's forecast, the temperatures wouldn't come close to the freezing mark, and they were due for heavy thunderstorms and hail.

"Yeah, the cold weather sucks. I heard Diaz and Secada talking about heading to the Panama house after the auction. Margaritas and señoritas in bikinis? I'm up for that."

"Me too," Darius agreed, wishing the man would shut the fuck up so Costello could tell him what was going on. He gestured to his right with the AK-47 he was carrying for guard duty. "I'm going to take a walk around the house–check things out."

"Knock yourself out. I'm going inside to get warm. Nobody's around. Come in for some tequila when you're done."

"Sounds good."

Darius strolled around the perimeter of the building as Carlos ducked inside the entrance to a mud room. Once he was sure he wouldn't be overheard, Darius spoke softly into his multi-purpose watch. "I'm clear, Costello. Sit-rep."

"For the past hour, the camera feeds have been in and out, just like the last time a storm rolled in—they'll probably get worse. But besides that, Diaz hasn't been spotted on the security cameras all day." Over the past six weeks, Costello and Romeo had been scanning through the recorded security tapes from the compound, looking for anything that could provide them with more intel. But since the teams had arrived yesterday, they'd been monitoring the live feeds. The only rooms that didn't have surveillance cameras installed were the master bedroom suite, Secada's suite, and Diaz's office. "He went into his bedroom this afternoon around

1300 and hasn't come out since. Secada went in there about a half hour later and stayed for about twenty minutes before coming back out. Nobody's gone in or out of the master suite since."

With his head on swivel, checking his surroundings, Darius responded, "I heard Secada tell the house staff this afternoon that Diaz had a stomach bug or something and didn't want to be disturbed. He gave them the rest of the day off. That was the last I heard from either Secada or Diaz."

"Secada was in Diaz's office for almost three hours after he left the master bedroom. He then went to the security office for a little bit before going to his own suite. That was about two hours ago. I don't know if he's still in there or if he's back in the office or with Diaz. The live feeds have been out more than they've been on."

"Damn storm," Darius muttered, a second before a lightning strike brightened the dark sky. It wasn't long before the crack of thunder followed. The storm was rapidly getting closer. "All right. I'll see what I can do about checking on them. I've got a bad feeling about this."

"So does Boss-man. He's already on his way to the compound with the second team. I'm turning over the surveillance feeds to Cookie and Egghead in Tampa, then headed your way too. If shit goes down, you'll have plenty of backup—just give them a few more minutes to get there."

"Got it."

Something was wrong. Emmanuel Diaz had taken over the family-run cartel after his brother had been killed, but he wasn't the intelligent and crafty businessman Ernesto had been. However, the family name, and the money behind it, had been enough to win over many of the men who currently worked for him. Truth be told, his right-hand man had become the brains of the operation. In fact, Darius was curious why Secada hadn't done a hostile takeover—maybe he was waiting until the timing was right.

Rounding the back of the house again, Darius looked up at the northwest corner where the master bedroom suite was located. The lights were out, and it was only 2000 hours. Emmanuel never went to bed before 10 p.m. Had Secada decided to stage a mutiny? There was only one way to find out.

Darius was just about to head inside when Ian's voice came through his earpiece. "Batman?"

"Go."

"We've got the compound surrounded, but it looks like things are going to go FUBAR. We're not the only ones out here. Looks like there might be a rival cartel trying to move in."

Another flash of lightening lit up the sky, and its accompanying crack of thunder indicated the storm wasn't far off. "Any chatter?"

"Egghead's looking into it but might not have the intel in time—not that it really matters at this point. You locate Diaz yet?"

"Negative. Going to scout out his bedroom. Just need a few minutes to get up there."

"Your safeword is 'snake'."

"Copy that, snake." Darius almost laughed—Boss-man was getting his two businesses' terminologies mixed up. But either way, Darius sure as hell hoped he wouldn't need to use the word "snake" to indicate everything had gone to shit and his cover was compromised. But it was nice to know there were now over a dozen team members ready to come to his and the female prisoners' rescue.

Instead of going in through the mud room and possibly running into Carlos, Darius hustled to the other side of the house to an entrance the house staff used. Once inside, there was a maid's staircase that lead to the second floor. He snuck up the steps on silent feet.

Upon reaching the top of the stairs, he stilled at the doorway leading to the hallway and listened for a moment. All seemed quiet. Even though the security cameras were flipping out, he hit the button on his watch to be sure they didn't come back on at the wrong time.

Peering around the door jamb, he checked to see if the long hallway was empty before he stepped out. To his left was the door to Secada's suite. Pretending as if he was just making the usual rounds, Darius turned right and strode past several guest rooms, the main staircase, a sitting area, and the Diaz children's rooms. He stopped outside the master bedroom suite, swung his AK-47 around to his back, and again, listened for a moment.

Outside, the storm had arrived. A clap of thunder sounded like it was right on top of the house, while rain began to pound on the roof and windows. Fuck, what more could go wrong? The weather was going to make it more difficult for him to hear his team out there and for them to see what the hell was going on with the unexpected company.

As far as Darius could tell, there were no sounds coming from the other side of the door. The hallway and foyer chandelier flickered off then back on again. Great, add in a power outage and this mission going FUBAR would be an understatement.

Trying the doorknob, he found it locked. He didn't have his pick set with him—hadn't thought he'd need one tonight —so he reached into his pocket to get the next best thing. While the locks on the house's exterior entry doors were all reinforced, the interior ones were easy to bypass. Pulling one of his alias's credit cards from his wallet, he slid it between the door and its jamb. Within seconds, he had his rifle back in his hand and was edging the door open. There were no lights on in the room, but a combination of foul and metallic odors hit his nose.

Aw, shit.

Darius pushed the door open enough to enter, then shut it again behind him, leaving the room's lights off. A thunderbolt gave him enough just enough illumination to see Diaz lying sideways on the bed, with his feet hanging off the side. Digging a small flashlight out of his pocket, Darius turned it on, stepped forward, and stared down at the dead man. Diaz and the black comforter were covered in blood, and he'd apparently lost control of his bowels and bladder as his life had drained from him. A narrow slit in his shirt to the left of his sternum told Darius a knife had probably been plunged directly into his heart.

Had Secada killed him? Most likely. But that conjured up a bunch of other questions, like who was getting ready to attack the compound and were they friend or foe of Diaz's second-in-command? Had murdering the bastard tonight been part of a larger plot to seize control of the cartel or had it just been bad timing as someone else staged a hostile takeover? Either way, it was fucking up the entire mission. They were going to have to get the women out of there tonight. The mission had been to get the names of as many human-trafficking scumbags as possible, but not at the risk of the prisoners' lives. At least Diaz wasn't part of the equation anymore, and Secada would be removed as well before the night was over, if Darius had anything to say about it.

Darius stealthily moved back to the door, opened it a crack to make sure the coast was still clear, then closed it again. He lifted his wrist to his mouth and spoke softly. "Boss-man?"

"Go."

"Diaz has been taken out—probably by Secada. No one else knows yet, as far as I can tell."

"Fuck. Things are about to go to shit here too. We grabbed one of the tangos in the woods and not-so-politely asked a few questions before silencing him. There's an attack coming your way, and the hostages are in the fucking middle of it. You've got to get them out of there, but with the fur about to fly, I can only spare two from the teams to help you. We're going to be taking fire from both directions, and this downpour isn't helping matters, but we'll clear the way for you to lead the hostages into the woods."

Well, hell. "Is Tampa on the line?"

Brody's voice sounded in Darius's ear. "Affirm, Batman, but not sure how much we'll be able to help. Video feeds are still down."

This night can't get any freaking worse, can it? "Who's backing me?"

"Costello, Romeo, you're on hostage detail," Ian ordered. "Babs, can you still fly in this mess?"

"That's a rhetorical question, right?"

A few chuckles came over the line at the female helicopter pilot's snark, but Ian ignored them. "Fine but change the exfil point to Bravo. You'll be caught in a crossfire here."

"Exfil Bravo, copy that."

The original plan had been for Babs to land the contracted UH-60 military helicopter to extract the hostages and most of the team in the large lawn area behind the main house. Now, they were going to have to figure out how to schlep the women a half mile through the jungle, in the cold rain and darkness, to reach a second area large enough for the big bird. To top it off, the women were poorly dressed for the foul weather and terrain.

"Romeo, Costello, you're going to have to come in through the mud room." He hadn't known what else to call it, so that's what they'd been calling it throughout the mission. "The entrance to the stairs for the dungeon is off that to the right."

While they'd been studying the floor plans of the estate and satellite photos of the grounds for weeks now, he wanted to make sure they were all on the same page. "Most of the guards are in the bunkhouse for the night. I'll take care of Carlos. There should be two others on the perimeter, but they tend to be slackers. The weather probably drove them to take cover."

The only other guard they'd have to worry about until the alarm was raised was the one in the shack at the front gate. With any luck, he'd be snoring away or distracted by boredom, but he wasn't Darius's problem. His team would take the guard out, quickly and quietly.

"Boss-man, how much time do you think we have before the tangos attack?"

"According to the guy we interrogated, you've got twenty minutes max."

Fuck!

Chapter Twelve

It didn't take long for Darius to ambush Carlos, put him in a headlock until he lost consciousness, zip-tie his hands behind his back, and then hide him in the mud room's closet. He was just closing the closet door when Romeo and Costello—both dressed in black and heavily armed—joined him inside the house. Aside from the storm outside, everything else seemed eerily quiet, but that wasn't going to last long.

Romeo handed Darius a black bulletproof vest. With the large amounts of ammo the cartels had available to them, every little bit of protection helped. He quickly pulled the heavy body armor over his head and secured it tightly against his torso using the Velcro straps.

Taking the lead, Darius grabbed the bulky cell door key from where it hung by the door to the converted basement, then descended the stairs, with his two teammates on his six. As usual, as soon as they heard someone approaching and the lights went on, many of the women retreated to the back of their cells, trying to make themselves as small as possible.

Darius now understood why all too well. He'd had no idea Secada had been raping some of the women, but he'd make sure the man suffered for it if it was the last thing he ever did.

While Romeo manned the door to the stairs, Darius stopped in front of the first cell that held two young women. When he inserted the key into the lock, they both whimpered, their eyes widening in fear. Knowing there wasn't much he could say that would reassure them he was one of the good guys, Darius glanced at Costello. "They'll be more comfortable with you talking to them."

She nodded then addressed the women. "We're from the United States, and we're getting you out of here, but you have to stay quiet and do what we say, okay?"

As Darius worked quickly to open the other cells, he could tell the women recognized him as one of the men who'd held them captive. They weren't about to trust him as far as they could throw him, but he had to, at least, try to put their minds at ease. "I was undercover and was never going to let them sell you."

When he reached the last cell, his hand froze an inch away from sliding the key in the lock. "Where's Princess Tahira?"

The younger woman, Nala, burst into tears, her body trembling forcibly. Her cousin, Lahana, slowly got to her feet. Her face, arms, torso, and legs were covered in bruises, some deeper than others. Darius fought to keep the rage those bruises inspired from his face, as she answered him. "That bastard took her. He's going to rape her, just like he did to me and some of the others."

Her voice was stronger than he'd expected. Whereas some of the women were timid and fearful, the others seemed to find their strength in the presence of their rescuers.

"Where?" Darius asked, although if he had to guess, the son of a bitch had taken Tahira to his suite.

Lahana shrugged. "I don't know. Somewhere upstairs."

A young blonde who'd stepped out of her now open cell, touched his arm, getting his attention. "He drugs them before he assaults them. You have to save her."

That was a given. "How long ago did he take her?"

Sorrow filled her pretty blue eyes. "Long enough."

"Shit." He spoke into his watch. "Boss-man?"

"Go," Ian replied.

"Her Highness is upstairs, probably on the second floor." He left out the fact she was most likely in Secada's suite. "I'm going after her." Ignoring the other man's string of curses, Darius turned to Costello, who'd finished coaxing the rest of the women from their cells. "Get them out of here—I'll get Tahira."

"I'll go with you," the female sniper said with fire in her eyes.

Darius had never seen her so pissed and almost said yes just to see her unleash a shit-ton of fury on Secada's ass. Instead, he shook his head and started for the stairs. "No. Romeo can't take care of all of them by himself—especially with the chance of crossfire. Get them out of here. I'll get Tahira and head for the exfil."

Knowing he was right, Costello immediately but reluctantly agreed. "Fine, but if you run into trouble, you better holler."

"Will do."

Leaving his teammates to do what they did best, Darius took the stairs two at a time. When he reached the first floor, he pulled his 9mm handgun from its holster on his hip. While the AK-47 on his back had more firepower, he had more control and accuracy with the pistol. Sweeping it back and forth in front of him, looking for targets, he quickly made his way to the second floor, then paused to listen for any movement beyond the doorway. To give himself a better range of motion, he quickly removed the heavy jacket he'd been wearing for guard duty and left it at the top of the stairs. It would be restrictive in a fight. The moment he stepped into the hall, there was a clap of thunder, followed by the reports of assault rifles and cursing coming through his comms unit. If he hadn't had the unit in his ear, he wouldn't have heard the shots over the loud storm, but it was clear all hell had broken loose. *Shit.*

Taking a left, he stealthily approached Secada's suite, while listening for anyone else moving about the house. It was highly unlikely any of the guards would make their way into the house with all the gunfire outside, but the mission had already gone FUBAR. And Darius had a feeling it was about to get worse, if that was at all possible.

With his weapon up and ready to fire, he gently tried the doorknob. No sense in kicking it in if it was already unlocked. The knob turned. Taking a steadying breath, Darius shoved the door open, stepped inside, and scanned the room, the muzzle of his gun always aimed in the same direction as his gaze.

His heart and stomach sank. Tahira was unconscious and naked on the big bed, her legs splayed open, a nasty bruise on her face, and her hair in disarray. Semen and blood painted the insides of her thighs and the sheet between them. He was too late.

But she was alone.

Movement to his left had Darius pivoting but not fast enough. Wearing only pants, Secada dove out the open bathroom doorway and tackled him. The two men tumbled to the floor, with Darius landing on his back with the AK-47 between him and the floor. His breath was knocked out of him as his handgun went flying across the room. Secada smashed his fist into Darius's face. He would feel the pain later, but Darius was running on adrenaline and rage. He blocked the next punch before it made contact. Grabbing the back of Secada's skull, Darius pulled him closer and head-butted him. Taking advantage of the stars the other man had to be seeing, Darius flipped him over and reversed their positions, but Secada recovered fast. They struggled, each trying to get the upper hand. Darius was surprised at the other man's strength, but the cartel lieutenant was no match for the retired Navy SEAL. Two jabs to the bastard's nose broke it, then sent the shards up into his brain.

Panting, Darius relaxed back on his heels, Secada's dead eyes staring up at him. "I hope you went straight to hell, asshole."

He stood and didn't give the other man a second thought as he rushed over to the bed. Tahira was still unconscious—probably from whatever drug Secada had given her, since the bruise on her face didn't seem bad enough to have knocked her out. Grabbing a blanket from where it'd been tossed to the side, Darius gently wrapped her abused body up in it, then picked her up in his arms. He had to get her out of there quickly but decided to take a moment to afford her some decency and warmth.

Swiftly carrying her out into the hallway, he headed for Diaz's master bedroom, snatching his own jacket from the top of the backstairs. The drug czar's widow was about Tahira's size and was about to donate some clothes.

He paused inside the suite, looking for a place to put her down—definitely not on the bed with the dead drug lord. There was a sitting area in front of an unlit gas fireplace across the room, and Darius laid the unconscious woman down on a chaise lounge.

He tenderly brushed a few strands of hair from her face, rage filling him when he got a better look at the swollen bruise on her cheek. Three small, oval discolorations along her right jaw and one on her left were just the right size to be made by fingertips, and Darius was tempted to go back to Secada's room and cut the fucker's dick off and shove it down his throat. Two reasons prevented him from doing so: Secada wouldn't feel a thing, and Darius was in a hurry. He didn't even have time to clean Tahira up, though he was afraid if he did, she'd be mortified when she realized he'd done so. Would that be worse than needing to clean herself? He didn't know.

"I'm sorry I didn't get there fast enough, Princess," he murmured, guilt plaguing his gut.

Hesitant to leave her for even a moment, Darius forced himself to find some clothing for her. Entering the suite's walk-in closet, he selected a pair of designer, dark-green, velour sweatpants, a long-sleeved, black knit shirt, and a deep eggplant-colored, zip-up sweater. None of it matched, but fashion wasn't a concern right now.

Next, he found some black socks, sneakers, and a warm parka, just in case. He'd be carrying her the half mile to the exfil site, but it might take longer than planned, and he wanted to reduce the risk of her getting hypothermia between the rain and cold temperatures if those plans changed. The blanket would have to do for now. It was dark blue and would keep her from being lit up like a Christmas tree if the beam of a flashlight hit her. Even a bolt of lightning would reflect white or light-colored fabric.

Finding a duffel bag on a shelf at the back of the closet, he stuffed the garments and shoes into it. There wasn't enough time to dress her now, but he'd take care of it as soon as he could. And since everything had already gone to shit on this mission, he wanted to have clothes for her in case they ran into another snafu.

As he bent down to pick her up again, an explosion

rocked the house under his feet, and Darius's eyes went wide. "What the fuck?"

It was then Darius realized he didn't hear any of the team chatter. His hand flew to his ear. At some point, probably in the fight with Secada, Darius had lost his earpiece. There was no time to go back and look for it. He glanced at his wrist and felt a small measure of relief. While he wouldn't be able to hear what his teammates were saying, they could still hear him.

Leaving Tahira, Darius hurried over to one of the windows and peaked out through the blinds.

Shit.

It was a war zone out there. Bright bursts of light indicated bullets being discharged from three directions. The bodies of several of the cartel's thugs lay where they'd been hit as they'd exited the bunkhouse. A fire was burning near the house below Diaz's bedroom, and a second explosion shook the house again. Someone had something stronger than handguns and rifles out there, and it wasn't coming from his own team. *Double shit!*

It would be impossible for Darius to cross the property into the wooded area that would eventually lead him to the Bravo exfil site, while carrying Tahira. In fact, even without her, it would still be too risky. That meant he had to come up with a plan C. What else was new? During his SEAL and Trident missions, things weren't truly FUBAR until at least a plan D or even E was needed.

"Batman to Lead One," he said, holding his wrist to his mouth. He paused for a moment, listening for a response before his brain kicked in, reminding him his earpiece was gone. "Batman to Lead One or Tampa Base. I've lost my comms. If you can hear me, I have the princess. Can't make it to Exfil Bravo. Will head to Rendezvous Oscar. Repeat, I have the princess, and we're heading to Rendezvous Oscar for exfil."

Hopefully, Ian and the others had heard him and would know he'd be taking Tahira to the orphanage, where Sister Patrice would be able to hide them, if necessary, until the team could get them out of there safely. The orphanage was about ten miles through mostly thick woods, which would give them cover in case they encountered any bad guys along the way. A ten-mile hike was not a problem for Darius, but the storm and Tahira's unconsciousness would slow him down. It was a toss-up if things would be a little easier had she been awake and able to run, but this wouldn't be the first time Darius had needed to exit a mission in a hurry while carrying someone.

Lifting the strap of the duffel bag over his head, he hung it from his shoulder, across his chest. He then adjusted the sling of his AK-47 and brought the weapon around to his right hip. Next, Darius pushed a button on his watch which would give him an open connection to his team without interfering with their transmissions. If things went further down the rabbit hole, at least they'd be able to hear him.

"Stop fucking jinxing yourself, you idiot," he muttered.

Turning back to Tahira, he quickly lifted her up and placed her over his left shoulder. It was a far cry from being a dignified way to carry a member of royalty, but fuck protocol. He needed at least one hand free to open doors and shoot if he had to. After making certain she was balanced correctly and wouldn't slip if he had to make any sudden moves, he hurried to the door leading to the hallway. After a quick check that nobody was out there, he opened the door all the way and stepped out. There was a sunroom downstairs at the opposite side of the house with reinforced French doors leading to the large flower and shrubbery garden Diaz's wife loved to enjoy. It would provide Darius with some cover until he was able to sprint across the manicured lawn to a small gate in the stone wall surrounding the property. From there, it was only two or three hundred feet before they'd reach the tree line that would provide a moderate measure of safety as they trekked through the woods.

Descending the stairs with one hand on the back of Tahira's thighs and the other holding his rifle ready, Darius could hear the gun battle again. The explosions must have blown out a few of the first-floor windows. As he reached the foyer, the front door flew open and two men with guns didn't wait to see if there was an enemy within sight. Their expressions of surprise were met with a hail of bullets from Darius's gun. The men never had a chance to fire their own weapons before death dug its greedy claws into them as they dropped to the floor.

Without hesitation, Darius moved quickly down a small hallway that led to the sunroom. With the glass walls and ceiling now surrounding them, it would really suck if one of those grenades or rockets someone was using came too close. Darius and Tahira would be cut to ribbons.

The torrential rains pounded against the glass, as if a thousand horses were in a stampede. It was almost deafening, but not enough to block out the thunder and continuing gunfire which seemed to still be coming from the other side of the property. Hopefully, that meant all the tangos were too busy to notice the retired SEAL carrying an unconscious woman.

Trying the handle of the door leading to the garden, he was relieved to find it unlocked. Peering through the darkness of the night, he didn't see anyone who might be in his way. Just to the left of the door was some equipment that must have been left by the gardener. A small, black tarp covered a portion of the pile. Darius grabbed it and hastily covered Tahira with it. The water-proof material would keep her dry until he could find them a defendable shelter for a few hours to wait out the worst of the storm.

After Darius reaffirmed Tahira was settled securely on his shoulder, he took a deep breath and darted out into the downpour.

CHAPTER THIRTEEN

T he pelting raindrops stung his face and hands, as Darius made his way through the garden, not giving a shit about all the colorful blooms he smashed with his feet along the way. He was grateful he'd covered Tahira with the tarp, since he'd been soaked within seconds of leaving the confines of the mansion, and the horrors it held, behind.

Tahira.

Darius forced his hand holding the AK-47 not to clench in rage. He'd failed her. The beautiful woman he was carrying had been violated in a way no one should ever have to endure. Darius wished he could kill Secada over and over again until the bastard had suffered enough for what he'd done.

His mind flitted to the night he'd surprised her in the kitchen at the Clearwater Beach estate. That was the real woman he'd met that night. Not the princess the public saw. Not the spoiled brat he'd dealt with on prior details. She'd been real that night. No makeup, no designer clothes, no sign of a privileged life most people could only dream of. When she'd smiled at him before returning to her bedroom, he'd felt it all the way to his toes. He remembered thinking later that it was too bad they came from two different worlds—he would have liked to get to know her better and maybe take her on a date. But Tahira would always be in the spotlight, surrounded by the chaos that came with being a crown princess, while Darius was the furthest thing from royalty one could get.

At the end of the garden, using a large shrub to conceal their silhouettes, he scanned the expanse and surrounding area between where he stood and the stone wall. The battle still raged on the other side of the property, and Darius wondered why this end seemed to be clear. Not that he would complain.

After checking his grip on Tahira's motionless body, Darius took off at a dead run. The muddied soil of the lush lawn tried to suck his feet into its depths as he zig-zagged across it, making each step more difficult than the last. Moving in a straight line made a person an easy target, and even though it seemed they were in the clear, Darius wouldn't risk going against his training.

Reaching the gate, Darius cursed when he saw a lock and chain keeping it shut. Pointing the muzzle of the automatic weapon at the lock, he fired a burst of bullets, destroying the hinderance keeping him from getting Tahira to safety. Hopefully the storm and gunfight on the other side of the property had muffled his shots.

He kicked open the gate, then glanced back to make sure they hadn't been spotted. Water rolled down his brow into his eyes, and he shook his head to clear his vision.

It was a short run to the tree line, but the mud he was now dealing with was worse than before. Each sinking step was a struggle to stay upright and moving. He'd give anything to have his favorite military boots right then. The construction boots he had on had been part of his cover.

He'd arrived at the Diaz compound with summer clothes. Apparently, the spoiled rich kid, "Glenn Hamilton," thought the entire continent of South America was sunny and warm all year round. Members of the cartel had laughed at the *estúpido gringo*. Carlos had been ordered to take him shopping the next day for more appropriate clothing.

Once he hit the edge of the woods, the ground was harder, and it was easier to maneuver. He jogged into the shadows of the tall canopy of pine, eucalyptus, and willow trees for about a hundred yards before, ducking behind a thick, bark-covered trunk and peering around to see if he'd been spotted or followed. There was no sign of life, human or otherwise. The wildlife was probably hunkered down against the teeming fury released by Mother Nature.

Turning his head into Tahira's hip, he put his mouth as close to his watch as possible. "Batman to Home Base. The princess and I are clear, heading to Rendezvous Oscar. Blow the place to kingdom come."

A few seconds ticked by as Darius wondered if his transmission had been received. Without his earpiece, he could only hope Egghead and Cookie were just making certain all the good guys were also out of the blast zone. Once they got the go-ahead, they'd send a signal to a satellite they were patched into, which would then set off the explosives Darius had hidden throughout the mansion the day before. Some might think it was overkill, but the less evidence a US-sanctioned agent had spent the past few months living there, the better. It had been a relief to know Diaz had sent his wife and kids out of the country, and Secada had dismissed the innocent housekeeping and kitchen staff for the day. Darius would have hated for any of them to have been killed in the destructive maelstrom taking place.

Just when he thought they hadn't heard him in Tampa, a tremendous roar filled the night, drowning out everything but its destruction of the house. Maybe he'd used a little too much C4 because even from that distance, he could feel the scorching heat of the fire.

Letting the rifle hang from its sling, Darius reached back and found Tahira's wrist and quickly checked her pulse. She was already ice cold, and her heart rate was too fast. *Damn it.* He could lose her to hypothermia before they reached the orphanage. It was too far a hike in the crappy conditions to risk it. He had to find shelter for the night and get her dressed and warm. Hopefully, she'd be awake by the time the weather cleared. If his teammates had gotten his transmissions, they'd start working their way from the orphanage toward the Diaz property, looking for him and Tahira when they failed to show up right away. But the team knew he'd do what anyone of them would have done and that was get the unconscious woman dry and protect her until it was safe for them to travel again.

Turning his back on the fiery ruins, he set out to find a shelter to hunker down in for a few hours.

Chapter Fourteen

Tahira clawed her way toward the light, desperate to escape the clutches of the demon intent on keeping her in the pitch-black abyss she'd fallen into. The heat was unbearable, her body sweating profusely as she struggled to get away from the heaviness pinning her down. Her mouth was parched, and her body ached, but she ignored the discomfort. She had to run away, if only she could just get to her feet. But where would she run to? She couldn't see anything in the darkness surrounding her.

A deafening explosion had her nearly jumping out of her skin. She screamed, but it was cut off when a hand clamped down over her mouth, making it even more difficult to breathe. A damp, putrid stench of decay assaulted her nares.

Make me hard, bitch.

One of her hands broke free of its confinement, and she struck out, trying to force her captor to release her.

Make me hard . . .

"Princess . . . shh . . . it's—"

She swung, kicked, and thrashed harder against whomever was holding her back, desperate to get away from

. . . from whom? She couldn't remember but knew she had to escape. She bared her teeth and sunk them into the hand covering her mouth as best she could. Blood tinged her tongue.

"God damn it," the man hissed in a low, insistent voice. "Tahira! It's Darius Knight. Stop fucking biting me."

The words penetrated her mind, and every muscle in her body froze. *Darius? Oh, thank God!* She quickly unclenched her jaw, releasing him.

She blinked several times, and it was then she realized her eyes had been shut the whole time. Her gaze darted around as she tried to figure out their surroundings. As her vision adjusted to the dimness, there was just enough light for her to figure out they weren't in a house or other building. She was lying on something hard. The air around them was bone chilling and damp, and a shiver chased away the last of the oppressive heat she'd felt during her nightmare. There was a tarp or something between her body and the ground.

Stretched out behind her, Darius's body relaxed. One of his legs was draped heavily over her thighs and his arm crossed her torso, immobilizing her. While his shirt appeared to be dry, his cargo pants were damp. He slowly moved off her, as if making sure she wasn't going to start fighting again, before he completely pulled away. She missed the warmth of his body immediately.

"Are you okay?" His voice remained low, but this time, it was calming and filled with concern. "I didn't hurt you, did I?"

Hurt her? She didn't think he had—however, she'd obviously hurt him. But as she rolled onto her back, Tahira realized she was aching—in a lot of places. From head to toe, her body felt like she'd been in a car accident or had tumbled down a rocky hill, although nothing seemed to be broken. She grimaced as she gently tried to get comfortable, then looked up to find Darius lying on his side, a few inches away, staring down at her. It'd been months since she'd seen him, and she'd almost forgotten how handsome he was—almost. His emerald-green-eyed gaze searched her face, and a mustache and beard covered his upper lip and jawline. She couldn't recall ever seeing him with more than a five o'clock shadow and decided she didn't care for the long, scruffy hair covering his face. Maybe if it was trimmed.

His brow was furrowed, and she almost reached out to soothe it with her fingers.

A torrential downpour registered in her mind, but they were obviously sheltered from the storm. "Where are—"

"Shh. Keep your voice down. I don't think anyone followed us, and it's unlikely they'd hear us over the rain, but we can't take any chances the bad guys might be looking for us."

Bad guys? Memories flooded her mind in short bursts, making it difficult to focus on just one. The cruise. Jamaica. The waterfalls. Men with guns. Her bodyguards shot. Waking up in an underground prison with her cousins and other women. Struggling against someone's grip. Pain. Then nothing but darkness.

"Oh my God," she whispered. "My cousins—"

"Are fine. Ian, Amar, and the rest of the team rescued them and flew them to safety on a helicopter."

Her eyes narrowed with confusion. Why wasn't she with them? She'd been in the cells with them, so it stood to reason she would've been rescued with them, right?

As if he'd read her mind, Darius said, "You weren't in the cell area when we went to rescue everyone. I had to take a different route to get you out of there. We're going to meet up with everyone after the storm lets up."

As though it was punctuating his statement, a bolt of lightning blazed outside for a split second, showing her they were in some sort of small grotto. They were back far enough from the entrance, and around a slight curve in the hollowed rock, so that the pouring rain she now heard wouldn't get them wet. She shivered, pulling the unfamiliar jacket and blanket covering her closer around her body.

After the lightening's accompanying thunder quieted, Darius continued. "Do you remember being taken to another part of the mansion?"

"Mansion? We were in a mansion?" Flashes of a large, unfamiliar, well-decorated house came to her, but they were mixed with rooms from the palace and vacation homes she'd grown up in. She was having trouble filtering her thoughts and making sense out of it all.

"Yes. In Argentina. I was working undercover in a drug cartel when you and your cousins arrived a few nights ago. I couldn't let you see me until it was time to rescue you and the others. I was worried you'd give away my cover if you recognized me."

He was right—even with his thick facial hair, she would have known him immediately and been unable to hide a reaction. But something he'd just said seemed odd to her—however, she couldn't zero on it. "Where are we now?"

"A cave I managed to find just before the hail started coming down, thank God. From the size of them, we both would've been knocked out cold." He hitched a thumb toward the wall behind their heads. "We're about eleven clicks—sorry, kilometers—northwest of where we're supposed to meet the team. Even without the hail, the rain and cooler temperatures were bad enough. I couldn't risk you developing hypothermia in your condition. The ground was also pretty slippery, and I didn't want to drop you."

"You carried me?" Her voice croaked on her words. "How far?"

"Yeah, considering you were unconscious at the time, I

couldn't very well ask you to walk the five kilometers from Diaz's compound to here." He stood and stepped around her. "Hang on. Let me get you some fresh rainwater. You must be thirsty."

Now that he mentioned it, she was parched. Gingerly sitting up, Tahira watched as Darius picked up a huge, green leaf from where it lay on a nearby rock, then strode toward the entrance of the cave. He was wearing black cargo pants, a long-sleeved T-shirt, and hiking boots. She glanced around and wondered if he had a jacket to keep him warm.

As he disappeared around the curve of the rock wall, Tahira assessed her current condition. Under the jacket and blanket, she wore someone else's sweater, knit shirt, velour lounge pants, socks, and trainers, or as the Americans called them, sneakers. While she would've been ripped apart by the press for the awful, fashion-less color combination, the clothing was much warmer than her bikini and wrap had been. The trainers were a half size too large, but she'd survive in them.

As she sat back against the wall, she realized there was something soft and warm folded up behind her. She looked closer and discovered it was a fleece-lined jacket that had pillowed her head as she'd slept. It obviously belonged to Darius, and Tahira's heart melted a little when she realized he'd given up his warmth and comfort for her. The black jacket she'd been using had probably come from the same place he'd found the other clothes for her. She briefly wondered who they belonged to, but it really didn't matter. There were many other things to be concerned about.

Wringing her aching hands together, she felt jagged edges along her formerly-manicured fingernails. Slowly, she ran her hands over her arms and shoulders, finding several tender spots. Her face was next, and she hissed when her fingers touched her left cheek and jaw. The aches were almost unbearable. What the hell had happened to her? She struggled to remember, but it was all a blur.

She took further stock of her injuries. Her breasts, ribs, back, thighs, and groin hurt. After making certain Darius wasn't coming back yet, Tahira lowered her hand under the jacket, between her legs, and brushed it over her mound. Pain flared, and nausea roiled. Her body trembled, and she slammed her eyes shut. *What—*

"Here. Drink this."

Tahira yanked her hand back, and her eyes flew open. She hadn't heard him return, holding the large leaf and using it as a makeshift bowl.

"It's rainwater, so it shouldn't bother your stomach. Open your mouth."

He eased it forward toward her mouth, careful not to spill any. Tahira leaned forward and parted her lips. Darius gently tilted the tip of the leaf, and cool water trickled onto her dehydrated tongue. It was so refreshing, she greedily drank it all, then glanced up at Darius, her cheeks reddening in the dim light, when she realized what she'd done. "I am so sorry. I should have left some for you."

The corners of his mouth angled upward. "It's okay, Tahira. You needed it more than I did, and there's plenty of rain coming down. Do you want anymore?"

Licking her lips, she shook her head, rattling her still foggy brain. "No, maybe in a little bit, but I really need to . . . um . . . to go . . . uh . . ."

Reading her thoughts, he chuckled wryly. "Well, unfortunately, the ladies' room is out of order, but you can go behind that boulder over there . . ." He pointed at the large rock against the opposite wall, halfway between them and the entrance to the cave. ". . . and take care of things. I'll get myself some water while you're doing that. Just let me know when you're done."

"Okay." While it hadn't been often in her life when she'd urinated somewhere that didn't have a toilet, she wasn't averse to doing it now. Her bladder was ready to burst. She tried to clench her thighs, but a sharp discomfort she felt between them forced her to relax her muscles again. Maybe she'd gotten a urinary tract infection—considering the conditions she'd been in and the limited amount of food and water the captors had given the women, it wasn't an impossibility.

Holding out his hand, Darius helped her stand and made sure she was steady on her feet before releasing her. She was grateful for his assistance because her head had spun a few times before she was able to right herself again. Now that she was moving, the aches in her body felt ten times worse. She wanted to know what had happened to her but feared the answer. Her mind was in self-preservation mode, and she needed a few more minutes before she questioned Darius. She'd a deep suspicion she wasn't going to like his responses.

Stepping behind the boulder, she waited until Darius disappeared from her line of sight. Leaning back against the wall for support, she widened her stance and pushed the waistline of the lounge pants down past her knees. She squatted down and waited for her body to relax so it could relieve itself. When the stream finally started, Tahira gasped at the harsh, hot sting that shot through her. A few tears seeped from her closed eyelids and rolled down her cheek. She clenched to stop urinating but that only made the burning worse.

Her legs trembled from being in a squat position. Tahira opened her eyes and looked down, but in the darkness, she could barely see anything, until several bolts of lightning lit up the sky and the grotto, in rapid succession, followed by cracks of thunder. The brightness lasted long enough for

Tahira to make out streaks of dried blood on the inside of her thighs.

Make me hard, bitch.

Secada. Struggling. Drugs. A bed. Fear. Force. Pain. Resignation. Darkness.

Tahira turned her head and retched the acidic, watery contents of her stomach. The heinous memories bombarded her mind and senses. Her head swam in a brutal ocean of despair. She'd been violated, in a way no one should ever experience, by that vile bastard. His mouth, tongue, and hands had roamed over her skin, as she'd lain there, unable to move. Unable to protest. Unable to fight. Her treasured virginity had been ripped from her core and tossed aside as if it had been a worthless piece of garbage.

A blood-curling wail of grief was wrenched from her lungs. Her life was ruined. She could never marry. Never have a child. When she met her soulmate, she would only be able to love him from afar. If anyone found out, she would be publicly disgraced.

Her rapist had not only stolen her veil of womanhood, but also her future. Her heart. Her soul.

CHAPTER FIFTEEN

After the improvised bowl was refilled from the pouring rain, Darius retracted his now soaking wet, injured hand and brought it toward his mouth. Damn, that hurt. In addition to a few small puncture marks, the area surrounding the bite mark was already starting to bruise. At least it was his non-dominant hand.

He took slow gulps, making sure he didn't drink too quickly and give himself cramps. That was the last thing he needed on top of everything else that had gone FUBAR.

Smiling, he let out a small snort. Nowadays, every time the acronym FUBAR came to mind, he thought of a furry Belgian Malinois with big ears and a derpy grin. FUBAR, formerly known as Glock, was a training failure from Trident's new K9 division—he'd been more interested in being a goofball than a badass. Babs had fallen for the dog and adopted him after he'd been dropped from the last class. His name had already stuck with everyone, and it fit him perfectly, so she'd kept it. He now hung out in the TS garage where his new mom was their mechanic when she wasn't piloting their Sikorsky MH-X Silent Hawk—a very expensive, stealth helicopter.

Not knowing if his team could hear him, Darius still tried to give them an update through his watch's transmitter. As soon as the worst of the storm was over, he and Tahira would head out. He hated making her trudge through the rain, mud, and underbrush, but the faster he got them to the orphanage, the better he'd feel. She was going to need treatment—at some point he was going to have to tell her what happened back in the bedroom he'd found her in. She would need to be treated for any possible STDs and be given a morning-after pill in case of pregnancy.

When Darius had found the cave over five hours ago, he'd been able to dress Tahira and make her as comfortable as possible. He doubted she'd ever slept on the ground in her life. After shaking the rain off his parka, he'd turned it inside out and tucked it under her head. While the tarp had given them some protection against the cold, damp earth, he'd spooned in behind her, using his body heat, her jacket, and the blanket to keep her warm. While he'd doubted any members of the cartels were in the woods looking for them, he'd remained awake while Tahira had slept, watching over her.

While the storm raged overhead, he'd worried about how much of the drugs she'd been given were still coursing through her system and when she'd wake up. Then he worried about what she'd remember after her mind cleared. He still couldn't shake the image of her abused body lying on that bastard's bed. He would give anything to go back in time to a point when he could've saved her before it had been too late. His hands clenched, and once again he wished he could kill Secada for a second time for what the bastard had done to the innocent woman.

A billion joules of energy crackled across the sky, illuminating the night, followed by several more streaking bolts that impacted the trees and ground less than a quarter mile away from their shelter. The corresponding cracks of thunder were close to deafening. Standing under the overhang at the cave's entrance, Darius marveled at the strength of the tempest Mother Nature had summoned. Ever since he was a kid, he'd loved thunderstorms, while his younger brother and sister had hated them. He recalled how, when Levi and Barrie had been eight and six, respectively, he'd tried to convince them it was just God bowling, but they never fell for it.

As the thunder dwindled away, a noise behind Darius had him turning his head to listen over the downpour. "Princess?"

A sharp cry pierced the air, and Darius drew his sidearm as he ran toward Tahira. Rounding the boulder, he stopped short when he saw she was alone—alone and crumbled into a ball where she remained squatting. Her long, black hair hung down over her face, which she'd covered with her hands, but they couldn't muffle her wails of despair. The curdling stench of vomit, combined with urine, reached his nose. There was only one thing that would cause this kind of reaction from her—she'd remembered. How much, he didn't know, but she'd remembered enough to know she'd been raped.

Holstering his gun, Darius crouched down. Wary of how she would respond, he kept some distance between them and didn't reach out to touch her. "Princess?" he said softly.

She didn't answer him. Instead she rocked back and forth, sobbing and keening. The sweatpants were down past her knees, but between her position, her arms crossed over her lower abdomen, and the dimness of their surroundings, Darius couldn't see anything that would embarrass her. However, another flash of lightening showed the bloody streaks on her thighs. Damn it. He wished he'd had time to clean her up, but it hadn't been a priority at the time.

He raised his voice a little louder but kept his tone soothing, as if speaking to a spooked horse. "Tahira? Sweetheart, are you in pain?"

A violent nod of her head morphed into a shake.

"Do you remember what happened?"

Her only response was to cry harder. Each tear that raced down her cheek carved another bit of regret into his soul. Although, by the time he'd found out Secada had taken her, it had already been too late, Darius still felt as if he'd failed her. He'd sworn to protect her and fallen short of his goal, something he'd never forgive himself for.

Slowly reaching out, he gently brushed her hair back over her left shoulder. "Tahira, I know there's nothing I can do to change what happened. I just want to comfort you, if you'll let me. May I hold you? Can I help you stand so you can pull up your pants? I won't look. I just want to help."

She grasped his arm as if it were a lifeline to keep her from drowning in despair. Sobbing, she used her other hand to wipe her nose. When he was certain she was ready, Darius stood and slowly helped her up. Her body trembled as he held her shoulders in support while she pulled the sweatpants back over her slender hips. As soon as she was decent, she leaned into him, threw her arms around his neck, and bawled.

Not knowing what else he could do, Darius tucked his arm under her knees and picked her up. She clung to him as he carried her back to their makeshift bed. Using the wall for support, he lowered himself to the tarp, settling her onto his lap and holding her close. "Shh. You're safe, Princess, and that bastard will never hurt you or anyone else ever again. Shh."

Pulling back just far enough to lift her gaze to his face,

she stared at him in horror. "Y-you kn-know what . . . what . . ." While searching for whatever words she was looking for, she hiccuped.

God, he hated this. Unwelcome tears pooled in his own eyes as his heart broke for her. His throat grew thick, and he had to force his words past it. "I was too late. I'm so sorry . . ." She wasn't the only one trying to find the right thing to say. "I—"

"You saw—"

He shook his head, not knowing exactly what she was referring to—it could be either the rape itself or her nude body. Compassionately, he answered for both. "It was over before I got there. I covered you and then grabbed these clothes, so I could get you out of there. I had to hurry. I'm sorry I didn't have time to clean you up." Yeah, he was leaving out a lot of information there, but there was stuff she didn't need to know just yet. Later, after she calmed down, if she wanted more details, he'd tell her as best he could with as little gore as possible.

"Oh, my God! It is true. He—he r-raped me, right? The—the blood?" Before he could answer, she threw her head back and wailed, balling up the front of his shirt with her fists. "Please tell me it is not true! Darius, please!"

Her begging twisted his gut into knots. As much as he wished he could say it never happened, he couldn't lie to her. His hand ran up and down her back, trying to soothe her. "I'm sorry, Tahira. I'm so sorry. But it's over. When we get you back to the States, we'll take you to the hospital to get checked out and—"

"No! You do not understand!" She pushed against his chest—not to get away from him but to emphasize her words. "My life is over—"

"It's not—"

"It is! I-I can never marry now." Letting go of his shirt, she buried her face in her hands and cried harder. "I can never marry!"

Confusion washed over him as her words tumbled through his mind. Why would she think she could never get married? He'd never known anyone who'd been raped—at least, to his knowledge—and wasn't certain if this was a normal reaction so soon after the assault. Pain, grief, disbelief, anger, embarrassment—those emotions he'd expected. But why it would affect her ability to marry was lost on him. "Yes, you can—"

"No!" Dropping her hands to her lap, she took a deep, ragged breath before continuing. "You do not understand our culture, Darius. I will no longer be a—a v-virgin on my wedding night. In—in my country, women can be publicly ostracized by their husbands if they are not pure on their wedding night. I will bring shame to—to my family. To my crown. I will be shunned by our people."

He was dumbfounded. How could someone blame her, or anyone else for that matter, for being raped? Darius would never understand that whole "she asked for it because of the way she was dressed" or similar bullshit explanation. And any man who was lucky enough to win Tahira's heart would be nothing but a fucking bastard if he announced to the world she wasn't a virgin on their wedding night. "But it wasn't your fault, Tahira."

"It does not matter, Darius. To many, it will not matter if it was my fault or not. I will be shamed either way."

Resting her forehead on his shoulder, she sobbed. His T-shirt absorbed her hot tears, which scorched his skin. Darius tightened his arm around her waist and just held her, unable to find any other words to console her. Somehow, after ten or fifteen minutes had passed, she'd cried herself to sleep—although the adrenaline crash and the drugs still in her system had probably helped.

Darius left her on his lap until pins and needles ran down his legs. Moving slowly, he lowered her to the tarp and tucked his parka under her head again. He covered her with her jacket before stretching out behind her and pulling the blanket over them both. Spooning her, he gave her what little comfort and warmth he could. He just wished there was something else he could do to help ease her pain.

CHAPTER SIXTEEN

"Tahira? Princess, I need you to wake up. The worst of the storm has passed. We need to get moving."

She fought to remain sleeping, unwilling to face her new reality, but Darius insisted she awaken. He gently shook her shoulder. "Tahira? I'll carry you, if necessary, but I'd rather have both hands free if we run into trouble."

Trouble. Her entire life was in trouble now. How could she return to Timasur and let her father choose her husband? She wouldn't even be able to choose a man to marry, knowing full well the union would crumble mere hours after the ceremony. And she couldn't confess to her parents *why* she couldn't marry. They'd be devastated. They were undoubtedly worried sick since learning she'd been kidnapped. Maybe Amar or Ian had already contacted her parents to let them know she was alive and no longer in the hands of her captors.

"Princess?" It was apparent from his tone he knew she'd heard him.

Sighing, she rolled onto her back but kept her eyes shut. "I am awake. There is no need to carry me, Darius."

"How are you feeling? Physically, I mean."

Because after her breakdown earlier, it was clear she wasn't faring well emotionally and wouldn't be for a long time. In fact, she was surprised she'd slept at all without any nightmares. Somehow, she'd found comfort and safety in Darius's arms. While she expected to feel embarrassed after having told him about her rape and loss of virginity, she didn't. While he was protecting and comforting her, he wasn't treating her like a helpless waif. Since the night she'd asked him to call her by her first name, she felt as if he'd been seeing her in a different light. She felt like they were equals. It was similar to what she experienced in Ian and Angie's presence. While they had to defer to her royal status in public, in private, she was on par with their friends and family members, and it was a feeling she enjoyed.

Tahira blinked until his face came into focus. He was kneeling next to her, concern filling his eyes. She swallowed and tried to keep from crying again. "I am sore all over, but I will be able to walk."

Nodding, Darius held out his hand. "That's my girl. You're tough, and you'll get through this, but first let's get the hell out of Argentina, hmm?"

She placed her hand in his and let him help her to her feet, groaning as her stiff muscles protested. Picking up her jacket, Darius held it for her to slip her arms into it. After drawing the zipper up to her neck, she turned to see him pull on his own parka. The large, semi-automatic rifle she'd seen earlier went over that, and she doubted that was the only weapon he had with him. With his dark hair, scruffy beard, and valiant determination, Darius appeared every bit the warrior she knew he would be if danger crossed their paths. He would do everything in his power to get her to safety, and she trusted him with her life.

The last thing he grabbed was the tarp. After shaking the

dirt from it, he used a knife to cut a large square from it. After tucking the knife and smaller section into his pocket, he folded the rest of the tarp in half, then draped it over her head and back. "It's still raining. The drier you are, the warmer you'll be."

"What about you?"

A small smile appeared under his facial hair. "After spending half my Navy SEAL BUD/s training in the cold ocean, this is a walk in the park, Princess. Don't worry about me." He glanced toward the front of the cave before his gaze returned to her. "I need you to promise me something, though. If I tell you to do anything out there—be quiet, get down, run, anything—promise me you'll do it without hesitation. I need to know you'll obey me if things go FUBAR out there."

His request wasn't unfamiliar to her. Bodyguard obedience, in times of danger, had been drilled into her since she'd been little. She knew any wavering in her response to their orders could result in herself or one of her guards being hurt, or worse, killed. She tilted her head. "I will do as I am told, Darius, that will not be a problem, but I do have one question."

"What's that?"

"What is fubar?"

The corners of his mouth lifted again, and she wished she could see the dimples she knew were there. A low chuckle rumbled from his massive chest. "It's an acronym often used in the military and law enforcement. It means messed up beyond all recognition, and that's the polite way of saying it."

It wasn't difficult to figure out which word he'd replaced, and she thought it was sweet he'd curbed his language for her —not that she hadn't been exposed to cursing before, but the people she knew did not use vulgarities in the presence of royalty, especially in public.

"Then you have nothing to worry about. If things go . . . FUBAR . . ." It was a funny thing to say and almost drew a giggle from her. ". . . I will follow your orders immediately."

"Good. And I want you to drink some more water to stay hydrated. Do you need to go and take care of anything before we head out?"

She knew what he was asking, but she had no desire to urinate again. Not if she had to deal with that burning pain again. Later, she would have no choice, but for now, she wanted to put it off for as long as possible. "No. I am ready."

Following him to the front of the cave, she waited while he refilled the leaf. He handed it to her to drink, then pulled out the section of the tarp he'd cut off. He rinsed it off in the rain. Stepping outside, he snatched a bunch of leaves, like the one she was holding, from a nearby plant and then cut a section of narrow vine that was clinging to the outer walls of the cave. Bringing everything back to her, he gave her the piece of tarp. "Hold that open for me."

When she complied, he laid the leaves on top of the tarp, overlapping them several times. Once that was done, he took it from her and held it under the rain again. It finally made sense what he'd done. It was a pouch that would hold water for their journey, since the rain wouldn't last much longer. Who knew if they'd come across a fresh stream that was safe to drink from?

Folding up the edges, he let the sack fill with water, then closed off the top with his hand. Again, he handed it to her. "Hold it just like that so I can tie off the top." Using the vine, he secured the improvised flask, then tied it to the belt at his lower back.

Readying his rifle, Darius led Tahira into the rain. This was the first look she had of what was outside their shelter. Tall trees, spotted underbrush, and uneven terrain surrounded them. The sun had risen a short time ago, but the clouds and trees hid it from view. They had to walk down a slight hill before the ground leveled out, and Darius held her hand until they reached the bottom.

"Stay behind me. There's no beaten path, so we'll have to make our own. Let me know if you have to take a break for any reason, and I'll find us some cover."

They silently trudged through the mud and foliage at a slow but steady pace. Tahira estimated it was about forty-five minutes before Darius veered to the right and stopped at a fallen tree behind some underbrush. The rain had stopped approximately fifteen minutes prior.

After giving her some of the water from the pouch, he took a few sips himself then secured it again at his waist. "I have to duck behind that tree over there. If you need to, you can take care of your own personal business here. I'll call out before I come back."

A short time later, Tahira had relieved herself, and now she was trying to force the painful flashes of her rape from her mind along with the scalding sensation between her legs. As much as she wanted to get back to civilization and the safety of Timasur or the United States, every step they took brought her toward her unwanted future as a spinster. She tried to focus on how to convince her father to retract his ultimatum. She could tell him the truth, but she couldn't bear to pass her pain on to her parents. They loved her unconditionally, but from the moment she told them of her assault, they would forever see her as a victim. She was damaged, and she feared the heartache and pity she would see in her parents' eyes when they looked at her.

After making sure she was decent, Darius returned. "Here. Eat this." Her eyes narrowed at the brown and ivory lump he held out to her. "It's a non-poisonous mushroom native to the area. They grow on tree trunks, just above the ground. I peeled off the surface, so it's clean to eat."

With his other hand, he held up a second mushroom, then took a bite out of it. Tahira accepted the large chunk of fungi and nibbled on the meaty flesh. The woodsy flavor exploded on her taste buds, causing her stomach to growl. It had been over twelve hours since she'd eaten her last meal, if it could even be called that. The scant serving of spicy rice and beans had barely been enough to fill her stomach. Right now, the mushroom tasted like the best thing on Earth, and she quickly finished it off. Darius pulled more out of his parka's pocket, handed her another piece, and gestured in the direction they'd been heading earlier. "We'll eat on the way. We've got a lot of ground to cover."

"How do you know we are going in the right direction?"

He tapped his watch with his finger. "This has a ton of features in it—a compass being one of them. I memorized the coordinates to our destination before I went undercover."

Falling in line behind him as he took off again, she remembered something. "When I first woke up after you rescued me, you said you had been undercover in a drug cartel, yes?"

"Yeah, I did." He pointed to the ground on his right side. "Watch your step. There's some scat."

Avoiding the brown lumps of feces from a large animal, she continued, "But if they were a drug cartel, why were we there—my cousins and I and the other women?"

He glanced over his shoulder with a grimace. "Because drugs aren't the only crimes bastards like that deal in to line their pockets—drugs, human trafficking, child pornography, guns, and anything else that they can make money on. Nothing is off limits to most of them. Although, every once in a while, we come across a crime boss with scruples, but it's rare."

They walked in silence for a few minutes, then Darius asked, "Princess, did you really mean what you said earlier?

About being ostracized if it's revealed what happened to you?"

Her eyes widened as she stared at his back. "Yes! Please, Darius, you cannot tell anyone—"

"Shh, Tahira. I'm not going to tell anyone. That's your secret, and I'll take it to the grave if I have to."

Relief filled her. "Thank you."

A few moments passed before he spoke again. "What if you married, your secret was not revealed, and somewhere down the line, you got a divorce? Would you be able to marry again? Is divorce even allowed in Timasur?"

"Yes, divorce is allowed in my country, but it is not as easily done as it is in the United States. I would be allowed to marry again, and my lack of virginity would not be a problem. Why do you ask?"

Darius stopped short and spun around. "What if you and I got married?"

THE WORDS CONTINUED TO TUMBLE OUT OF DARIUS'S MOUTH before he could stop them. "I would keep your secret, and we could divorce a few months later. Then you'd be free to marry a man you fall in love with and not have to worry about not being a virgin."

Tahira's jaw dropped as she stared at him as if he had five heads and was speaking in tongues. Her eyes were even bugging out. Yeah, he'd shocked the shit out of her. Well, that was only fair since he'd shocked the shit out of himself too.

Ever since she'd cried herself to sleep in his arms, his mind had been spinning out of control. He cared for her. Somewhere during the time he'd first been assigned to be her occasional bodyguard, she'd become more than a client or an asset. She'd become a friend, and Darius would do anything to help a friend in need. But suggesting marriage? Yup, that was definitely a first for him. He'd never come close to asking a woman to marry him, not even Sara Ainsley who he'd dated for over eighteen months five years ago, and here he was proposing to Tahira—sort of. It was probably far from the "down on one knee" proposal she'd dreamed of having all her life, but from where he stood, she truly believed that would never happen now anyway.

He had to be insane. There was no way she would agree to this, and it was probably just making things worse for her and super awkward between them. Still, he couldn't seem to stop himself from continuing. "Look, I know it sounds crazy, but think about it. No one would ever have to know it's a marriage of convenience and that we never had sex. We could stay in Clearwater Beach. After a few months, we'll say that we made a mistake and we're getting a divorce but staying friends. Then when you want to get married for real, you're covered. Your husband will know going in that you've been married before, so he'll know not to expect to be . . . to be taking your virginity."

When her fingers covered her mouth, he finally stopped rambling and waited for her to say something.

She shook her head. "Why? Why would you even suggest that? Why would you do that for me?"

At first, he thought she'd been offended by his unexpected offer, but then he saw a mixture of disbelief and gratitude in her watery eyes.

Closing the distance between them, he gently cupped her cheek and thumbed away a tear that had fallen. "Why? Because you've experienced something no woman on Earth should ever have to, Princess. I can't imagine what's going through that pretty head of yours and how you'll deal with the aftermath of what happened to you. But if I could do this one thing to help you heal and have the happy life you deserve with a man you love someday, then I'm willing to do it. It's one less thing you have to worry about."

"But—but, I do not . . . I do not understand. What—what would you get out of it?"

"I said no sex, and I meant it, sweetheart. I wouldn't expect that from you. Not after what you've been through. You save that for the man you fall in love with. As for what I would get out of it—I'd know I did the right thing to help a friend. That I helped save her from the anguish she would be facing if the truth came out or it was assumed you lost your virginity by choice just to have some selfish bastard tell that to the world. I can't put you through that, and I can't have you believing you'll never get married for real. Let me help you, Princess," he pleaded.

Darius knew they needed to get moving again, but this was important. The more he stared into her glistening eyes, the more he knew this was the right thing to do. Despite his earlier uncertainty about the plan, he didn't want her to say no.

"You are not dating anyone? There is no one who will be heartbroken if you do this for me?"

He smiled. "No, I'm not dating anyone, and there's no one out there pining for me. Someday I might get married for real, but probably after I retire from Trident. For now, I want to do this for you, okay? Will you let me?"

Seconds ticked by before Tahira took a long, shaky breath, before slowly letting it out. Rising on her tiptoes, she placed a soft kiss on his cheek. "Thank you, Darius. You do not know how much this means to me. If you are really certain about it, then, yes, I will accept your help. Just promise me that if you change your mind, you will let me know."

Leaning down, Darius brushed his lips across her forehead. "Then it's settled. Now, let's get the hell out of here."

CHAPTER SEVENTEEN

D arius leaned against the wall in the sitting room down the hall from Tahira's hospital room in a secluded and guarded wing. When she'd fallen asleep from exhaustion on the Trident jet, he'd asked Lindsey to watch over her while he jumped into the onboard shower. Once there, he'd stripped out of his wet and dirty clothes, cleaned up, shaved, and put on a clean pair of BDUs, a black tank top, and fleece pullover he'd borrowed from McCabe. There at the hospital, though, it was too warm for the heavier shirt, so he'd removed it a few minutes ago and hung it on the back of a chair.

After Tahira had agreed to his half-baked plan to marry her, they'd trudged through the woods for another two miles or so, before they'd heard ATV motors getting louder as they approached. At first, Darius had grabbed Tahira and hid them both behind some thick foliage, but when he spotted Romeo and Tristian on the first vehicles to pass them, he ran out and flagged down Lindsey and Amar on the next two. Within two hours they'd all rendezvoused with the rest of the team at the orphanage and hightailed it to a private airport to get the hell out of Dodge.

Now, members of both Alpha and Omega teams were scattered about the room, finally giving him some space and solitude after he'd responded with short, terse answers to all their questions since he'd left Tahira's room. King Rajeemh, Queen Azhar, Ian, and Amar were in with the princess, talking about God only knew what. At least he knew what they wouldn't be talking about.

The doctor who'd examined Tahira had been sworn to secrecy about her rape. In addition to being a practicing physician at Tampa General Hospital, the gray-haired man was also on the government's payroll for when patients required covert treatment. In the past, he'd seen numerous members of the FBI, the CIA, Deimos, and other agencies, and high-profile dignitaries who, due to the nature of their injury or illness, and how it'd been obtained, needed to be treated "off the record."

When Dr. René Moreau had arrived in Tahira's private room, minutes after she'd been admitted, the princess had insisted Darius stay with her for the interview and exam, while everyone else had left to give them privacy. Once the three of them were alone, Tahira had given Darius permission to fill the physician in about her assault and the fact she didn't recall much of it.

"From what I understand, Doctor, you'll be able to keep all references to the . . . attack from Her Royal Highness's record." Darius used her title as he'd been instructed to do while in public during his previous stints as her bodyguard. After saying it the first time in a conversation, it was proper to drop the middle word for ease. "If anyone finds out, it will not only have devastating effects on Her Highness and her family but will also cause an international uproar."

The bespectacled man frowned. "I can certainly keep it

quiet, but who else knows?"

"Her Highness, me, you, and the bastard who did it. Since I sent him to Hell, just us three know now. I expect you'll keep it that way. It didn't happen on US soil, either, and where it did occur, the authorities have no clue what happened and never will, so there won't be any investigation that Her Highness will be drawn into."

"So, we don't have to worry about a trial then. Fine—my lips are sealed. I'll have to test for STDs, but I'll do the pathology myself, so no one else needs to be involved. I'll also come back with a dose of Levonorgestrel—the morning-after pill to prevent any pregnancy . . ." His gaze shifted to his patient. ". . . that is, if that's what you want, Your Highness."

Still looking overwhelmed, Tahira blinked several times before answering. "Forgive me, Doctor, but I was not paying full attention. What did you say?"

Instead of letting the physician respond, Darius stepped closer to Tahira and took her small hand in his large one. His gaze met hers, silently telling her he'd support whatever decision she made. "There's a medication he can give you—a pill. If there's even the slightest chance you could be pregnant . . . the medication would stop it."

"N-no!" Her eyes went wide, horror filling her voice. "You are talking about an—an abortion. I-I cannot, Darius. It is against our religion. Please understand . . . I cannot. Please."

With the doctor behind him, Darius sighed and placed his other hand on her forehead, smoothing her hair back in a calming motion. He lowered his voice so the other man wouldn't overhear him. "Shh. It's okay, Tahira. It's okay. You don't have to do anything you don't want to do." He paused, then said, "I know this is personal, but where are you in your monthly cycle?"

As she thought about it, her gaze had flickered away for a moment, then returned to his face. A splash of pink had appeared on her pale cheeks, giving them a livelier color that'd been absent the past few days. "That . . . that time of the month, as your American women say, is due in a few days."

"Okay." He quickly did the calculations, trying to remember if that was good or bad, then glanced at the doctor for confirmation, but his words were directed at Tahira. "So that means you have about another two weeks or so before you ovulate again?" The doctor shrugged and moved his outstretched hand back and forth in front of him in a more-or-less gesture. Darius decided to go with the "more" option and turned back to Tahira. "That means there's a very, very slim chance you're pregnant. But if you are, we'll deal with it, okay? I promise. One step at a time."

Her eyes welled up, causing his gut to clench. "I-I am so sorry, Darius.

He shook his head. "Shh. It's okay, Princess. This is not your fault. I don't want you to worry about anything but healing and getting your strength back."

Moments after the physician had finished his exam, the king and queen of Timasur had hurried in to see their only daughter. Darius had excused himself to give them time alone, but before he could leave the room, King Rajeemh had embraced him and kissed Darius's cheek and then the other, thanking him profusely for saving Tahira.

A few minutes after Darius had joined the two teams in the waiting room, the king had requested Ian and Amar to meet with him in Tahira's room. Darius knew the shit was going to hit the fan soon, and he was going to have to lie through his teeth to his bosses and teammates. He'd sworn to Tahira he wouldn't tell a soul the truth, other than the doctor, and he couldn't, *wouldn't,* break that vow. He'd follow through with the nuptials, then when it was safe for her to do so, they'd get a divorce. He cared about Tahira, and if this sham marriage helped her avoid the scandal and stigma that awaited her if anyone found out she wasn't a virgin on her wedding night, then he'd go through with it.

Darius had no immediate plans to get married and settle down. Yeah, he'd figured someday down the road he'd look for a woman who would put up with him for three or four decades, if he lived that long. At thirty-eight, he probably had seven to ten years left with Trident, unless, God forbid, an injury pulled him out of the field. While many of his friends now had kids—hell, some of those kids were already teenagers—Darius had always been fine with not having any of his own. His parents should've divorced long before they had. They'd stayed together "for the children," when in reality, they all would've been far better off if the two had gone their separate ways. Darius never wanted to put any children in that position—either dealing with divorced parents or ones that should be but weren't. A wife was one thing, kids were a whole other ballgame.

From where Darius stood, he could see straight down the hallway, and it was impossible to miss when Ian stormed out of Tahira's room and headed right for him, rage etched on every inch of his taut face. *Oh, shit.* He'd never seen Ian Sawyer this pissed before—not even on missions with their SEAL team. Darius almost expected to see steam coming from the man's ears. His long legs ate up the distance as he marched into the room and tossed aside a plastic and metal chair from a small dinette table, almost hitting McCabe who barked in surprise, "Hey! What the—?

Ian paid no attention to anyone else in the room, his sharp, blue eyes throwing daggers at his target. Darius straightened but saw the fist coming at him too late to avoid it. Pain exploded in his jaw as Ian kept him from hitting the floor by grabbing him by the shirt and shoving him against the wall. Darius grasped Ian's wrists, his own anger peaking, but he knew the worst thing he could do right now was to fight back. He'd expected this, but it didn't mean he was going to stand there and get his ass kicked. If Ian took another swing at him, Darius would counterattack with one of his own.

Around them, there were low-volume shouts of "What the fuck?" and "Boss-man, what're you doing?"

Ignoring all of them, Ian growled. While he kept the volume of his voice down, the intensity was loud and clear. "Everybody but Devon get out—shut the door behind you."

From the corner of his eye, Darius could see the bewildered looks on everyone's faces. Jake Donovan was the only one brave enough—or crazy enough—to step forward, cautiously, as if trying to soothe a wild animal poised to attack. "Boss-man, ease up. Whatever—"

"I said, get the fuck out! Now!"

With obvious confusion and reluctance, everyone but Devon filed out of the room. Jake and Nick were the last to leave, and after one last glance back at the three men, they stepped outside and closed the door. Devon stood nearby in silence, his gaze shifting back and forth between his brother and teammate, clearly trying to figure out what in the hell was going on.

As soon as he heard the door click shut, Darius said, "Ian, look, I—"

Ian shoved against his chest, pinning him harder against the wall. "What the fuck happened out there? You couldn't keep it in your fucking pants? Is that it?"

"That's not what happened—"

"Well, something fucking happened! You want to tell me why Tahira just told her parents you two are engaged?"

Devon's eyes bulged, and his mouth fell open before his head dropped back on his shoulders and he groaned. "Oh, shit."

Finally letting go of Darius's shirt, Ian stepped back, rage still painted on his face. "'Oh, shit's right, brother." He crossed his arms over his chest and glared at Darius. "Less than twenty-four hours in the forest, and you what? Fell madly in love with her? I don't fucking buy it. What I can buy is that adrenaline caused things to get out of hand and now she thinks you're getting married."

Swallowing hard, his gaze never leaving Ian's, Darius let a moment pass before he dropped the bomb. "We are."

Ian's nostrils flared. "You are, what?"

"Getting married."

"Shit," Devon murmured again as he and his brother stared at Darius in shock.

He waited, expecting to block another punch, but then Ian just shook his head in disgust. "I hope your fling was worth it because you're fired."

His stomach dropped as the man he respected the hell out of turned on his heel, strode to the door, and flung it open hard enough for it to bounce off the wall. Ian stopped in front of Cain and Tristan who were waiting just outside the room. "Get all his equipment, IDs, and shit from him—he no longer works for Trident."

Dumbfounded, everyone split their attention from the pissed-off man stalking back toward Tahira's room and the other man whose career with them had just ended. As Darius slouched against the wall, Devon ran a hand down his face, then shook his head. "Batman . . . Jesus, you fucked up big time, but I'll talk to him. Go home for now and get some shut-eye—we'll work this out tomorrow, after he's had time to calm down."

With his jaw and fists clenched, Darius nodded and grabbed the discarded sweatshirt before taking off for the elevator, not saying a word to any of his teammates . . . former teammates. *God damn it!*

CHAPTER EIGHTEEN

"You what?" Angie screeched, making Ian's headache pound even harder as he sat down on the couch with Beau at his feet. "How could you friggin' fire Darius?" It seemed his pregnant wife was doing a much better job at curbing her cursing than he was as their first child's due date approached. "What the heck did he do?"

That was the big question Ian had been rolling over and over in his mind for the past three hours. He'd been livid when Tahira had quietly told her parents she'd fallen in love with her rescuer during their ordeal over the past several days, and they were now engaged. Ian had reacted without thinking it through and let his anger get the better of him. Tahira's parents had been equally stunned but, surprisingly, not mad or upset. Amar had just raised his eyebrows at Ian in a "what the fuck?" reaction but had kept his mouth shut.

Now, as Ian gave his wife a short summary of the day's events, something felt off. He'd known Darius for years, working side-by-side with the man in some of the biggest hellholes on Earth. His employee and teammate had always been a stand-up kind of guy, one you could trust when shit went down. Which was why Ian was now thinking he was missing something.

"I don't believe it." Angie rubbed her round belly as she shook her head. "Darius would never take advantage of a woman like that—especially Tahira. You drilled it into everyone's head at Trident that she was off limits, no matter what, and you'd fire them if something happened. I vaguely remember a threat about letting King Rajeemh castrate them too. The contract operatives you get from Chase? Yeah, there's a couple I could see doing something like that—not many, but there are a few—but not anyone on Alpha or Omega. If you trust them with my life, then you have to trust them with Tahira's." She sat on the couch next to him and put her hand on his shoulder. "Something's wrong with this whole scenario, Ian. Why would he ask her to marry him out of the blue like that? Maybe they did fall in love out there in the jungle. Stranger things have happened when two people are thrown together in unexpected situations."

Mulling Angie's words in his head, Ian knew she was right about one thing—something was definitely wrong with the entire sequence of events.

"Any news from Lady Cara?" Angie asked, changing the subject.

Ian nodded. "Yeah, she called me earlier. Her sister's friend is back with her family, and Cara is making sure she gets whatever help she needs. Said she owes us one. I'll be saving that card for when we really need it." Cara Webb was what the black-ops community called an information broker. She was also a member of the BDSM community. She had underground connections that would someday prove handy, no doubt. Ian wasn't going to waste her IOU on something trivial.

Leaning over, he brushed his lips across his wife's mouth.

"I've got to run out. I'll pick up some takeout from Donovan's on the way home, okay?"

"You're going to talk to Darius, aren't you?"

"Yeah. I'm not promising anything, but before I go through with firing him, I want all the facts. He just better be willing to give them to me."

When he stood erect again, she held out her hands for him, letting him help her up from the couch. She wrapped her arms around his waist, her baby belly between them. "He will. Just don't threaten him with the castration thing again. And text me when you want me to call in the order to Donovan's, because I don't know what I'll be craving yet."

He kissed her forehead. "I will. Love you, Angel."

SITTING ON HIS COUCH, A HALF-EMPTY BOTTLE OF BEER IN HIS hand, Darius stared at the big screen TV that took up an entire wall in his living room, having no clue what channel it was on. It could've been a Spanish soap opera, and he wouldn't have even noticed. Cain and Tristan had left a few minutes ago, after unsuccessfully trying to get him to tell them what in the hell was going on. While Ian and Devon knew part of it, and it wouldn't be long before the news spread, especially since Tahira's parents now knew they were engaged, Darius hadn't been ready to talk about it with his teammates.

He'd known Ian was going to be pissed, but honestly, he never expected the guy to fire him. Dev said he'd talk to his brother, but Darius wasn't sure his former lieutenant was going to hire him back. He'd betrayed their trust—well, at least they thought he had.

Now, he had to figure out what he was going to do next for a job. He could call Chase Dixon at Blackhawk Security, but he and Ian were good friends, and Chase wouldn't go behind Ian's back and hire someone the man had just fired.

After showering again and changing into sweatpants and a T-shirt, Darius had called the hospital to check on Tahira. He'd left without saying goodbye, and he didn't want her to think it was anything she'd said or done. She'd been sleeping when he'd gotten through, and Amar had taken the call at the nurses' station. While Darius had expected the head of the royal security team to ream him like Ian had, the man had sounded friendly, telling him he'd have Tahira call him back when she woke up. He'd also said the king and queen had retired to their estate in Clearwater Beach to catch up on some much-needed sleep as well. Darius took that as not to bother them today, but at some point tomorrow, he was going to have to meet with them—after all, they were about to become his in-laws. And wasn't that a fucking kick? Damn, he really hadn't thought this whole thing through, but it was too late to back out now.

As he took another swig from the bottle, someone knocked on the front door to his condo. At first, he was going to ignore it, thinking it was someone else from the Omega Team wanting to talk, but whoever it was kept pounding, harder and harder. Slamming his beer down on the coffee table, Darius stood and strode to the door. Yanking it open, he barked, "What?"

He was shocked to find Ian on his doorstep, holding a six-pack of beer. "Hey, twatopotomus, I brought a peace offering and a new nickname. You gonna let me in or just stand there?" The guy wasn't smiling, but he also didn't look like he wanted to rip Darius's head off.

"If you're going to try to hit me again, this time I'll fight back."

Ian snorted and pushed his way into the foyer, forcing Darius to take a step back. "I might, but that's still up in the air. It depends on you." His boss ambled into the living room, put the six-pack on the coffee table, took one for himself, then sat in the recliner.

"Whatta you mean?" Darius asked, retrieving his own beer and returning to his spot on the couch.

Ian glanced at the TV. "What is that? A Spanish soap opera? Damn, you spent too much time in South America, didn't you?"

Grabbing the remote from the coffee table, Darius shut off the TV, then waited for the other man to state why he was there. Seconds ticked by before the question he didn't want to hear was thrown at him.

"What happened in Argentina?"

He took a drink from the bottle and swallowed. "You read my report."

"Yeah, I did. I want to know what you didn't put in the report. Don't fucking lie to me again, Batman. You and I go way back. I didn't blink an eye when you tossed your name into the hat for the Omega Team. I also took one look at the name on your resume and automatically put it in the hire file without reading the rest of it. I trusted and respected you like a brother—still do, if my suspicions are correct." Ian leaned forward, staring at Darius with those piercing, blue eyes of his. "So, let's try this again. What *wasn't* in the report? Something happened to Tahira before you got her out of there, didn't it?"

Biting his bottom lip, Darius didn't respond. As much as he trusted the man, Tahira had also given him that same trust. It was killing him to have to decide which one he had to betray.

Leaning back again, Ian sighed. "I figured out quite a while ago Tahira only flirts outrageously with the single men she trusts not to take advantage of her. That, and learning more about her and the religion and customs of Timasur, made me realize she was still a virgin. But that's changed, hasn't it? And not because you and she had a jungle fling." When Darius remained silent, Ian pushed again. "Damn it, Batman. I might be a little slow on the uptake now and again, but I'm not fucking stupid. Look me in the eye and tell me I'm wrong, and I'll let it go. But if I'm right, it won't leave this room—I would never, *ever* do anything to hurt that girl. She's like a little sister to me and Angie. I care about her—I care about you too—but I can't help both of you if you don't talk to me."

Taking a deep breath, Darius let it out slowly and made his decision. His friend had pretty much taken the choice away from him by being too damn perceptive. Darius also knew this conversation would never be repeated if Ian said it wouldn't be. "There's nothing you can do about it. When I got to the cell area to help the girls escape, I didn't know she'd been taken upstairs by Secada. After leaving Costello and Romeo there to get the rest of them out, I ran upstairs, but I-I was too late." He cleared the frog that had suddenly taken up residence in his throat, while picking at the label on the beer bottle with his thumbnail. "I killed the mother-fucker, got her wrapped up in a blanket—she was still uncon-scious from the drugs—grabbed some clothes for her, then got her the hell out of there. By that point, everything had gone to shit.

"Later, when bits and pieces started coming back to her, and she figured out what'd happened, she freaked—under-standably—but it was more than that. She told me she'd been a virgin, and if she wasn't one on her wedding night, she'd be disgraced. Apparently, in their country, it's not unheard of for assholes to tell the world their bride wasn't pure on their wedding night and demand a divorce. It would've destroyed her parents and her reputation. Despite being a princess, many would treat her as an outcast—not her immediate family, but she would lose her respectability and everything she'd ever worked for—all her charity work would crumble. She'd be publicly humiliated." He took another sip of beer. "She was so lost, so heartbroken, man, I couldn't let her go through that. So, I came up with the plan to marry her. Then, when it wouldn't cause a scandal, we'd get a divorce. If she married again after that, the virginity thing wouldn't be an issue. No one would know that we never had sex during the marriage, and she'd be safe."

"Remind me again why you think you're not a Dominant?" When Darius rolled his eyes, Ian said, "No, I mean it. Okay, so you're not into whips and chains and some of the darker shit, but it's so much more than that. If you're really serious about this marriage thing, and there's nothing I can say or do to change your mind . . ." Darius shook his head—the whole thing sounded crazy, even to him, but he couldn't retract his promise to Tahira. "Then down the road, maybe sooner than you think, you should consider using aspects of the lifestyle—the milder ones—to help her through this. She's going to need counseling—Doc Dunbar would be ideal—but there are things you can do to help her too—non-sexual things. Dev and I can mentor you."

Darius had met Dr. Trudy Dunbar several times. She was a psychologist The Covenant used to counsel its members if they needed it, and she was also on the government's approved list to treat veterans from the special-ops community for PTSD. Those guys had a lot of sensitive intel in their heads, so the shrinks had to be fully vetted in order to help them. Cowboy was one of those vets and had been seeing Trudy since joining the Omega Team.

After downing the rest of his beer, Ian stood and put the empty bottle back into the six-pack carton. "Think about it. In the meantime, you're hired again. But don't be a twatopotomus next time. Tell me what the fuck is going on, so I don't feel the need to punch your lights out.

"Now, I've got to go get my wife and unborn kid some dinner from Donovan's. Get a good night's rest—you earned it. I'll meet you at the hospital at oh-nine-hundred. We've got some security details, among other things, to work out with Amar."

The man had finally said something Darius agreed with one hundred percent—he needed at least twelve hours of sleep before he could feel human again. Getting to his feet, he walked his boss to the door. "I'll see you in the morning."

Ian smirked. "Be prepared for the Trident women to take over your life once they hear you're getting married. Five words—bridal shower and gift registry." He shuddered dramatically, almost making Darius laugh. "Enough said."

Chapter Nineteen

D arius jarred awake as his cell phone came alive on the nightstand next to his bed. Red digital numbers on the clock on his dresser announced it was 0210 hours. Without turning on a light, he grabbed the phone and checked the screen. An unrecognized local number was his only clue to whoever was calling. Stabbing the connect button, he then put the phone to his ear. "Knight."

"It's Amar. I'm sorry for the late hour—"

"Is Tahira okay?" He tossed aside the covers and swung his legs off the bed to sit up.

The head of the royal guard sighed. "Physically, yes. But I'm afraid she awoke from a nightmare and is very upset. She threatened to scream if they tried to sedate her. She is asking for you and ordered me not to contact her parents. Can—"

"Tell her I'm on my way." Getting to his feet, Darius reached for the T-shirt he'd been wearing earlier and a pair of jeans from a pile of clean laundry he hadn't put away yet.

"Thank you, my friend. I will see you shortly."

Disconnecting the call, he tossed the phone on the bed and quickly got dressed, securing his holstered weapon at his lower back and letting the shirt cover it. His wallet went into his back pocket before he snatched up his phone and car keys. He'd only gotten about four hours of sleep, but years of being in the SEALs had taught his body how to regenerate itself quickly during combat naps. While he could still use another solid eight hours, he was awake enough to safely drive to the hospital.

Tahira had asked for him—needed him. For some strange reason that sent a jolt to his heart, causing it to pound. Butterflies took flight in his gut. What the fuck? The woman was a battered rape victim, and yet his body was acting like a horny teenager who was going on a date with the head cheerleader. *Get a grip, Knight.*

After taking a quick trip to the bathroom, he stopped in the kitchen and grabbed a cold bottle of water from the refrigerator on his way out the door. At the late hour, it only took him ten minutes to reach the hospital. He parked in the lot and hurried inside. When a skinny, male security guard sitting at the front desk tried to tell him that visitors weren't allowed at this time of the night, Darius pulled out his wallet and flashed his Trident Security identification. "I'm with the detail on the fifth floor, private wing."

The pimply-faced guard, who couldn't he more than twenty years old, sat up straighter in his chair and nodded. "Uh, sure. Go on up."

Darius frowned and leaned forward. "Don't you want to check my name against the list of approved people who are allowed in that wing?"

The kid's Adam's apple bounced several times. "Uh . . . um, yeah." He shuffled through some papers until he found what he was looking for. This was the best security the hospital had at night? "Um, w-what's your name again?"

"Darius Knight." He held his ID closer to the guard's face. "And if I catch you allowing anyone up on that floor without checking the list, I'll guarantee it will be your last shift here. Understood? There's a reason that's a private wing."

His eyes widened. "Um, y-yeah. Sorry, sir. It—it won't happen again." He ran his finger down the list of names of the royal guards, TS operatives, Tahira's parents, and a few members of the king and queen's trusted personal staff who'd accompanied them to Florida. "Um, h-here you are, Mr. Knight. Y-you can go up."

Glaring at the guard a moment longer to make sure he'd gotten his point across, Darius finally dipped his chin once and put away his wallet. Without saying anything further, he strode toward the elevator. Arriving at the fifth floor, he stepped out into the hallway. Travis "Tiny" Daultry, the head of security at The Covenant and occasional TS bodyguard when needed, was stationed at the door to the private wing with one of the royal guards. Both men were on high alert, their holstered weapons in full view of anyone wanting to challenge them. While the six-foot-eight, former professional football player towered over his companion by a good seven inches, Darius was sure the man from Timasur could hold his own if the two sparred.

A smile spread across Tiny's face as Darius approached. "Morning, Batman. This is Haji Mellouk." He gestured between the two men. "This is Darius Knight."

Darius wasn't offended when the other man didn't offer a hand. Instead, they each gave the other a curt nod before Mellouk's attention returned to the quiet hallway. Amar's men took their responsibilities seriously, even more so since the kidnapping.

Meanwhile, Tiny opened the door to the private wing for Darius. "Amar told us you were coming. He's waiting for you in the princess's room."

"Thanks. When's Henderson due in?" Doug "Bullseye"

Henderson was the head of the Private Protection Division at Trident and, in this case, Tiny's superior.

"Said he'd be here at eight to check on things." The big man's eyes narrowed. "Something wrong?"

"Tell him to talk to the head of hospital security and get that kid at the front desk off the overnight watch. He's young, green, and useless, and would probably pee in his pants if shit went down. Tell him not to get him fired but put him where he won't have to confront anyone, like monitoring the security cameras or something."

"You got it."

As Darius strode down the hall, the heavy wooden door shut behind him. While it was still quiet in that area, there was some activity going on. It appeared someone else had been admitted to the private wing because a uniformed Florida state trooper stood outside one of the previously-unoccupied patient rooms. Darius didn't bother to ask about who the new patient was, since it was highly unlikely he'd be given the information.

At the nurse's station, two women and one man, all dressed in scrubs with their identification tags hanging from lanyards around their necks, were working their way through their shifts. There were only four patient rooms in this section of the hospital, but they were more like five-star hotel suites. Each had a full bath and attached living rooms where family members had access to refrigerators, small convection ovens instead of microwaves, coffee machines, large screen TVs, couches, and recliners. The rooms where the patients recovered from their illness or trauma were soothingly decorated in soft earth tones, with expensive art on the walls. The wider beds were the nicest ones Darius had ever seen in a hospital, but they still functioned like their commercialized counterparts.

Outside Tahira's room, two more royal guards stood

sentry. Darius recognized them as men he'd met before at the Clearwater Beach estate. When they both gave him curt nods of their heads, it was obvious they remembered him as well. Neither stopped him as he pushed open the door just enough for him to ease into the room. Only one soft light over the bed was on, illuminating the beautiful woman curled up on her side. She looked so small amid the white sheets and blankets. Her long, dark hair covered the pillow her head was lying on. Even though he hadn't made a sound entering the room, her eyes flew open, and her terrified gaze met his worried one. Darius's heart clenched, and his gut felt like he'd been kicked by a mule.

Subtle movement from a dark corner of the room caught his attention as Amar emerged from the shadows. "If you need me, Your Highness, I'll be in the other room."

The man mutely shook hands with Darius before disappearing into the attached living room, closing the door behind him. He was probably going to catch up on some much-needed sleep, but that wasn't Darius's concern right now. He stepped forward and took a seat next to the bed. Tahira's face was ashen, and a tear rolled down her cheek. "Th-thank you for coming, Darius. I am sorry to have Amar call you so late."

She reached out, and he grasped her tiny, trembling hand in his big calloused one, rubbing his thumb over her soft skin. "Shh. There's no need to be sorry. What happened?"

"I had a nightmare. I was back . . . back in th-that bedroom. It was happening all over again. I-I don't remember most of it, but what I do remember . . ."

As her words trailed off, he leaned forward, resting his elbows on the mattress. "You're safe. I'm here, and I'm not going to let anything happen to you." He brushed a lock of her hair back from where it had fallen in front of her face. "Try to get some sleep. I'll watch over you."

Tahira hesitated, then tightened her grip on his hand and tugged. "Would you please lie with me? Like you did before. I-I just need you to hold me."

He really shouldn't, for so many reasons, including the fact this was a hospital and the nurses would probably have a fit, but he couldn't refuse when he saw the pleading in her gorgeous, brown eyes. Giving her hand a squeeze, he let go, stood, and rounded the foot of the bed. Her troubled gaze followed him. After making sure he wasn't disturbing any monitor wires or IV tubing—they'd apparently all been removed since he'd last seen her—he kicked off his sneakers and climbed onto the bed, on top of the covers she huddled beneath. As he spooned in behind her, making sure there was some distance between his groin and her backside, Tahira reached for his hand again. She pulled it until his arm was over her waist, then held it against her torso, just under her breasts. He tried to ignore the fact she was wearing a thin hospital gown over nothing but bare flesh.

Sighing, Tahira closed her eyes. "Thank you, Darius."

He shifted to get comfortable on the full-sized bed, then settled. "Go to sleep, Tahira. You're safe."

Her body relaxed as she whispered, "Only with you."

CHAPTER TWENTY

Tahira stirred in the warmth cocooning her. This time when she awoke, it wasn't in fear and hysterics, but in safety and contentment. Before she opened her eyes, she inhaled, and the familiar male scent she'd grown used to over the past few days tickled her nose.

Darius.

His arm was curled around her waist, and she wondered if it had moved at all since she'd drifted off to sleep. Turning her head slightly, Tahira felt his steady breaths against her cheek. She wanted very much to turn over and watch him sleep, to study his handsome face, but she knew that much movement would have him waking instantly.

When he'd arrived after her nightmare, one of the first things she'd noticed was he'd shaved. The coarse, heavy beard was gone, and in its place was soft, smooth skin over his firm jawline. She'd wanted to reach out and see what it felt like against her palm, but she'd held back. It would have been far too intimate, something she still wasn't ready for, even with the man who would soon be her husband.

Relief warred with dread in her stomach. She should relieve him of his promise to marry her, but having anyone find out she wasn't a virgin on her wedding night scared her almost as much as the thought of being sold in a slave auction. She and Darius could make the farce a success. Since he lived and worked in Florida, it wouldn't seem odd to anyone when she moved there permanently to be near him. They'd live in the Clearwater Beach estate and pretend to be a happily married couple. Whether or not they ever consummated their marriage would only be between the two of them. She trusted Darius to keep his word. He was a man of honor, something she'd known the first time she'd met him and the others on his team. Once an appropriate amount of time passed, the palace would announce the couple decided to divorce and remain friends. She wouldn't have to worry about her virginity after that.

The muscles in Darius's arm tensed, and he pulled her closer to his chest. One would think that after her sexual assault, Tahira would be afraid to be in a man's arms this way, but Darius would never hurt her, of that she was certain.

She was about to close her eyes again and relax into his embrace once more when the door to the hallway opened and one of the nurses walked in. Behind Tahira, Darius was instantly awake. He rolled away from her and stood, stepping back from the bed. She immediately missed the heat, strength, and safety of his body. She was also grateful it'd been a nurse who'd walked in on them in bed together and not her parents. That wouldn't have gone over well—engaged or not.

A flash of jealousy coursed through her when the pretty nurse smiled brilliantly at Darius, her eyes filling with interest at the sight of the handsome man. "No worries. I could tell you stories of things I've walked in on while working on this floor."

While the woman's words seemed kind, she was clearly flirting with Darius, and Tahira felt the need to subtly stake her claim. "My *fiancé* was comforting me. I sleep better when he is by my side."

Okay, maybe not so subtly.

Sad to say, that seemed to backfire when the nurse's gaze blatantly roamed Darius's lean, muscular body. "I don't blame you. I'd sleep better with him by my side too."

Tahira's eyes narrowed, and a tone of disapproval crept into her voice. It was one she'd learned from her mother when dealing with those who were rude to others or didn't remember to follow proper protocol in the presence of royalty. Neither Tahira nor her mother used it often, but it came in handy now. "Unfortunately, for you, I do not share. Please leave and have another nurse assigned to me—one who will give her full attention to me, her patient, and not my fiancé."

Her words had the desired effect when the blonde woman's mouth fell open and her spine stiffened. Her gaze flittered back and forth between Tahira and Darius. The princess had to fight back a smile when Darius cleared his throat and said, "I suggest you do as Her Royal Highness says. I really don't want to go over your head and get a supervisor, but I will."

The nurse's eyes widened, but then her jaw tensed. She spun on her heel and stormed out the door, pulling it shut behind her. She must have said or done something in the hallway because one of the guards knocked a second before he pushed the door open again and stuck his head in. "Your Highness, is everything all right?"

Sighing, Tahira nodded. "Thank you, Zareb. I am fine.

Please do not allow that nurse to return. I would prefer someone else."

"Understood, Your Highness." The man ducked back out into the hallway and shut the door.

Rolling on her back, Tahira stared at Darius, who was now leaning against the wall next to the window. "I am sorry."

His brow furrowed. "Sorry? For what?"

"For behaving like a bitch."

He snorted and chuckled. "You had every right to tell her off. I was pretty shocked by her forwardness myself."

He ran his hand through his longish hair. Her parents would probably want him to get it trimmed for an official engagement photo, but she kind of liked it this way. He was incredibly handsome and could easily grace the cover of one of the novels Devon's wife wrote.

After finding out Kristen Anders-Sawyer was a romance author, Tahira had purchased one of her books. She loved the woman's style, and after finishing that first one, she'd quickly downloaded and devoured the rest of them. Kristen's debut series had been . . . tamer—Tahira guessed that was the right word to use—than her Seductive Sensations series, which had the BDSM lifestyle as a backdrop in the story lines. Even though she'd been a twenty-five-year-old virgin before her assault, Tahira was far from naïve. She loved reading romance novels—going through ten to fifteen in a month—in every genre except for dark erotica. She'd tried reading it once but had found she didn't care for it.

A thought occurred to her. She'd once overheard Brody Evans and Marco DeAngelis discussing a club the Sawyer brothers had founded that was apparently on the same property as their security business. She'd been surprised when she realized it was a BDSM club they'd been talking about as she eavesdropped on their conversation at her family's beach estate. But then she'd realized the original TS team members were very much like the alpha heroes written by her favorite authors like Kristen, Cherise Sinclair, Avery Gale, Lexi Blake, Kallypso Masters, and more. She could easily picture the former SEALs as Doms. Now, she wondered if any of the members of the Omega team were in the lifestyle—specifically Darius.

"Princess, are you all right?"

She hadn't realized she'd zoned out for a moment. Lifting her gaze from her lap, she looked at him. She didn't correct his use of "Princess" in private because, for the first time in her life, it sounded more like an endearment than a title to her. It was probably just wishful thinking on her part, but she liked to think it was true. His soft, moss-colored eyes stared at her in concern, and she gave him a small smile. "Yes, I am, but I would very much like to be discharged and spend the rest of my recovery at the beach house. Could you please find my doctor and ask if that is possible?"

The corners of his mouth ticked upward. "Sure, I think we can arrange that. Anything else?"

"No, thank you."

She watched as he strode to the door, opened it, and turned the corner into the hallway. Part of her was sorry she'd interrupted his sleep in the middle of the night, but she was also grateful he'd come quickly. He hadn't asked for the details of her nightmare. Instead, he'd held her hand and then her body when she'd asked him to. As soon as his arm had wrapped around her waist, she'd felt safe enough to fall back into slumber, knowing he would watch over her. But the more she got to know her hero, and relied on him to keep her safe, the more she wondered who was going to protect her heart from falling in love with the man.

Tahira wished she could read Darius's aura better, but the colors surrounding him were mixed, and the ones that stood out the most said he was guarding himself. The real Darius was hiding behind a mask—not an evil one, but one that kept the rest of the world at bay. Would he ever let down the walls he'd erected around himself? And if he did, was Tahira ready to discover who he really was?

CHAPTER TWENTY-ONE

"Gentlemen, please have a seat." King Rajeemh gestured to a sitting area as Ian, Devon, and Darius walked into his large office in the Clearwater Beach estate. "Can Semira get you something to drink? Coffee, tea, or something else?"

Darius followed his bosses' leads and requested a coffee from the woman wearing a black skirt and crisp, white, button-down shirt, standing next to a table laden with anything they might be in the mood for. He then sat on a couch next to Devon, while Ian took an upholstered wing-back chair, opposite the leather one the king was sitting in. The only other people in the room were Amar, who was standing behind and to the left of the king's chair, and the king's chief of staff, Sebak Fahim, who was sitting on a loveseat across from the couch. His Majesty waited as the drinks were served and a platter of finger sandwiches and pieces of fruit was set on the coffee table between them.

It had taken a little more than an hour to make all the arrangements for Tahira to be released from the hospital. Dr. Moreau would be making a house call tomorrow to check up on his patient. He'd also strongly suggested to Darius that Tahira speak with a psychologist experienced with sexual assault victims. When Darius had mentioned Dr. Trudy Dunbar, Moreau had agreed she'd be a good choice. Darius would call Dunbar's office after this meeting and make an appointment.

When they'd first arrived at the estate a short time ago, Queen Azhar had whisked her daughter up to the younger woman's bedroom, insisting she get more rest. The bags under Tahira's eyes had belied her attempts to convince everyone she wasn't tired.

The server glanced around and then addressed her employer. "Is there anything else I can get for you, Your Majesty?"

The king gave her a kind smile. "No, Semira, thank you. That will be all. I will call for you if we require anything else. Please make certain Princess Tahira is settled in her room."

"Of course, Sire." She bowed slightly at the waist, then left the room, quietly closing the door behind her.

Once she was gone, Rajeemh glanced up at the head of his security. "Amar, please sit and tell me where you are in the investigation."

The man took a seat next to the chief of staff. "While I've held off on interviewing Princess Tahira until she was released from the hospital, I have spoken with Lahana and Nala. Neither recall ever having seen the men who kidnapped them in Jamaica before, and they didn't see those same men at all once they awakened in Argentina. They couldn't give anything further than what we'd learned from the few witnesses at the park. Their memories of the actual abduction are blurred, most likely due to a combination of fear, shock, and whatever they were drugged with. On that matter, the drug used to sedate them was out of their systems by the time the blood tests were done at the hospital, as expected."

Lahana and Nala had been treated and released from the same private wing at the hospital where Tahira had been. They'd boarded a private jet to return to their families in Timasur yesterday morning, hours before their cousin had arrived on US soil. Lahana would receive all the help she needed to get past her sexual assault as Tahira would.

"As far as we can tell," Amar continued, "the kidnappers were not on the cruise—all other guests and staff were accounted for before they left port. Ian sent Jake and Nick to the ship to recover the women's belongings, and they didn't find any clues as to who may have abducted the them. Farid, Daillo, and my other men assigned to the princess did not notice anyone suspicious paying attention to the women. Any attempts by other male guests to interact with them were discouraged by Farid and Daillo, and there were no altercations as a result."

Darius noticed that whenever Amar mentioned Farid and Daillo, the king frowned but didn't say anything. Since Farid was his nephew, it was probably Daillo he disapproved of. Darius made a mental note to find out more about the man who'd joined the cousins on their cruise.

"The Jamaican police are doing their best to try to identify the kidnappers, however the trail has grown cold. They are still trying to track down the final three jets that left the private airport during the timeframe we believe the women were flown off the island. If any further information comes to light, I will let you know immediately."

The king acknowledged him with a nod before his attention turned to the man sitting directly across the coffee table from him. "Ian, my friend, once again, I must thank you, Devon, Darius, and the rest of your employees for rescuing Tahira and her cousins."

"No thanks necessary, Your Majesty," Ian responded. "I'm just glad Darius was in the right place at the right time."

"As much as I would like her to return home with her mother and me, she has asked to remain here during her recovery. I would appreciate if you handled increasing the security measures, so her mother does not worry. We will be leaving for Timasur in the morning. Unfortunately, we are hosting the President of South Korea for a state dinner and trade talks. It took a long time to arrange, and to cancel would cause more questions and problems than I want to deal with at this time. Tahira's privacy is my utmost concern, and if that means I must return home, so be it.

"Sebak, has the official press release been prepared to announce the rescue of Tahira, Nala, and Lahana and deaths of Amar's men?"

"Yes, Sire. I have it here for you to approve." Opening a manila file he'd been holding, the squirrelly-looking man handed Rajeemh a piece of paper. "Amar has already reviewed it. We thought it was best to not hide the abduction but have kept many of the details out, including Lahana's assault. However, there is a chance further information will eventually be revealed if any of the other women rescued talk to the press, and we are prepared to deal with it if that happens.

Once the other hostages had been rescued, the Deimos operatives had made sure they were returned to their families. The women were told their captors had been killed, including the man who'd sexually assaulted some of them. They were also asked to remain silent about the princess, her cousins, the rescue, and the rescuers, however, there was no way to guarantee they would remain mum. His majesty instructed his staff to make certain all the rescued women received any aftercare necessary to help them deal with what had happened and he would quietly pay for it.

Fahim consulted his notes. "I have mentioned the guards' funerals are being arranged by the palace and their families will be taken care of during this difficult time. We are requesting that the press allow them to mourn in peace. We are also requesting they allow Princess Tahira and her cousins a chance to recover from their ordeal. No interviews will be granted, and an updated schedule of Her Royal Highness's public events will be posted within the week.

"As for the rescue, all we are saying is it was done by the royal guard's special forces team and nothing more will be released about the mission. Mr. Sawyer . . ." he nodded in Ian's direction, ". . . requested that Trident and its operatives not be mentioned." There had been no need to ask Fahim to not mention Deimos since the man, nor the king, had any knowledge of the US black-ops agency's existence.

"To avoid overshadowing the state dinner, I'll hold the press release until the day after. And as you requested, I have left out the news of Princess Tahira's engagement for the moment."

Over the tops of his wire reading glasses, Fahim glared at Darius. The man clearly did not approve of the princess marrying a non-royal from America. Too bad, Darius thought. The little shit didn't have a say in the matter.

Clearing his throat, Rajeemh read the press release then handed it back to his chief of staff. "Very good. That will be all for now Sebak."

Dismissed, the man gathered his papers, stood, and left the room. The king turned back to Amar. "Unfortunately, I need you to accompany Azhar and me home. The security for the prime minister's visit requires your full attention. Who will you be leaving in charge here?"

It was at that moment that Darius remembered Tahira's bodyguard, Kojo, who'd been killed, had been one of Amar's executive guards and in charge of Tahira's detail for the past year or two. Darius had met the man on a few occasions and had liked him.

"I've assigned Jabari Bastide to fill the position, sir," Amar responded. "He was already in line for a promotion and has been on the princess's detail for the past eighteen months."

"He was one of the guards left behind on the cruise when the women went ashore, correct?"

"Yes, he was. I've interviewed him and the other guards extensively. The princess and her cousins insisted on going ashore with only two guards. They didn't want to attract attention with a large entourage. Farid and Diallo also confirmed this. Since Her Royal Highness is often accompanied only by two guards, unless she is attending a highly-publicized function, they did not see any harm in her request. Either way, Jabari had been on duty overnight and scheduled to be off until later that evening. There is no record of him leaving the ship while it was docked in Jamaica, and I trust he had no part in any plot to kidnap the princess."

"But you believe one of her guards was involved?" Darius asked, incredulously. He hadn't been fully debriefed yet, so he hadn't heard what had been reported by Tahira's cousins, Diallo, and the other guards yet. He also hadn't read the witnesses' accounts of what they'd seen at the park where the abduction had occurred—a fact he planned to remedy later today.

Amar shrugged. "Honestly, I don't believe any of them were, Darius. To ensure there was no coverup, I've asked Brody and Nathan to do a complete check into the finance, computer, and phone records of the five guards assigned to the princess on the cruise. They've uncovered nothing suspicious."

"We also have to deal with the possibility someone on the ship was involved and had the women followed from the ship to the park," Ian added. "With the amount of tourist traffic on the roads from the port to the park, it wouldn't have been difficult to blend in and go unnoticed by the guards. But we're talking about just over twenty-four-hundred passengers and eleven-hundred crew members. It's going to take weeks, if ever, to narrow down that list to something reasonable for us to investigate."

"Also, according to Nala, Lahana, Farid, and Daillo, the women had only decided that morning at breakfast where they wanted to visit once they went ashore," Amar said. "There were three attractions they'd been considering. They played 'Rock, Paper, Scissors,' and Princess Tahira won. She decided on the waterfalls."

The corners of Darius's mouth ticked upward as he remembered her challenging him to the hand game that morning while they'd been waiting for her to be discharged. The winner got to choose which news program to watch. Darius preferred CNN, while Tahira—who'd won again —liked BBC.

From his right, Devon chimed in. "After all that, there's still the possibility it was a random kidnapping and Diaz just happened to recognize Princess Tahira. You said the women were there for about an hour before you went down to the cell area. Diaz could have been down there prior to that and figured out who she was or one of the kidnappers could have recognized her during the flight and let Diaz know. There's a helluva lot of questions with too many probables to answer them right now. With Diaz, Secada, and the rest of the lieutenants dead, we're left with interviewing a few low-level peons who were left behind. Some friends of ours are locating and interrogating anyone still alive who'd been there in the days leading up to the raid. We just might have to face the fact we'll never find out all the details behind the abduction."

Darius knew his bosses were right. There were far too many unknowns, and they might not ever be cleared up. The friends Devon mentioned were probably members of Deimos. If they'd been any of the Trident operatives, he would have said so.

"Please keep me and Amar updated on your investigation, and he will provide you with any new information his men uncover as well." The king's gaze fell on Darius, but his next words were for everyone else. "Gentlemen, again, I thank you for all your help in bringing my daughter and nieces home, but I would like to spend some time alone with Mr. Knight, if you do not mind."

It was a good thing Darius had been trained how to not give away what he was thinking or Rajeemh would have known how nervous he'd suddenly become. *What the hell?* He'd known the man would want to talk with him—after all Darius was going to be his son-in-law soon.

Holy.

Shit.

How had he not been hit over the head by that fact before? Regardless that it was a sham marriage, Darius was going to be the son-in-law of a fucking king!

Holy.

Shit!

If only Donna Ellsbury, who'd turned him down for their senior prom, could see him now. Darius had only been the second-string quarterback in high school, and that hadn't been good enough for her. He'd gotten a sick sense of satisfaction when the star quarterback had turned her down the following day. When she then tried to suck up to Darius, suddenly agreeing to go with him, he'd told her she'd had her chance and had blown it. He'd ended up taking his friend's sister, who'd been a junior, and they'd had a blast—just as friends. He hadn't gotten laid that night, like some of his friends had, but he'd never regretted his decision one bit.

Ian, Devon, and Amar all stood, and the Sawyer brothers bid the king goodbye. Since Darius had his own vehicle sitting in the estate's driveway, they didn't need to wait around for him.

Once they were alone, King Rajeemh got to his feet and stepped over to the bar that had been built into one of the bookcases lining the wall next to the door. Without saying a word, he picked up a decanter of amber liquor and poured it into two small, delicate-looking glasses. Returning to the seating area, he handed one to Darius before sitting in the recliner again. Darius was a little surprised at the gesture since it was still well before noon.

"This brand of anisette originates from Timasur and has become quite popular in other countries over the past few years. I don't often partake this early in the day, but today, I'll make an exception."

He took a sip of the liqueur, and Darius followed suit, letting the licorice flavor assault his taste buds. It was quite smooth and enjoyable.

Rajeemh leaned back in his chair and crossed his legs. "So, Darius, tell me about yourself."

"What would you like to know, Your Majesty?"

"Anything that is not in the file Amar and Ian put together for me after my daughter announced you two shall marry. Convince me to ignore the fact you bypassed several of my country's traditions, one being it is proper to ask a father for his daughter's hand in marriage, whether the union has been arranged or not."

Oh, boy. It didn't surprise him at all that Amar and Ian had given the king a detailed file on him. Any man in Rajeemh's position would have demanded the same. This wasn't an ordinary, blue-collar man having a conversation with the guy who wanted to marry his daughter. This was a man who ruled an entire country and had his image on its damn currency for Christ's sake. Nope, nothing ordinary about him at all.

Darius let out a long breath as he leaned forward and rested his elbows on his knees. He looked the older man in the eye. "I apologize for not speaking to you first, Sir. Asking for a woman's hand in marriage is a tradition that many still follow in the States as well. My only excuse is that, due to the circumstances, contacting you at the time was impossible. Yes, I should've waited until I had time to ask your permission, but the words had come out before it was too late for me to consider traditions." At least that was a full truth. "Tahira is a beautiful, strong, and courageous woman, and I care for her very much, Your Majesty. I'll provide for her and protect her from harm. I would lay down my life for her."

He wasn't lying to the man. Protecting innocents was an instinct he'd been born with, and it had been cultivated and strengthened during his time in the military. He treated women the way they were supposed to be treated—with respect and honor. And he did care for Tahira—that wasn't a lie either—but he hoped King Rajeemh had missed how the word love had been purposely omitted.

"My marriage proposal to Tahira may have been on the spur of the moment and a product of the situation we found ourselves in, but it is one I plan to follow through—that is, with your permission, sir." It suddenly occurred to him that the king could throw a huge monkey wrench into Darius's plan.

Rajeemh nodded as he paused the conversation for a moment. Darius waited patiently. He couldn't screw this up. Tahira would be shunned by many of her countrymen and women if the news of her rape got out. No, it wasn't fair to blame the victim, but even in the US, that's often what happened. In a country where women were still fighting for equality, despite new laws declaring they deserved the same treatment as men, there were still far too many traditionalists who would ostracize Tahira. Her royal title would not make her an exception to their rules—they would say because of it, she should have set a better example, as if she'd had a decision in losing her virginity in such a brutal manner. Darius knew her family, especially her parents, would support her, but unless she was willing to brave releasing the news of her assault, he was willing to provide her with an alibi.

"You do realize this union may cause problems with your career with a company that relies on its operatives remaining anonymous in many ways, correct?"

Darius took another sip of the anisette. The king's question was a valid one. Tahira was in the public eye, and as a result, the media would be trying to uncover every detail about her intended husband once the engagement was announced. "I spoke to Ian and Devon about that earlier, Sir. As we speak, Nathan Cook is at the Trident compound making sure there will be no links between me and any of the black-ops missions I've been on, either with the Navy or Trident, that can be found on the internet or the Dark Web. As far as the media is concerned, I'm a veteran who now works as a bodyguard and private investigator for a security firm—we're keeping it as close to the truth as possible. With the public side of Trident that's been cultivated throughout the years, they've done a very good job of hiding the black-ops side of things." Before the palace had hired Trident Security, the company and its employees had been vetted at great length. The king was aware of the fact they held numerous government contracts—including ones from several allies of the United States. "I have great faith in Nathan's abilities to cover all the bases and make sure the media only finds what we want them to find. Anyone who knows me, outside of my SEAL team and Trident, has no idea what missions I've been involved in—that includes my family. All they know is that I can't talk about the stuff I did with the SEALs and I now work in private security. And on that matter, we'll be using the fact I've been on Tahira's detail several times while she was visiting as the story of how we met and got engaged, as we can't say I was part of her rescue and what I was doing in Argentina in the first place. Again, it's best to go with something that's as close to the truth as possible."

"Good." The man stood and held out his hand, causing Darius to jump to his feet as well. "I believe this is where I am supposed to say something along the lines of if you hurt my daughter, they will never find your body." His easy grin didn't hide the certainty that he would probably do everything in his power to make Darius disappear if he needed to.

Darius shook the king's hand. "Understood, Your Majesty."

"Then welcome to the family. Over the next several days, you'll need to meet with a member of my staff to be schooled in proper protocol and traditions that will be part of the wedding. I'm sure Azhar will want to have a date set for the nuptials for when the engagement announcement is made, but I will leave that up to you and Tahira to discuss with my wife. I would like to make arrangements to have your immediate family join us in Timasur soon, so we can all get to know one another before the wedding."

Oh, shit. Another thing Darius had failed to think about. While his mother had died a few years ago, his father was still alive. Since Ian and Amar had put together his dossier, the king would know those facts, but how much had they told him about Darius's father? "I'll see what can be arranged, sir."

"Good. Then if you will excuse me, I have a meeting

online with my staff in Timasur to make certain the arrangements for the state dinner are complete."

"Of course. I have things I need to do at the office as well. I'll check in later to see how Tahira is doing." He shook the man's hand again, bowed his head, and waited for him to turn away. Darius then strode toward the door. He had some phone calls to make that he wasn't looking forward to—the first one being to his father. On second thought, maybe he should put that off for another day or so, because he knew it wasn't going to go over well. Most conversations with his dad these days never went well.

Face it, Darius, you stepped in a heap of shit this time.

Chapter Twenty-Two

I n public or in the presence of King Rajeemh and
Queen Azhar, the following will not be allowed:

**Kissing on the mouth, holding hands, hugging, or
flirting.**

That's fine, I guess.

Lewd gestures or spoken innuendos.

Doable—as long as Egghead isn't around.

Cursing.

Shit.

**Extending your hand for the king or queen to shake. If
they decide to shake your hand, they'll extend theirs first.**

Knew that one already.

Certain protocols had been drilled into the heads of the
Trident operatives for assignments involving the royal
family.

**Turning your back on the king and queen. They must
turn away first.**

Yup. Knew that one too.

Expressing political views in public.

Easy enough.

Posing for "selfies" with commoners.

No problem. Never do them anyway.

Walking in front of the king or queen. Always walk at least two steps behind and to the right side if possible.

Sigh. I guess that means when I'm with them in a civilian capacity and not guarding any of them.

Royal protocol:

Always use "Your Majesty" or "sir" or "ma'am" when speaking to the king and queen.

Duh.

Bow your head in respect when first approaching the king and/or the queen and again after you've been dismissed.

Got that one down.

If the king or queen is standing, then so shall all who are present. If they sit, wait for permission to also sit. If one is sitting and the other is standing, those present shall stand.

Knew that one too—also goes for POTUS. Love that episode of The West Wing. *"When the president stands, nobody sits."*

When dining with the king or queen, never start eating before they do. Once they are done with their meal, so is everyone else.

Eat fast—got it.

Other rules that must be followed:

All social media posts and pictures must be approved by the palace.

Not on social media, so don't need to remember that one.

Always accept gifts graciously.

Common courtesy.

Whenever in the public view, even if it is only for a few moments, your clothes must always be modest and appropriate for the circumstance.

Seriously? Doubt there'll be many circumstances for my BDUs and sweatpants.

Members of the royal family must learn more than one language.

I speak three—English, Arabic, and Spanish—four if they count Pig Latin.

Sighing, Darius scanned the next few pages of protocols he'd been given by one of the royal staff members, before tossing the stack on the coffee table in the royal estate's reading room. The engagement hadn't even been announced yet and already he felt like he was living in a glass bubble.

"It is a lot to learn, yes?"

Tahira's voice startled him, and he jumped up from the couch, turning to face her. He hadn't heard her walk into the room. Between her fuzzy pink slippers and the plush carpet, she hadn't made a sound. Her straight, silky hair was pulled up into a messy bun, and she was wearing heather-gray lounge pants and a matching T-shirt with baby-pink trim. The dark circles under her eyes were much fainter now that she'd slept a majority of the last twenty-four hours. As far as he knew, she'd left her bedroom only twice during that time —last night for dinner, and again, this morning, to have breakfast with her parents before they returned to Timasur.

Darius shrugged as she took a seat on the couch. "Half of it is common sense."

She patted the seat cushion next to her, that was still

warm from his body heat. "Please sit, Darius. When we are alone, you do not need to follow any protocol. I prefer when you are relaxed and just being you. It makes *me* feel more relaxed."

Her smile lit up her face, and it annoyed Darius that his body had a physical response to it. He quickly sat and willed his dick to behave. Shit, he was thirteen years older than her, and she was a rape victim—he shouldn't be thinking about her in any sexual way. But when she smiled at him like that, all thoughts of him treating her like she was a kid sister fled his mind. The next few months were going to be an exercise in mind over body.

"Darius?"

He nearly jumped across the room when she placed her hand on his knee. Gulping, he tried to ignore the heat being transferred through his jeans to his skin. "Hmm?"

"I asked you a question."

She had?

His brow raised. "Um, sorry, I—uh—zoned out for a moment."

She giggled. "Apparently. I asked if we could spend some time together, when you are not working. Now that we are not running for our lives, we will need to get to know each other better—our likes and dislikes. When the palace announces our engagement, the media will want to see us in public and will be asking questions. It is best that we know how to respond."

Darius couldn't think with her hand on his leg. He laid his on hers, tucked his fingers under her palm, and moved both their hands to the couch next to him. Before he could let go, Tahira set her other hand on top of his. Darius lifted his gaze to hers and was startled to see tears welling in her eyes while her bottom lip trembled.

"I am sorry, Darius. You—you do not have to go through

with this. We will tell my parents it was a mistake and not to announce—"

The despair in her voice and eyes was his undoing. Using his free hand, he quieted her by setting two fingers on her lips. "Shh. I made you a promise, and I'm not going to back out now. I care about you, Tahira. We'll get through this —together."

Her tongue peeked out to moisten her lips, but it caught the pads of his fingers as well. He knew it hadn't been intentional on her part when her eyes widened, and she pulled back a few inches. But it was too late. Darius's dick was throbbing as he stared at her mouth. What he wouldn't give to find out if her pillowy lips were as soft as they looked.

Her youth wasn't a problem for him—he'd dated women over ten years his junior before, as long as they were mature beyond their years—but Tahira's innocence *was* an issue. In almost every way, she was still a virgin. She didn't remember most of her assault, and he assumed she'd never actually seen a naked man in the flesh.

A thought occurred to him. After they divorced and if she remarried, how would she explain her naïveté to her new husband?

Seriously, asshole? You're looking for an excuse to get her into your bed?

Well, technically, she'll be in your bed after the wedding. How would you both explain why you're sleeping in separate bedrooms?

It was a good thing Darius could sleep almost anywhere, because it looked like he'd be spending the months after their wedding sleeping on the floor next to her bed.

Shit! Every time he thought this scheme of his was going to be easy, his mind found all the reasons why it wasn't going to be. But he couldn't turn his back on Tahira now. Without revealing the reasoning behind the sham marriage, Darius was the only eligible male candidate. Ian and Dr. Moreau were already married.

"I care about you too, Darius." She hesitated, seemingly uncertain, but then, before he knew what she was doing, she closed the distance between them and brushed her lips against his.

His cock jumped for joy, but a stunned Darius held himself still. The last thing he wanted to do was scare the hell out of her. Maybe Ian had been right. Darius could use the time before the divorce to help Tahira get past her rape—if she was willing. They wouldn't need to have intercourse— she would probably want to wait and share that particular intimacy with the man she eventually fell in love with—but kissing and petting would give her some experience. He could even show her what it was like to have an orgasm, if she wanted him to. He would just have to take care of his own needs when he was alone.

Her voice was so soft, he almost didn't hear her. "I am sorry. I have never been so forward with a man. I do not even know how to kiss a man—I have never done it before. I am sorry if I did it wrong."

What?

Tahira moved to stand, but Darius squeezed the hand he was still holding, causing her to freeze. Her gaze was on the floor as a blush bloomed on her cheeks. He squeezed her hand again. "Tahira, look at me."

When her bottom lip quivered and she didn't move, he brought his hand to her chin and turned her head so she was facing him. Her cheeks grew even redder—her bruised one and the finger marks on her jaw still enraging him—and her gaze was on his chest. He tilted her chin up and dropped his voice to what he hoped was the commanding tone he'd heard his Dom friends use on their women. "I said, 'look at me,' Princess." When her eyes finally focused on his, he continued in a soothing tone. "You didn't do anything wrong, and being innocent is nothing to be ashamed of." His thumb caressed her jawline. "In fact, I think it makes you that much more attractive."

Seconds passed as they stared into each other's eyes, and Darius found himself bewitched by her wholesome expression. Her pink tongue darted out again, and his gaze zeroed in on her plump mouth.

"Would . . . would you teach me how to kiss? I-I mean, we will have to kiss once for the public after the ceremony, and I—"

Not letting her finish, Darius leaned forward and cupped her jaw with both hands, drawing her closer. He was going to hell, but damned if he could stop himself from saying, "I'd be honored, Princess. Close your eyes."

Instead of her lids shutting, her eyes grew wide again. "Why—"

"Do you trust me, Tahira?"

She nodded as best she could with her head in his hands. "More than anyone, Darius. I know you would never hurt me."

She was right. He'd cut off his left nut before ever intentionally hurting her. "Then close your eyes."

Shit, if that tongue of hers peeked out between her lips one more time, he was going to suck it into his mouth. She was killing him, but a gentle kiss was as far as they were going to go tonight. As he patiently waited, her eyelids finally dropped.

Darius shifted closer and grinned when Tahira's mouth opened, as if anticipating when his would make contact with hers, but she was going to have to wait a little while longer. It had been at least twenty years since he'd been a teenage girl's first kiss, and he didn't think he'd ever been a woman's first. He wanted to make this special for her—something she would never forget. She deserved it after all she'd been through.

One of his hands went to her temple and brushed back a few of the stray hairs that had escaped her bun. Reaching up, he released the clip at the crown of her head, letting the black, silky strands fall free. He ran his fingers through them, loving how they tickled his palm.

"What—"

"Hush, Princess. I'll kiss you, but we're doing it my way."

He dipped his head down and lightly kissed her closed eyelids. Her hands came up and found his wrists, holding onto them like a lifeline.

"You're so beautiful. So sweet." His lips left butterfly kisses across her discolored cheek, over her pert, little nose, to the other cheek. He felt her shoulders sag and her grip ease.

"That's it. Relax and just feel," he whispered into her ear. His cock became harder when a shiver went through her body.

Down, boy. This isn't about you.

Darius nuzzled Tahira's ear a moment before kissing his way to the corner of her mouth. He brushed her lips with his own. She inhaled sharply but didn't pull away. Darius kept the kiss chaste, moving his closed mouth over her slightly parted lips, tilting her head a bit to get a better angle. A moan escaped her, and the sexy sound went straight to his groin.

Without encouragement, Tahira opened her mouth further. Keeping his control on a tight leash, Darius ran his tongue over her lips, then sucked the bottom one gently into his mouth. Her hands ran up his arms and encircled his neck. Slowly and tentatively, she began to explore him with her tongue. He flicked his own against hers.

"Oh! I'm so sorry, Your Highness! Please forgive my intrusion!"

Tahira jumped back at the interruption, breathing heavily, unwilling to face the staff member that neither of them had heard open the door. Darius had been just as affected by the kiss, but he managed to find his voice a lot quicker. Unable to stand without showing off the bulge in his pants, he turned his head toward the door. "It's okay, Semira. Did you need something?"

The young woman's gaze was on the floor in front of her feet as she stood by the door, fidgeting. "I'm so sorry to interrupt, but Her Royal Majesty is on the phone and would like to speak with you, Your Highness. They arrived home safely a short time ago."

Tahira ran her palms over her heated cheeks before glancing over her shoulder. "Thank you, Semira. Please tell her I will be right there."

"Yes, Your Highness." She hurried out the door, closing it softly behind her.

Tahira covered her entire face with her hands. When her shoulders started to shake, it took Darius a moment to realize she was laughing and not crying. The corners of his mouth pulled upward as he chuckled and relaxed back into the couch cushions. "It's been a long time since I was caught sitting on a couch, necking with a woman like that."

"Necking? Is that what we were doing?"

Not really, considering it had felt like a hell of a lot more than that to Darius, but he was keeping that to himself. Instead, he shrugged. "Some people call it necking, which is a little passé, others call it making out."

"*That* is the phrase I have heard Americans use before—making out." She hesitated, then slowly lifted her gaze to his. Her cheeks flamed brighter. "I liked it very much, Darius—necking with you. Maybe we could do it again sometime?" She quickly added, "To practice, I mean."

He cupped her chin and grazed his thumb across her

bottom lip, which was red and swollen from their kiss. It took everything in him not to lean in and pick up where they'd left off a few moments ago. His voice came out low and husky. "I'd like that very much, Princess."

Yup, I'm going to hell.

CHAPTER TWENTY-THREE

After assuring her mother she was okay and wishing her well, Tahira hung up the phone in her father's office. It had been a mostly one-sided conversation, because Tahira couldn't get Darius and the kiss they'd shared out of her mind enough to concentrate. She'd lied to him earlier. As a teenager, she'd kissed two boys—but those had been experimental and juvenile attempts to figure out what all her friends had told her *they'd* felt when they'd kissed boys. Some of her friends claimed it was just like the romance novels they'd read, which, of course, they'd hidden from their parents at that age. Fireworks, burning passion, unable to catch their breath—things like that. But after those two sloppy endeavors with the opposite sex had left her feeling empty, Tahira had wondered if something was wrong with her.

Having no interest in women, she knew she wasn't gay, but had wondered if she might be asexual—someone who didn't have any sexual desires. But as she'd gotten older and matured more, she knew that wasn't the case either. Men definitely interested her, they made her crave intimacy, but not with anyone in particular—until now. When Darius had kissed her—hell, before he'd kissed her mouth—he'd ignited something deep inside her that she'd never known existed. It was as if the missing piece of a puzzle that was her womanhood had fallen into place and her body had rejoiced. She finally understood what gave authors the inspiration for writing romantic scenes that left readers panting and wanting more. If Semira hadn't interrupted them, how far would Darius have gone? How far would Tahira have let him go?

What had startled her even more were the flashes of color that'd surrounded the man as they both recovered from the kiss. He'd always been one of those people she couldn't get a read on, but she'd known instinctively he was one of the "good guys." He would never hurt a woman—not intentionally—*that* she'd known. But for a few moments there, she'd gotten a glimpse of his aura. There had been reds, pinks, and purples, swirling together, each color fighting for supremacy. However, she'd also seen flashes of brownish mauves, which she'd come to associate with confusion or an internal battle being waged. She would have loved to have known what had been going through his mind at the exact moment those flashes had appeared, but before she'd been able to fully analyze his aura, Darius had pulled back, emotionally. Then his colors had faded, and once more, she had been unable to read them.

There had been a brief moment of hope blooming inside her during their kiss—she'd felt a connection with him. One she'd never felt before. One that had made her wonder if she'd found *him*. Her soulmate.

"Your Highness?"

Tahira turned toward the door. "Yes, Semira?"

"Is there anything you need me to do?"

Glancing at a clock on the wall, she was surprised to see the late hour. It was just after 8:00 p.m. The woman who managed the Clearwater Beach mansion, and its house-keeping and kitchen staff, had been working over twelve hours today—much longer than usual, unless there was a special occasion. "No, you may turn in for the night. Thank you for your assistance today."

"It was my pleasure, Your Highness."

As Semira left the room, Tahira yawned. She'd dozed on and off in fits since they'd boarded the jet in Argentina. She'd expected some insomnia in the hospital—no one ever slept comfortably in those places—but she still hadn't gotten more than a few hours of sleep at a time even after arriving at the beach house. Each time her body and mind lapsed into the REM phase, her nightmares surfaced. And each time, it felt the same. A heavy weight was pressed down on her chest, making it difficult to breathe. Perspiration coated her skin, causing goosebumps to appear all over her body. A putrid aroma of sweat and cigarettes would taunt her sense of smell until she thought she would vomit. Grunts that seemed to come from a feral animal resounded in her ears. Flashes of sharp pain between her legs had caused her to awaken more than once with a scream pursed on her lips, ready to be released for everyone in the house to hear. Somehow, she'd always managed to swallow it back down before it pierced the air. Once fully awake, she would realize she was panting and crying quietly, and the images would fade, almost as if they'd never existed. But they had—and they continued to exist—and Tahira was desperate to put them behind her.

Tomorrow, she would be meeting with Dr. Trudy Dunbar. Hopefully, the psychologist would be able to help Tahira to get past her nightmares. While much of that awful night was still a blur, her body remembered its responses to it. Would they eventually fade, or would she begin to recall all the horrible details that were locked away somewhere in the far recesses of her mind?

Getting to her feet, Tahira strode to the door and headed toward the kitchen for some herbal tea. She'd always found the brew soothing, but she suspected that would not be the case tonight. If she could only force herself to stay awake forever, never to relive the horrors of her attack again, but that wasn't an option.

Passing the door to the library, which was ajar, she paused when Darius's deep, rumbling voice filled the air. He was talking on his cell phone, but other than the name "Levi" she couldn't hear what he was saying due to the distance between them and his back being toward her. A shiver went down her spine while her gaze caressed his broad shoulders, strong back, narrow waist, and very fine backside. Her hands itched to touch every inch of him, as she remembered how he'd whispered in her ear, leading up to their first kiss.

. . . we're doing this my way . . . relax and just feel.

Oh, she'd definitely done just that. She hoped she hadn't been imagining the way her body had seemed to surrender to Darius. How he'd taken possession of her mouth like it was his to own and do with it as he pleased. How every nerve in her body had come alive at his touch and begged for more. Part of her couldn't wait to experience all that again, while the other part was terrified about what would happen if they became even more intimate. How would she react? Would her nightmares attack her conscious mind? Would she panic and force Darius away? She didn't want to disappoint him if he wanted to have sex with her on their wedding night, as was his right to expect.

She knew their marriage would only be temporary and

one of convenience, but she wanted to reward him for helping her, for rescuing her. What better reward could a woman give the man who was her husband than to offer him her mind, body, and soul?

CHAPTER TWENTY-FOUR

D arius fiddled with his cell phone, trying to figure out the right wording for the call he was about to make. He had to tell his siblings about his "engagement" before the news became public. If he was going to pull this off, he would have to make everyone believe he and Tahira had fallen for each other. One slip-up and the media would be all over it, desperate to figure out what the couple was hiding. He was still trying to decide the best way to avoid having the press going after his father—it wouldn't go over well for any reporter who tried to step on the man's property. Darius would have to make sure his brother and sister did extra sweeps for the shotgun shells their father always seemed to find a way to get ahold of and hide in the double-wide trailer he lived in. Once a week wouldn't cut it after the media frenzy started. The last thing they needed was for the old man to kill a trespassing reporter.

Hitting one of the speed-dial buttons, Darius placed the first call. When his brother picked up, Darius said, "Hey, Levi—let me get Barrie on the other line." The siblings often had three-way phone chats with each other—it was easier than having to repeat things twice.

"Don't bother," his brother responded, sounding like he had a mouthful of food. There was a pause when he must have swallowed because afterward his voice was back to normal. "She's right here. Hang on, I'll put you on speaker."

There was a click and then his sister came on the line. "Hey, big brother! What's up?"

Darius couldn't help the grin that appeared on his face. He loved his younger siblings and missed them at times like this. They'd grown up close, huddling together in one of their bedrooms while their had parents fought about everything under the sun. While the mismatched couple had never hit each other, sometimes their words had been worse than fists. Surprisingly, Phillip and Jacqueline Knight had only taken their frustrations over their unhappy marriage out on each other. Darius had wondered at times if the doting affection they'd lavished on their children had been a sort of one-upmanship to see who could earn the title of "favorite parent." He would never understand why they hadn't divorced. Darius and his siblings hadn't thought things could get any worse, but they'd been wrong. One night had changed everything.

Darius would never forget the call he'd received from his brother five years ago. A drunk driver had run a red light, hitting their parents' car, killing Jacqueline instantly. In a way, she'd been far luckier than her husband. His head injury had robbed him of ten years of his life leading up to the accident. The last thing he remembered was one of the fights he'd had with his wife when she'd stormed out of the house, threatening to never come back. While she had returned a few hours later, as she'd always done, in his mind, she'd abandoned him.

Now, Phil thought his children were fifteen years

younger than they were. Paranoia had also set in. He rarely left the trailer he insisted on living in on the outskirts of Brookford, a small town dwarfed by the Smoky Blue Mountains in Tennessee. The townspeople knew well enough by now not to disturb the old man, who would rant and rave and threaten anyone who stepped on his small half-acre of property. The only reason he hadn't been arrested for making threats was Levi was the town's police chief. Barrie, a midwife, and Levi would check on their father, making certain he had food and supplies and hadn't hidden any shotgun shells he could use to hurt someone. They still hadn't figured out where he was getting the damn things every few months, but at least they'd managed to find most, if not all, of his hiding spots. They would just convince the old man he'd done some target practice recently whenever he discovered his new ammo missing. Yeah, they were conning him, but whatever worked.

"Hey, sis. What'd you make for dinner?" Once or twice a week, Barrie and Levi had dinner together. With both their busy jobs, they sometimes sat down for the meal later than most people did. Barrie loved to cook, and Levi liked to reap the benefits of letting her use the spacious kitchen that had come with the house he'd purchased a few years ago.

"Momma's beef stew."

That was all she had to say to get Darius's stomach grumbling. Their mother had been an accomplished cook and left behind a well-used box filled with all her favorite comfort-food recipes handwritten on index cards. Barrie treasured the box and its contents, often recreating their mother's culinary masterpieces.

"One of these days I'm going to convince you to make a pot of that and ship it overnight to me." He paused. "How's Dad doing?"

"Ornery as ever," Levi responded. "I was out there

yesterday because a few teenagers wanted to see who was brave enough to poke the bear. Thank God I confiscated Dad's new stash of shells the day before. He scared the crap out of those kids with an empty shotgun. I doubt they'll try to take him on again. I think two of them pissed their pants when he circled around and snuck up on them."

"Who called it in?" Darius couldn't see the kids calling 9-1-1. That was the type of stuff you kept under your hat in their neck of the woods—messing with the local loon. Not that Phil Knight, a former lumberjack, had always been crazy and paranoid, but after the past five years, that was how he'd be remembered by many people when he passed away.

"No one had to. I was on the phone with him when the Russians invaded."

"Oh, jeez." This time it had been the Russians in their father's mind. The last time it had been the North Koreans, and before that it had been the Viet Cong, not that Phil had fought any of them during his four years in the Army after enlisting at eighteen. As far as his kids knew, the man had served all his time stateside.

"Yup. I hightailed it over there with two of my deputies. You think these stupid kids would learn." They wouldn't, and both brothers knew it, so Levi changed the subject. "So, are you back in the Sunshine State?"

"Yeah, got back a couple of days ago but had to deal with a debriefing and stuff." Darius's brother and sister had learned and accepted long ago there were many things about his work in the SEALs and Trident Security that he couldn't discuss with them. While sometimes their curiosity got the better of them, and they asked questions he wasn't always able to answer, they were used to him saying "no comment."

"Listen, I've got something to tell you . . . I'm . . . uh . . . getting married."

Levi's shocked "holy shit" was barely audible over Barrie's

squeal of excitement. "O.M.G.! Get out of here! I didn't even know you were dating anyone. What's her name? Where's she from? What does she do? How did you meet her? When do *we* get to meet her?"

Chuckling, Darius shook his head. Barrie had always had a habit of rattling off a string of questions without waiting for an answer to any of them until she ran out of things to ask. Once there was a break in the interrogation, Darius responded, "Her name is Tahira. She's from a small country in North Africa called Timasur, and she's a . . . um . . . a princess." Damn, that sounded so weird, even to him.

There was silence over the phone, and Darius pulled it from his ear to check the screen and see if he'd gotten disconnected. Nope. They were still there. "Guys, say something."

A roar of laughter came from Levi. "Good joke, big brother. A princess? Right, like you could ever hook a princess. Maybe in a fairy tale."

"Darius, damn it! I was all ready to start planning a wedding. That was mean."

Darius sighed loudly. He should have expected their reaction, but then again, how many men from Tennessee called their family to say they were marrying into royalty. Not many at all. "I'm telling you the truth. You can Google her. The palace will be announcing the engagement in a few days, so I wanted to give you both a heads up. I've got my computer geek trying to lay some groundwork to keep the media vultures away from Dad, but I don't know if we'll be able to prevent anyone from making the connection. As soon as the news is released, it won't be long before it's all over town. Someone will see dollar signs and contact the press with info on me and my family."

"You're fucking serious, aren't you?" Levi asked, the disbelief in his tone had been cut in half.

"Yeah, I am. I've been on her security detail a few times, and we kind of hit it off."

Barrie finally found her voice again. "You really *are* serious. Holy shit! Does this mean you're going to be a prince? Will we have to bow or curtsey or something when we see you? Oh my God! Are we going to meet a king or queen? I'll have to go shopping! What should I wear when I meet them? Oh, and where will the wedding be? In . . . what's the name of her country again?"

When his sister finally took a deep breath, Darius did his best to answer all her questions. Ten minutes later, he finally disconnected the call, only to have the phone ring almost immediately. Seeing it was Cain Foster, he swiped the screen. "Knight."

"We've got company—three media vans just pulled up. One of them is CNN and another is the BBC."

"What? The press release hasn't gone out yet. What the hell do they want?" From his pocket, he pulled out a comm unit that was connected to both the TS team and the royal guards and stuck it into his ear. He could listen in on everyone doing their jobs.

"I don't know, but we're going to need a little backup. There are more coming." Foster must have opened the door to the vehicle he and Morrison had been sitting in outside the front gate because Darius suddenly heard a bunch of people shouting questions. "This is just the tip of the iceberg, brother."

Darius looked up as Jabari Bastide, the new head of Tahira's detail, stuck his head into the library. "Where is Her Royal Highness? The press is at the gate."

Disconnecting the call, Darius strode toward the doorway. "I know. She was talking to her mother on the phone in the office a little while ago. I'm not sure where she went from there. If you want to handle things out there, I'll look for Tahira and keep her inside."

If the man took offense to Darius speaking so informally about the princess, he didn't show it. Darius was going to have to remember when a situation called for him to refer to her as Her Royal Highness or, at least, Princess Tahira. In such a short time, he'd gotten used to just calling her by her given name.

"No, my men have already joined your teammates. Princess Tahira is my responsibility, and I just checked the office—she's not there."

A flash of sadness and guilt appeared in the man's dark eyes, and Darius felt bad for him. The reason he'd been promoted was because his two teammates and friends had been murdered protecting their charge, while Bastide had been sleeping on the cruise ship. He took his new position even more seriously than his old one and would lay down his life for the princess, of that Darius was sure. As bratty as she used to be, over the past few years, as she'd matured, Tahira had won the respect and loyalty of her guards. She now knew about their family members and inquired about them often, which made the men like her even more.

"Okay. If you want to check upstairs, I'll see if she's still down here somewhere." With twenty-nine rooms in the three-level, main house, it would take a few moments to find her. Darius hoped she hadn't gone outside. He didn't think she was in any danger, but he still wanted to make sure she was safely out of view from any telescopic camera lenses.

Bastide nodded, then turned on his heel and hurried toward the foyer to take the stairs. Darius double checked the office on his way past it and found it empty. So were several other rooms. Finally, he found her in the kitchen, reading a fashion magazine and drinking a cup of tea.

Tension he hadn't realized had crept into his neck and shoulders released at the sight of her. "There you are."

Startled, she looked up at him. "Darius." Her mouth turned downward as she studied his face. "What is wrong?"

"Nothing for you to worry about. Hang on." He tapped his earpiece. "Bastide, Her Royal Highness is safe in the kitchen."

"I'm on my way."

"Safe? Darius, what—"

Tahira's started to stand, fear blazing in her eyes, and he held up a hand, trying to calm her. "It's okay, Tahira. The press just showed up at the gate. Apparently, word got out about our engagement."

Her mouth gaped. "B-but Sebak was not supposed to release the statement until the day after tomorrow."

Stepping over to her, Darius pulled her into his arms. She was shivering, and he doubted it was because she was cold. "I'm not sure what's going on and why they're here, but you're safe, Princess. I won't let anything happen to you. The press won't get anywhere close to you."

Behind him, he heard Bastide enter the room, but Darius didn't release Tahira. He didn't know why, but he suddenly didn't want to entrust her safety to anyone else. Bastide had asserted she was his responsibility, but ever since that relatively chaste kiss they'd shared, Darius wanted to claim Tahira as his in a completely different way. One word seemed to resonate through his mind—*mine.*

Chapter Twenty-Five

Tahira paced back and forth in front of the windows overlooking the Tampa Riverwalk with her arms clasped around her torso. Dr. Trudy Dunbar's office had a gorgeous view that unfortunately didn't alleviate the nervousness rolling around in Tahira's gut. Taking a deep breath, she turned to face the psychologist who was sitting in a chair next to a couch. This was the moment she'd feared—talking to someone other than Darius about her assault. Patient/doctor confidentiality made it a little easier—Dunbar could lose her license if she repeated anything they discussed behind closed doors. Ian and Darius also trusted her, which helped Tahira trust her as well.

She'd been appalled and embarrassed when Darius had told her Ian had figured things out, but then the head of Trident Security had stopped by to let her know her secret was safe with him—he wouldn't even tell his wife. Ian had become like a big brother to Tahira, and from their private conversation, she knew he didn't think any less of her for what had happened. In fact, she was certain if her rapist were still alive, he would suffer a long, torturous death at the hands of the retired Navy SEAL. Ian had ensured her that any help she needed to get past the rape, he and Darius would make sure she got it.

After leaving the estate two hours ago, Darius's team-mates and Tahira's guards had played an intricate game of cat and mouse with the press. They'd driven all around Tampa, leading a parade of vans with satellite dishes on the roofs, and changed vehicles twice, while Lindsey wore a wig, impersonating the royal princess. Tahira had donned her own wig—one with short, medium-brown hair, makeup to cover the bruises on her face, and large sunglasses. Once the coast had been clear, she and Darius had slipped out the back of the house, hurried to the estate's dock on the bay, and boarded a boat Tristan McCabe had waiting for them. The man ferried them across the bay where an SUV was parked for them. With all the subterfuge, the press had no idea Tahira was now talking to her new psychologist, and she was grateful.

"I was raped." There . . . she'd said it, and in doing so, it made it all too real. Tahira covered her face with her hands for a moment. Her heart pounded in her chest, and she gulped several times, trying to fill her lungs with oxygen. She blinked back a few tears, then circled around the desk and took a seat on the couch.

"Take a deep breath, Tahira. That's it. One more." Dr. Dunbar's voice was soothing, filled with empathy and under-standing. Once Tahira's shoulders relaxed, the doctor contin-ued. "I can only imagine how you must have felt. Your presence here means you want to move forward. I'll be here to help you get through this, and we'll take it one step at a time. When you're ready, please tell me what you remember."

Tahira was glad she felt comfortable enough with the

other woman to talk to her. She couldn't keep it all inside. She'd been raped, and even if she was afraid of it becoming public knowledge, she wouldn't downplay what had happened to her with the people trying to help her. "I-I do not remember as much when I am awake—I was drugged at the time—but when I am asleep, the nightmares come. I see and feel bits and pieces, but my body's response to them is what I fear."

"What do you fear?"

Tahira realized what she'd said could be misinterpreted. "I mean, I am afraid I might die while reliving what happened. My breathing and heart rate become out of control. I have heard people can die of fright, and it scares me. That and my screams might have someone finding out I was . . . I was raped."

It was still difficult to say out loud. Darius had been trying to convince her there was nothing to be ashamed of, but Tahira felt conflicted. As a woman who'd been sexually violated, she knew it was not her fault and she shouldn't feel guilty. But as the daughter of the king of Timasur, a country where a woman's lack of virginity on her wedding night was considered by many to be a crime worse than murder, she couldn't let anyone else learn of her assault. More than two centuries ago, Timasur had been another country altogether, and Tahira could've been stoned to death if her secret had been discovered, even with her royal status.

The two women spent the rest of the hour-long appointment discussing what had happened—what Tahira did remember and what she didn't but had learned from Darius. Dr. Dunbar also taught Tahira some relaxation techniques for when she felt a panic attack coming on, assuring her it was very rare to die from fright.

When a soft ding sounded from a small table next to Dr.

Dunbar, she took off her reading glasses and looked at Tahira. "I'd like to see you three times a week to start with, if that's okay with you. As you work your way through this, we'll drop that down to twice or once a week."

Tahira nodded. "Yes, that is fine. I-I appreciate what you are doing for me."

The psychologist smiled at her. "I'm just listening. You're doing all the work."

After they scheduled her next few appointments, Tahira exited the office to find Darius sitting in the waiting room, reading something on his smart phone. When he heard her, he jumped to his feet, concern filling his handsome face. "How'd it go?"

"It went well. I like her—she is very nice."

The tension in his features eased. "Good, I'm glad. Are we all set?"

She smiled and handed him the business card Dunbar had given her. "Yes—these are my next few appointments."

As he led her to the elevators, Tahira was shocked when he slid his hand down to hers, entwining their fingers. When she looked up at him, he seemed to be just as startled by what he'd done. Before he could have any regrets and pull away from her, she squeezed his hand. "Thank you for bringing me here, Darius. I hope Dr. Dunbar will be able to help me."

He hit the call button for the elevator with his free hand, then turned and cupped her chin. His penetrating gaze sent a shiver down her spine. "I hope so too, Princess."

The doors to the car opened, and they stepped inside. Tahira was disappointed when Darius released her hand to push the button for the lobby. She immediately missed the warmth and safety she felt whenever he touched her. She wished she could see his aura, but after a brief flare of red had surrounded him, he'd shut down, causing it to disappear. How was she supposed to know if what she was starting to feel for him was reciprocated if she couldn't see his aura? She was in uncharted territory here. It had never bothered her before when she couldn't see someone's colors, but then again, it'd never happened with someone she was attracted to. Somehow, she had to figure out if what she felt was one-sided or not because she hoped like hell it wasn't.

Chapter Twenty-Six

After turning into the driveway of the estate, Darius kept going and pulled into the open garage and hit the remote to shut the overhead door. The press was back at the gate in full force. He hadn't wanted to return by boat, giving away their ruse in case they needed to use that route again. Let the damn bottom feeders stew and wonder about how they'd been tricked.

Escorting Tahira into the attached kitchen, he nodded when she said she was going to change out of the dress pants and blouse she'd worn to her appointment. Darius forced himself not to imagine her peeling off her clothes until she was standing there in just her bra and panties—which in his mind were baby pink and lacy. Damn it—so much for pushing down that thought because it was now front and center. He had to think of something else quickly before he had a raging hard-on.

"Hey, how'd it go?"

Relief coursed through Darius when Cain walked into the room. *Work. Yes. Work. No baby pink lace over soft, bronzed skin. Work, work, work. Focus.*

Clearing his throat, Darius sat on one of the stools at the island in the middle of the huge kitchen, which could be part of a five-star restaurant. "Good, I guess. Tahira liked Trudy, and she's got appointments set up to go back."

As far as his teammates, the Deimos agents, and the royal guards knew, Tahira was having nightmares from just the kidnapping and her time in captivity. Neither Lindsey nor any of the men from Trident had questioned Darius further when he'd said he'd rescued Tahira from Secada before anything could happen to her. None of them had given him any indication they thought he'd glossed over the truth.

"How was the parade?" he asked.

Cain snorted. "All that was missing were the bagpipes, fifty-foot balloons, and the ticker tape."

"Any idea what they know and how they found out?"

Leaning on his hands against the island, the team leader bent at the waist and stretched his back. "Well, they know about the kidnapping, but how they know is the question. Tried interrogating a few, but they just waived their First Amendment rights in our faces, citing anonymous and confidential sources." He stood straight again and shrugged. "Could've been one of the other captives, one of the Jamaican cops—although I don't think it was them since the press had details the cops didn't know, like knowing about Argentina. Hell, it could even be a leak in the palace. Who knows? While it came as a surprise, they didn't have anything that wasn't going to be in the press release. Maybe one of what's-his-name's public relations people let it slip."

That was a possibility Darius hadn't thought of. Sebak had no reason to pull something like this—his ass would've been fired, and Darius suspected the man liked his position as right-hand man to the king too much to do something to jeopardize it. But someone on his staff could have easily been bribed.

"Anyway," Cain continued, "Bastide called and updated Amar, and the official release will go out first thing in the morning, Timasur time."

"Good. Hopefully, we'll be able to keep the rest of it under wraps."

The other man paused and then tilted his head. "You're really going through with this, huh?"

Darius didn't have to ask what Cain meant by that, and he tried to sound convincing in his response. "Yeah, I'm getting married. Go figure. I'd always thought Skipper or Romeo would be the first from Omega to fall."

"Alpha sure fell like dominoes." Cain frowned. "I hope this isn't the beginning of a trend for Omega, because I have no intention of taking that plunge any time soon. Someday, maybe, if the right woman comes along, but I'm starting to think fate doesn't want me to go down that road. Being a Secret Service agent and now a black-ops one doesn't exactly make for an easy marriage with 'Hi, honey, I'm home. What's for dinner?'"

"You never came close to having a wife, two point four kids, and a white picket fence?" Darius asked.

The other man shook his head. "Nope. Hell, the longest relationship I've had since graduating college and joining the Secret Service was three months, and that'd been with a sub I'd collared with a contract. She was moving to Paris, and we knew going into it there was an end date."

Cain had been in the lifestyle for years after being on the detail of someone who'd been in it and had figured out he was a Dom after going to several clubs while playing body-guard. That was all Cain had told Darius, keeping his charge's name out of it. Privacy and secrecy were apparently big things in the BDSM community, and most members kept their mouths shut about who and what they saw in clubs.

"Doesn't that feel weird, having a contract with an end date with someone you're dating?"

"In the beginning it did, but once you get used to the fact there are no expectations beyond the end date, it works out."

"What if a Dom or a sub falls in love with the other and doesn't want an end date?"

Cain's eyes narrowed. "Why are you suddenly asking about the lifestyle? I thought you weren't interested."

Busted. If he were honest with himself, he hadn't been able to stop thinking about Ian's offer to train him, but he still wasn't convinced the lifestyle would help Tahira get over the trauma of her rape.

He shrugged. "I didn't think I was, but after hearing about it so much, I'm just curious, I guess. Isn't the point of starting a relationship with someone to see if you're compatible or not before taking it to the next step? You ask her out on a date. You figure out what you do and don't have in common and if there's any chemistry between you, then you decide if you want a second and third date. If you do, you probably eventually end up in bed together. As the relationship reaches each phase, you have to decide if you want to take it to the next one or end it, right?"

"But the lifestyle takes a lot of the guessing out of that equation," Cain said. "Everything is negotiated up front. There are very few surprises. If you wind up attracted to a submissive, in more than just a D/s way, and want to see where it goes, then you discuss it. There're no head games or wondering what the other person is thinking. Open, honest communication is key. Yeah, there's the occasional stalker type out there or someone who's in the lifestyle for all the wrong reasons, but with experience, you learn to spot and avoid them. And there are plenty of stalkers outside the life-style too."

Footsteps in the hallway told them someone was about to

enter the kitchen seconds before Tahira appeared. She'd changed into a pair of knee-length yoga pants and a matching tank top. The makeup she'd been wearing earlier had been cleaned off. While the bruises on her arms, neck, and face were visible, she'd forgone her usual running shorts which would have shown the bruises on her thighs.

Darius couldn't keep his gaze away from all the gloriously deep bronze skin of her legs, arms, and shoulders. Her hair was up in a ponytail again, and he wanted to wrap the long strands around his wrist and pull her to him. His cock twitched in his khakis. Damn, she was fucking gorgeous, becoming more so each time he saw her.

Stepping over to the refrigerator, she opened the door and retrieved a bottle of water. Then she hesitated before looking over her shoulder. "I am going to work out on the treadmill. Anyone want to join me?"

The mansion had a well-equipped gym in one of its many large rooms, complete with a sauna. While the question had been addressed to both of them, her gaze had held Darius's. Cain glanced between the two of them, then shook his head with a small smirk. "I'll pass, Your Highness—I'm still on duty. But I'm sure your *fiancé* would be more than happy to join you in getting all hot and sweaty."

As his teammate strode out the door with a chuckle, Darius fought the urge to flip him the bird and call him an asshole. It clearly hadn't escaped Cain's notice there was electricity arcing through the air between the engaged couple. Well, that's the way it needed to look to convince everyone this engagement was on the up and up.

What the hell was happening, Darius wondered. He'd never had such a feeling of awareness with any woman he'd dated then what he felt when he was in the same room as Tahira. Maybe Ian and Cain were right, and parts of the life-style would do both Tahira and Darius some good. They could learn how to help her heal, maybe give each other some mutual pleasure, and have a contract that had an end date—the day they announced they were getting divorced. They'd sit down and negotiate everything and renegotiate as needed. No exceptions beyond what they'd agreed upon. Sex could be on or off the table, although he would prefer it on. And, damn it, now he had an image of her laying on the island in front of him, beautifully naked and spread wide while his tongue and fingers did wickedly delicious things to her pussy.

"Darius?"

He realized he'd been staring at Tahira in silence and forced himself to focus. And, damn it, he had to remember she was a rape victim. She probably didn't even want to have sex with him or anyone else for that matter. The woman was still healing, physically and emotionally.

Right now, she was holding up a second bottle of water and waving it at him. Licking his lips and swallowing hard, he stood, glad the island hid his semi hard-on from her, as he nodded. "Head to the gym. I'll get changed and meet you there."

The smile that spread across her face was almost blinding, and it stirred something within him. He'd pleased her and that simple fact made him feel ten-feet tall. Now Darius just had to figure out how to run on the treadmill next to her without coming in his fucking shorts.

CHAPTER TWENTY-SEVEN

Grabbing a towel, Tahira stepped out of the shower and dried herself off. While she hadn't been able to do her regular run on the treadmill after a warmup—she was still aching all over—she'd been able to walk slowly for three-quarters of an hour. Her and Darius's trek through the woods would've been much worse if she hadn't been on a five-day-a-week exercise regimen for years. However, she hardly remembered any of today's session—except the man who'd run several miles on the treadmill beside her.

Darius was a beautiful specimen of a man. Today was the first time she'd seen some of the tattoos that decorated his upper arms, shoulders, and chest. She'd known he had at least one on his left bicep, since she'd seen him in a short-sleeved shirt before, and the black design had extended just below it. But she'd suspected that wasn't the only one he had. In the gym, his khaki-green tank top had revealed several others, and she'd longed to trace each one with her fingertips to catalog them in her mind. Most men in Timasur didn't tattoo their bodies, but on Darius, Tahira found the ink attractive.

With his broad shoulders, defined chest and back, narrow waist and hips, muscular legs and arms, a chiseled jaw, and expressive eyes, more than one woman had drooled after Darius in Tahira's presence when he'd been her occasional bodyguard. But it wasn't until they'd returned from Argentina that the attention he drew from other women had bothered her, even if they just looked at him from afar. At the hospital and coming and going to Dr. Dunbar's office, there'd been several women silently flirting with him with their appreciative and hungry gazes.

Tahira was being naïve and selfish. Darius was doing something incredibly nice to help her. He wasn't hers to keep . . . she was only borrowing him. She would have to give him up after their charade was over, and as each moment with him passed, she worried if she would be able to do that without having her heart ripped out.

Standing in front of the vanity mirror, Tahira frowned. They would have to wait until her bruises could be completely covered by makeup before taking an engagement photo to be released to the press. If anyone noticed even a hint of discoloration in the photo, there would be questions Tahira didn't want to have answered.

She'd wanted to invite Darius to join her for dinner that evening, but then thought better of it—he'd gone home after their workout. She was still rattled about the kiss they'd shared. While she wanted to do it again, after her session with Dr. Dunbar, Tahira didn't want to use Darius as a crutch. She had to deal with her assault, not push it aside as if it'd never happened.

While kissing Darius had been an unforgettable experience, Tahira wasn't sure what would've happened if he'd tried to do more than just that. Would he have even wanted to do more? Or would that have taken them out of the friend-zone they seemed to be in. "Friends" was a word

Darius had used often since her rescue. He'd also said he cared for her, but that's what friends did, right?

Sighing, Tahira grabbed her favorite body lotion and massaged it into her skin. She couldn't bear to look at the bruises on her thighs and bypassed them with her hands. After they faded and then disappeared, she was certain she would still always see them. They were a vivid reminder of her rape, even though much of the assault was a jumble of bits and pieces in her mind. She couldn't recall the actual penetration, but it had happened, of that she was certain, even without Darius's confirmation.

Snatching a silk robe from the hook on the back of the bathroom door, she pulled it on while walking into her spacious bedroom. Her phone rang from where it sat on her nightstand. Glancing at the screen, she was happy to see it was Nala. She hadn't spoken to either of her cousins since their rescue but had been playing phone tag and texting with Nala earlier in the day. Lahana had not returned any of the calls or texts Tahira had sent.

Sitting on her bed, she answered the call. "Hello, cousin! How are you?"

"Thank goodness! I'm so glad to hear your voice! I'm okay, I guess. Jumping at sudden noises, and having trouble sleeping, but hopefully that will pass. How are you?" Nala sounded much younger than she had before their abduction.

"Bruised. Achy. Exhausted. But I will be okay. How is Lahana?"

"Oh, Tahira, I don't know. She is very . . . angry, I guess I would say. I told her I would never reveal what that man did to her, and she yelled at me, said it didn't matter. Her mother said she has barely come out of her bedroom. They have been letting her rest."

She was worried about Lahana. She'd been raped and had her virginity stolen from her just as viciously as Tahira. "She needs to speak to a counselor. I will make certain one is arranged for her. For you too. Talking with a trained professional will help you both heal from this."

"What about you?" Nala hesitated. "I mean, wh-what happened when . . ."

While she trusted her cousin, Tahira couldn't bring herself to confide in anyone else. Too many people already knew—Darius, Ian, Dr. Dunbar, and Dr. Moreau. In her mind, that was more than she was comfortable with, even though she knew her secret was safe with them. "I was rescued by Darius. He—he killed Secada before anything happened, then got me out of there." She swallowed the bitter taste that lie left in her mouth. "He found us a cave to shelter in for hours during the storm before the rest of his team found us. I have some bruises, but other than that, I am fine."

"Oh, thank goodness. I am so glad he got to you in time."

If only that were true.

"I heard congratulations are in order too. I can't believe you are marrying Darius! I mean, you never mentioned him other than that he was one of your bodyguards in the States."

Yet another lie fell from her lips. "Well, we talked a lot during the times we were together. Then after he rescued me, I knew he was my knight in shining armor, as they say."

"It is just like a fairy tale," Nala responded, her voice suddenly filled with wonder. "That is so romantic."

Tahira didn't want to discuss her impending, bogus marriage with anyone right now. Glancing at the clock, she saw it was a little after three p.m. That meant it was just after seven in the evening in Timasur. "I should try Lahana's phone again. Maybe she will talk to me."

"I hope so. Tell her I'm here for her if she needs anything."

"I will, cousin. And before I forget to tell you, I want you to know I am proud of you. You were very brave."

A sob came over the line. "No—no I wasn't. All I did was —was cry and cower."

Tahira wished she was in the same room with the younger woman, so she could comfort her. "That does not matter. We all cried and cowered. But you survived, and you will recover from this a much stronger person. Of that I am certain, cousin. I love you."

"I love you too," Nala responded through her tears.

"I will see you soon. Let me call Lahana and try to talk to her."

After disconnecting the call, she hit a speed dial button. After three rings the voice mail picked up. Having already left two messages, Tahira didn't bother leaving a third. Instead, she sent a text. "I am here for you. Please call me so I can hear that you are okay. I love you."

Setting the phone on the nightstand, Tahira brought her legs up and relaxed back on the bed. She couldn't remember the last time she'd taken a nap in the middle of the day before yesterday, but her ordeal had taken a toll on her body and psyche. Between her session with Dr. Dunbar, the walk on the treadmill, and her conversation with Nala, the energy had drained from Tahira, and she couldn't stay awake any longer. Closing her eyes, she brought up an image of Darius in her mind, then floated off to sleep.

Chapter Twenty-Eight

"My parents would like to know when they can meet your family."

Darius swallowed the piece of bacon he'd been chewing and reached for his coffee, trying to put off responding for another moment. To help with the engagement pretense, Ian had assigned him to Tahira's detail for the next few weeks. After being undercover in South America for months, Darius didn't mind the easy assignment one bit. Aside from dodging the press to attend her therapy sessions, Tahira had opted to stay sheltered behind the walls of the Clearwater Beach estate, not wanting to appear in public until the bruise on her cheek was completely gone. The finger marks had faded, and the right style of clothing could hide the discoloration on her arms, shoulders, and legs. Every time Darius saw one of the contusions, he wanted to kill Secada all over again.

With permission from the palace, Darius was staying in one of the guest rooms in the main house, which helped keep him out of the media's eye. It also meant he was spending a lot of time with Tahira—on and off duty. This morning, they were sharing breakfast on the patio, while two guards maintained their privacy from down on the dock.

As expected, after the formal engagement announcement last week, the press had done everything they could to find dirt on the man who'd reportedly won Princess Tahira's heart and hand in marriage. Outside of his SEAL teammates, very few people knew Darius had been one too. Those that did could be trusted to remain quiet about the Trident he'd earned and worn proudly yet secretly. Most of the people in his hometown thought he'd been working on a submarine during his time in the Navy, and that was the way Darius wanted it. As for his teammates, former and current, they had been a given—none of them would ever speak to a reporter.

However, although his black-ops life was protected, thanks to Brody's and Nathan's bad-ass computer skills, his personal life was up for grabs. There was only so much they could hide in this day and age, and it hadn't taken the media long before they'd descended on Brookford to harass its residents into telling everything they knew about Darius Knight. Levi had assigned an around-the-clock detail to sit outside their father's trailer to make certain no reporters ambushed the man and ended up on the wrong end of a shotgun. Unfortunately, the tabloids were now running stories about how the Knight patriarch lived in squalor, while Darius was marrying a wealthy princess. Thankfully, Darius had already explained the situation to King Rajeemh during a telephone call the other night. It was Phillip Knight's wish to reside where he did, and he resisted any attempt by his family to upgrade his living arrangements. Since he wasn't a threat to himself, only anyone stupid enough to ignore the "Trespassers Will Be Shot - This Is Not a Joke" signs Levi had put up along the property lines, their dad remained where he was—peacefully, most of the time.

As if sensing his reluctance, Tahira added, "I mean, your brother and sister. They realize meeting your father might not be possible. My grandfather had dementia for years before he passed away, so we understand what you must be going through. My father suggested we could meet Levi and Barrie within driving distance of your hometown. He does not want to invade Brookford with the royal entourage that must always accompany them. What would be the nearest city that would be convenient for them?"

The more time he spent with Tahira, talking about anything and everything, the more she tunneled her way into his heart. He was attracted to her, there was no denying that. And they got along great. She was more fun to be around than he'd realized—at least when he wasn't on bodyguard detail. Then, she seemed to disconnect from him, and that confused the hell out of him. But it also put him back in his place. He wasn't royalty and never would be. He was a military man who'd seen things Tahira could never imagine—the worst of humanity. Yes, she'd suffered through her own barbaric assault, but the things Darius had seen and done, in the name of God, country, family, and the innocent, should never touch the beautiful woman sitting across the table from him. He wasn't worthy of her. Despite the rape, she was still virtuous and naïve, and he would only sully that.

But, damn, he wanted her. Maybe it was because he shouldn't. Or maybe it was because in any other lifetime, the princess wouldn't be caught dead with such a lowly peasant. No, that wasn't it—he suspected Tahira would be the same person even if she'd grown up poor—gorgeous, funny, sweet, caring, generous, and intelligent. Most of those traits he'd never noticed before, simply because he'd been a hired gun who only needed to be ready to take a bullet for her.

The first time he'd been on her protection detail, while she'd attended an AIDS research fundraiser, he'd seen a ravishing young woman, dressed to the nines, with curves that would have a comatose man sitting up to take notice. But he'd also seen a woman so far out of his league that they were on two different playing fields. She traveled the world and stayed in the most luxurious resorts and palaces available. Hell, the woman wore a fucking crown on certain official occasions. Darius had also traveled the world, but he'd done it while wearing combat boots, a KABAR, and camouflage. And "luxurious" accommodations for him meant anywhere he didn't have to sleep on the floor.

Yup, they were the complete opposite, but as they say, opposites attract. And he was attracted to her—big time. Hell, he'd taken to jacking off almost on a daily basis. Being so near her and not being able to do more than kiss or hold her was wreaking havoc on his libido. But the last thing he wanted to do was push her into something she wasn't ready for. And she wouldn't be ready until at least after they were married. She'd held onto her virginity for so long, and just because it had been ripped from her didn't mean it no longer mattered. To him, she'd be a virgin in every sense of the word until after the wedding, and then it was her decision where they would go from there.

"Darius?"

He shook his head and gave her a small smile. "I'm sorry. I zoned out there for a little bit. Um, yeah, I guess we could arrange that. I'll call Levi and Barrie and ask them what day and place would be good for them. We have Levi's officers and some family friends who can watch our dad for a few hours. We'll have to figure something out so they can both attend the wedding."

As much as he didn't want his siblings and teammates flying to Timasur to attend the event, he hadn't been able to come up with a good enough reason for them not to. There was no way he could tell them the marriage would be over in a few short months. When he'd suggested the ruse to Tahira three weeks ago, he'd thought the whole thing would be easy-peasy—just another mission. Marry, wait a few months, get a divorce or an annulment, then go on with the rest of their lives—simple, right? But every time Darius turned around, there was some other issue he hadn't considered. There were more speed bumps in the road than he'd expected, but their destination stayed the same. The wedding would take place, hopefully without a hitch, and he'd deal with the fallout of the divorce when the time came. In another year or two, when Tahira met someone worthy of being her husband for the rest of her life, everyone would forget her first marriage had ever existed.

They had five more weeks until the wedding took place—apparently, everyone involved, including the caterers, the wedding planner, the florist, and the dress designer, had dropped everything to be involved in the Timasur wedding of the year. It was going to be a huge shindig that Darius couldn't even comprehend, even though Tahira had insisted on a having much smaller event than her brother's wedding the year before. The day before the official Christian wedding was a huge affair, including traditional Timasurian dress and festivities. Their culture and customs incorporated bits and pieces from other countries in Europe and Africa, including Mali, Egypt, England, France, Portugal, and Morocco. Darius would be wearing a tuxedo for the church service and a silk shirt, silk pants, and sash for the cultural ceremony. He would also be barefoot for the latter.

Yeah, he couldn't wait to hear how much shit Levi was going to give him when his younger brother saw the outfit. Hell, he was already taking a ribbing from his teammates after McCabe had walked in on Darius being measured for both outfits by a royal seamstress who'd brought several versions to the estate for him to try on.

"Have you spoken to Lahana lately?" It had been a week since Tahira had spoken to her cousin, who was spending time at her family's vacation home in the French Riviera.

Tahira sighed. "No, I have not. She will not return my calls or texts anymore."

Things hadn't gone well the first time she'd finally gotten Lahana on the phone. Even though her cousin had been raped and assaulted too, Tahira hadn't been comfortable admitting her truth, especially over the phone where there was always the possibility of someone listening in. After their terse conversation, Tahira had told Darius that Lahana blamed her for getting them into the mess in the first place, which was ridiculous. The cruise and destinations had been Lahana's idea, and there was no way they could have foreseen the abduction. Apparently, Lahana was also resentful over the fact Darius had saved Tahira, while Lahana had no white knight—her words—who'd rushed in to rescue her before she'd been raped. The woman had ended the call by hanging up on Tahira when she'd been in mid-sentence.

"Maybe I should tell her we do have something in common, that we were both . . ." She glanced around, wary someone might overhear her. "You know."

Darius reached across the table, took her hand, and kept his voice low. "That's completely up to you, sweetheart. I'll support you in whatever way I can. But the more people you tell, the better chance there is that it gets out."

"I know. I will have to think about it."

"Well, whatever you decide, I'll support you."

A brilliant smile spread across her face. "Thank you, Darius, for everything."

When her gaze dropped to where their hands were, Darius's followed. Without him realizing it, his thumb was caressing her soft skin. Heat flared in his groin, making him hard, and he cursed inwardly. He had to stop thinking about her in a sexual manner, but she was making it very difficult. Aside from a few chaste—in his opinion—make-out sessions, he hadn't pushed her any further. Then, again, with the increase in staff at the estate, between the security guards and the people assigned to help plan the wedding, among other things, Darius and Tahira hadn't had much time to themselves except for moments like this. But here and there, they'd been able to share a few intimate moments. After all, they had to appear comfortable and in love in the presence of others—at least that was what he'd told himself every time they'd kissed.

He was about to pull his hand away when she squeezed it and then released him. Shy passion simmered in her eyes, stirring his own desire, but she changed the subject. "So, what movie is on the agenda tonight?"

They had a mutual love of horror movies, much to Darius's delight. Tahira hadn't seemed like the Stephen King or M. Night Shyamalan type, but Darius had been off on most of his assumptions about the pretty princess. Three or four times a week, they could be found in the mansion's sixteen-seat, movie theater-style, viewing room with its ninety-eight-inch screen, watching a classic or newly released horror film. Some nights, it was just the two of them. Other nights, Tahira had invited some staff members and Darius's teammates and significant others to join them. The Omega team got a kick out of it because there was a popcorn cart, a stash of the usual snack bar candies, a soda fountain, leather reclining seats, and a surround-sound system to rival a commercial movie theater—talk about the lifestyles of the rich and famous. And that was only a *quarter* of the size of the one at the royal palace in Timasur, Tahira had told them.

After wiping his mouth with his napkin, he said, "I was going to talk to you about that. They're having a small get-together at the Trident compound—nothing fancy, just a barbecue. Would you like to go with me? We wouldn't have to worry about the press, even if they do follow us. The security over there is top-notch. Any reporter that manages to step foot on the property will have to deal with armed guards and BDS&M."

Her eyes widened. "Excuse me?"

A chuckle vibrated from his chest. As far as he knew, she wasn't aware there was a sex club at the compound, having never been on the property. "Sorry. Not BDSM as in kink. BDS&M is the nickname for the four guard dogs Kat Michaelson trained for Trident. Their names are from the military alphabet—Bravo, Delta, Sierra, and Mike." He shrugged. "Ian's weird sense of humor."

"Oh." She relaxed back into her seat and smiled. "Yes, Ian does have an odd sense of humor sometimes, although, I think he curbs it around my family, as we are clients as well as friends. And to answer your question, I would love to go. I have wanted to see the yard Angelina designed for Ian. I hear it is wonderful."

"Great, then it's a date . . ." He mentally smacked himself. "Sorry, I mean—"

"Please do not be sorry, Darius. If it is okay with you, I would like to consider it a date. But if that is not what you want—"

God, he was going to hell. Before now, he'd been able to talk himself out of the feeling they were dating. But it did make sense—after all, in a few weeks they'd be husband and wife. Being a couple should proceed that, right? "Then a date it is."

CHAPTER TWENTY-NINE

"May I hold him?" Tahira asked Kristen. Little JD—John Devon Sawyer—had just woken up from his nap, and she was dying to cuddle with the infant.

"Of course!" Devon's wife didn't hesitate to hand over the little boy.

Cradling him in her arms, Tahira gently swayed back and forth, inhaling his sweet baby scent. He studied her with a piercing blue gaze that'd been passed down from his paternal ancestry. JD was going to be as handsome as his father. "He has your nose and mouth and Devon's eyes."

"I wish he had Devon's nose too. Mine's shaped weird."

"That's five, Pet," her husband responded from a few feet away, causing Kristen to blush.

Pivoting toward him, she placed her hands on her hips. "Darn it. You weren't supposed to hear that. How the heck can you talk and listen to a conversation five feet away at the same time?"

"It's a gift. Want to try for ten? Just roll your eyes like I know you want to, Pet, and it can be arranged." When she didn't respond, he smirked and went back to his conversation with Val, Tristan, and Cain—Darius's teammates who'd helped rescue the women in Argentina.

Tahira's eyes narrowed when the woman turned back to her. "What do those numbers mean?"

"They mean I'm going to have my rear-end spanked five times because I put myself down." She sighed. "Actually, I put my nose down, but it doesn't matter. Dev doesn't like it when I talk about myself in the negative sense."

Having read all of Kristen's books, and those by other BDSM authors, Tahira knew Doms didn't tolerate their submissives denigrating themselves. And Devon was definitely a dominant, as was his older brother, Ian. Their younger brother, Nick, was all alpha too, except when it came to his husband, Jake Donovan, his brothers' friend, employee, and teammate. Then Nick's submissive side came out. If Tahira hadn't read numerous gay and ménage romance books over the past few years, she probably wouldn't have noticed the change in the man when his Dom was near or the charm that Nick wore on a chain around his neck. Tahira had been curious about the Triskelion after reading about it in several books. It was similar to a Yin Yang but had three equal parts instead of two and was commonly used in BDSM communities.

While Tahira had gotten to know her Trident bodyguards better over the past two years, especially since she'd grown close to Ian and Angie, she'd learned a lot more about them and their significant others over the past few weeks. With Darius living in Clearwater Beach with her, his co-workers came by often and not always to work. When they were off duty, they let down their hair, so to speak, in a way they usually didn't do around her. She felt herself being drawn into their extended family and was enjoying it. She loved how, while still respectful of her title and her status as a client, they treated her like she was one of them.

However, this was the first time she'd heard Kristen mention she participated in the lifestyle. Well, it did make sense, since on the other side of the compound there was a sex club that Ian, Devon, and their cousin Mitch had founded. Tahira had only learned about that a little over a year ago, but she'd never been to the compound before, so she'd never seen the inside of the club. She had to admit her curiosity was getting the better of her. Was it similar to the way Kristen described her opulent fictional club, Leathers? Or was it more of a dark dungeon like she'd read about in other books?

Someone moved in behind her, and Tahira had an unfamiliar urge to jump away. When Darius's head peered over her shoulder, her body almost sagged against his in relief. His hands rested on her hips in a way she was beginning to get used to. When others were around, the couple did their best to appear in love and engaged—that meant they needed to show off a certain level of intimacy. While in the public eye, there were rules about displays of affection for members of the royal family, but those rules were tempered while among only family and friends.

Now, she felt the heat of Darius's body against her back and through her jeans where his palms and fingers made contact. A stirring of want and passion swirled in her lower abdomen. What she wouldn't give to have this attraction she was imagining between them be real. She'd never met a man she wanted more than her next breath. Her body responded to Darius in a way she'd never experienced before. It tingled when it felt his gaze upon it. Desire made her panties wet— something she never expected with the aftereffects of her rape. Maybe it was because she couldn't remember the way she'd been violated. Everything after being thrown onto the bastard's bed that day was a blur.

But maybe, it was Darius himself, who made her feel safe,

who was the reason her body felt like this. The kisses they'd shared over the past few weeks were wonderful, yet she knew he was holding back. While she would not have sex with him until after they were wed, it was getting frustrating that they hadn't gone any further than making out.

"You look comfortable holding him. You'll make a great mother someday."

Tahira smiled at him and then down at the baby again. "I hope so. Despite my royal upbringing, I am very close to my parents, and they were good role models for my brother and I throughout our childhood." While she and Raj had grown up with several nannies and teachers always around, the king and queen had made certain they were an active part of their children's daily lives. One of Tahira's favorite memories was being tucked in at night by either her mother or father and having them read a story or two for her. That was probably why she'd developed a deep love of books over the years.

In Tahira's arms, JD squirmed and grew red-faced.

"Uh-oh," Kristen said as she reached for him. "That's his I'm-going-to-scream-because-my-tummy-is-empty   face." Sure enough, the little boy opened his mouth and let out a wail for everyone to hear. "If you'll excuse me."

She stepped over to one of the many sitting areas of the grass-covered backyard, set between two of the four ware-house buildings that made up a large portion of the compound's structures, and sat down. Ian's lab/pit mix followed and laid down beside them. Within seconds, JD was suckling on his mother's breast. Nursing was something Tahira had never seen in person before—in her country, that took place behind closed doors—but, of course, she'd seen it on the internet and in movies. Kristen and her child looked so connected and peaceful that it almost took Tahira's breath away.

A giggle from Angie had Tahira turning to look at the

other woman, who was due with her own child in about six weeks. "What?"

"I can hear your biological clock ticking from here," she said with a grin, rubbing her swollen belly. She glanced back and forth between Tahira and Darius, who was now standing close to her side. "You know, I was worried about the two of you—I thought maybe you were rushing into this marriage thing in the heat of . . . whatever heat you were in. But as I watch you two, you look good together, and you definitely can't keep your eyes off each other. Tahira, you just about melt when Darius looks at you. And Darius, you have that possessive Dom stare down pat, even though that's not your thing."

Choking on the beer he'd been drinking, Darius coughed harshly, before blushing. Tahira felt her own cheeks warm. After wiping his mouth, Darius shook his head at Angie. "Seriously? I mean, I doubt Tahira even knows what that means."

Tahira crossed her arms, cocked her hip to her side, and lifted her chin. How dare he make her seem immature. "What do *you* mean, Darius? Of course, I know what she meant when she called you a Dom. I may be a princess, but I am not that naïve. I have read all of Kristen's books and many more like them. I know what Doms and submissives are. I also know there is a sex club on the other side of the parking lot."

His jaw dropped as Angie snickered at him. "Hey, Ian. I think Batman needs some Dom lessons—fast!"

◇◇◇◇◇

DARIUS DIDN'T KNOW IF HE WAS SHOCKED, MAD, AROUSED, OR just plain going insane. One thing he did know, he was proud of Tahira. She'd stood up for herself. He'd been stupid to assume she was so innocent she didn't know what the lifestyle was about. Hell, it sounded like she knew more about it than he did, and he was surrounded by people who lived it. He stared at Tahira, seeing her with a new set of eyes, like he'd done several times since he'd found her in Diaz's prison. She continued to amaze him and that made his attraction to her grow even more.

"Damn it, Batman. Stop digging a fucking hole and apologize for whatever you just said to piss off your fiancée," Ian chastised from his grill station, where he was cooking hamburgers, hot dogs, and shish-kabobs.

Ignoring his boss, Darius nodded. "You're right, sweetheart. It was wrong of me to make that assumption. I'm sorry."

Her expression softened. "Apology accepted. Thank you." She pivoted back to Angie. "Now, what are the chances of me seeing the club? I want to know if it is similar to my expectations after reading Kristen's books."

The pregnant woman's eyes widened. "Um . . . that you're going to have to ask my husband. I have no say in the matter when it comes to non-members seeing it. Ian!"

"What, Angel?"

"Tahira wants to see the club."

Ian glanced over his shoulder and stared at them a moment. "Sure. But ask someone else to take them over there. I don't want you walking more than necessary."

From the looks of things, Darius didn't know who was more surprised at Boss-man's response—him, Angie, or anyone else attending the impromptu party, who all seemed to have stopped talking at the same time. In fact, the only ones who didn't appear shocked were JD, Marco and Harper's toddler, Mara, and Tahira. It wasn't often anyone who wasn't a member was allowed in the club. But, then again, Darius knew what Ian was thinking—the same thing he'd suggested to him a few weeks ago. Tahira might benefit from them both learning about the lifestyle. Darius didn't miss how the man had said, "take *them* over there." Clearly, Darius was supposed to go with Tahira to see the place. It wasn't that he'd never been in there—as an employee of Trident, he'd needed to sign the club's non-disclosure agreement like all its members. He'd been in there several times, both while it was closed and open, though he usually stayed at the bar during the latter.

"I can walk you over," Harper said, handing her sleeping daughter to her husband. "I have to get something out of my locker anyway."

"Tahira." She looked at Ian, who was pointing the spatula he was using at her and eyeing her intently.

"Yes?"

"Anything you see in there, stays there. Privacy is a big part of our world. I'm trusting you by not demanding you sign a non-disclosure agreement before going in there."

A broad smile crossed her face, and her eyes twinkled with delight. "Thank you, Ian. I will not tarnish that trust."

"Batman." Ian nodded his head to the side, indicating he wanted a word in private with him. Darius approached and stopped in front of his boss, who glared at him and lowered his voice. "You do *not* play in any way, shape, or form without training. I so much as get a hint of you messing around without knowing how she might get hurt, I'm going to hurt *you* like you've never been hurt before. Got it, twatopotomus?"

Oh, yeah. He got it.

Five minutes later, Harper led them down the grand staircase to The Covenant's "pit" as the members called it. Apparently, it felt more like one than a dungeon, with the balcony that encircled it so people could watch the fun from above.

"This is beautiful." Tahira's assessing gaze was everywhere, taking in the burgundy, dark green, and gold color scheme, the iron lighting fixtures and accents, the leather chairs and couches in numerous seating areas, and, of course, the BDSM apparatus in cordoned off sections around the expansive room's perimeter. "Ian and Devon designed this themselves?"

"From what I'm told," Harper responded, "their cousin, Mitch, who manages the club, came up with the original, two-story design after Ian had purchased the compound for the security business. I think this was originally slated to be a training building. Ian and Devon didn't make many changes to Mitch's plans. From there, the three of them traveled to many upscale lifestyle clubs around the world and incorporated the elements they liked best. The only parts that were added later were the garden, which is upstairs at the far end, and the twelve new theme rooms below that. I'll have to show you the garden—you'll love it. It's my favorite place now."

Darius watched as the submissive took Tahira on a tour of the place. Her face was filled with awe and enchantment, things he hadn't expected. He was also seeing the club from another perspective for the first time. It was elegant, sensual, and a bit forbidden, and it stirred something within him. Suddenly, he could imagine Tahira sitting on the floor next to his chair, with her head resting on his thigh as he stroked her thick hair. She wouldn't be naked like some of the Doms preferred their submissives to be in the club. Instead, he'd have her wearing a harem costume or something like that. With the culture she'd been raised in, she'd probably be more comfortable that way. He also wouldn't want any other man seeing what was his.

Shit. Get a grip, Knight. She's not yours! In a few months this will all be over, and you can go back to your occasional one- or two-night stands.

The thought made him frown. When had he gone from "casual affairs" with no entanglements to thinking of a woman as his and his alone? And not just for the moment, but for a very, very long time. Like forever. *Shit.*

Chapter Thirty

The huge indoor "garden" was stunning. Tahira felt like she'd stepped onto the four-square-mile tropical island her family owned in the South Pacific. Its faux-grass, potted plants, shrubs, and tall trees, cabanas with sheer, white curtains and daybeds to lounge on, a non-alcoholic tiki-bar—alcohol was only allowed at the main bar above the pit—and a retractable roof gave it an outdoor atmosphere. When the roof was open, a mesh screen was in place to keep out bugs and thwart camera lenses. Apparently, two of the club's well-known members, fraternal-twin brothers, and their wife had their lifestyle plastered all over the internet, because of the men's jealous ex. Afterward, the press had been trying to get a glimpse of the inside of The Covenant and had used drones. But the screen was coated in a way that let the fresh air and light in, yet nothing else. Any images that were taken while the roof was open just showed a layer of black and nothing more.

Tahira loved the little paths that wound around the foliage to hidden areas where people could have a sense of privacy even though anyone could walk by at any given time.

"Harper De . . ." she paused, trying to curb her habit of using the first and last names of those people she didn't know well in order to remember them. She was getting better, but there were times she faltered. Darius grinned and winked at her, obviously knowing she'd caught herself. She winked back and then looked at the other woman. "I can see why you love it so much. It is beautiful. I would probably want to spend most of my time here too. Although, the rest of the club is magnificent too. May I ask how long you have been in the lifestyle? Or is that too personal a question?"

Harper snorted and waved her hand. "Oh, nothing's too personal to me. I tend to be a bit of an exhibitionist, at least when Mara isn't around. I went to my first munch in college and have been involved in the lifestyle ever since. Marco started while in the Navy and introduced Brody to it when they both ended up on the same team with Darius."

"They were on the team a few years before I was assigned to it," he said. "There were a bunch of guys besides them who were into the lifestyle, but I never saw the draw. I've learned a lot more about it since I started with Trident—it's hard not to with the club right next door. But what's a munch again? I've heard the term before but never really paid attention to what it meant."

"It's a get-together where people interested in the lifestyle can meet experienced Doms and subs and ask questions and learn what it's all about. There should be no play allowed at munches, but sometimes you'll see some non-sexual videos, defining different types of play, to give people a taste of what they might see at a club."

"I find Shibari fascinating," Tahira exclaimed, much to Darius's surprise, as she sat on the edge of one of the daybeds under a cabana. "Does anyone do that here?"

"Oh, yes. In fact, Master Stefan is an expert at it. He teaches some classes a few times a year and will do demonstrations. And you're right—it *is* fascinating. I love to watch it, although I'm not too keen on being suspended like that. I trust Marco—I don't trust the ropes."

Darius had seen one of Coast Guard Lieutenant Stefan Lundquist's rope demos. It really was kind of mesmerizing to see him bind his submissive, Cassandra, one of the club's waitresses, then suspend her from the ceiling using a pulley system. The woman was usually zoned out—subspace was what they called it—by the time she was raised into the air.

Harper gestured to the large, inviting space with her hands. "Look around some more, if you want. I'm just going to run down to the women's locker room. I'll be back in a few minutes."

As the other woman left them alone, Darius sat down on the bed next to Tahira. "When have you seen a Shibari demonstration?"

"I've never seen one in person, but I have seen videos of it on the internet."

"Yeah, I guess you can find anything on the internet these days." He paused. "Can I ask you something?"

The seriousness in his voice had Tahira shifting her body to face him. She placed her hand on his where it rested on the mattress. "Of course, Darius. You can ask me anything."

He took a deep breath and let it out slowly. "Before I ask it, just know that this would be your decision, okay?"

"Okay." She had no idea what he was leading up to.

"After Ian figured out what was going on with us, he suggested there were things about being in the lifestyle that might help you deal with what happened better. He's willing to train me to be a Dom for you. Nothing wild and kinky, but there are aspects of BDSM that are more psychological in nature than sexual. He mentioned that giving you control might help you overcome the fact things had been out of your control. Does that make sense?"

Tahira bit her bottom lip and thought for a moment. She'd been reading one of her favorite BDSM authors' books over the past few days and had wondered about the same thing Ian had suggested. While there were parts of the lifestyle that did not appeal to her—exhibitionism being one of them—she'd been pondering how the submissives in the books willingly relinquished control to their Doms. After they felt safe enough to do it, they didn't have to worry about making any decisions. They only had to get lost in how their Doms made them feel—with or without sexual contact. With their safewords, lists of limits, and trust in their Doms, the submissives still controlled the scene. There was no worry that their Doms would go beyond what was safe, sane, and consensual.

"Yes, it does, and I think it might be a good idea." She paused. "But what about you, Darius? How do you feel about it? Is it something you are interested in? I do not want to impose on you any more than I have already."

"You're not imposing, sweetheart." He sighed. "If you'd asked me weeks ago if I was interested in it, I would've said no. But after talking to Ian, I've been doing a little research on my own, and I think it really might help you. But it's totally up to you. If you say no, then that's the end of it. This is not something I *need* like some of the other guys. But it might be something you can benefit from, and if you're willing, then so am I." He reached up and cupped her cheek. "I worry about you. You're still having nightmares." When she opened her mouth, he stopped her. "And don't deny it. What I want to know is why haven't you come to me for comfort? You have to know I'd do anything to help you, Princess."

"I do know that, and I thank you, but I did not want to disturb your sleep."

"Princess, I sleep very lightly after all my years in the

Navy. If you need me, please don't shut me out. I'm one of the few people you can talk to, and I want to be here for you."

She held his hand to her cheek and closed her eyes for a moment, wishing they had a real romantic relationship and not one based on a lie. Blinking, she focused on his soft green eyes. Something had changed between them within the last few moments, and she pulled back a bit to concentrate, seeing something she'd never seen with him before—his aura!

Multiple colors swirled around Darius, and Tahira zeroed in on each one and their meanings. Shades of green for healing and compassion; indigos for benevolence; and reds for passion and strength. Tahira's breath hitched. His aura was just as beautiful as the man.

"Tahira, what's wrong?"

His voice drew her back into focus. "I am sorry, Darius. As you say, I zoned out for a moment. Nothing is wrong. In fact, I think a lot of things are suddenly right. Yes, I would like for you to help me explore this lifestyle, and I hope I can give you something back in return."

Without hesitation or waiting for him to respond, she closed the distance between them and pressed her mouth to his. He stiffened for a split second before he took over the kiss, his hand going into her hair and holding her there. A groan escaped him as his tongue demanded entry to her mouth. She parted her lips for him, her arms going around his neck as she moved even closer. Whatever had just happened between them released a hunger she'd never experienced before. Up until now, their make-out sessions had been relatively tame. But now, she silently urged him to release whatever he'd been holding back from her.

His hands slid down her sides and grasped her hips. Tugging them, he pulled her closer until she was straddling his lap. She grew wet as she felt his erection pulsating against her sex. Once she was settled, his hands stroked the contours of her back. Taking his cue, she let her own hands roam over the sinewy muscles of his shoulders, upper back, and arms. As their lips melded together, his tongue dueled with hers, and his hand snaked around and cupped her breast, causing Tahira to moan in pleasure and need.

A clanging sound in the main club had Darius breaking the kiss. They were both panting heavily as he stared at her with lust-filled eyes, seconds before regret filled them. "I'm sorry, Tahira—"

"Hush, Darius. Please do not say that. I very much enjoyed what just happened between us, and I want it to happen again. It proves that what that bastard did to me has not made me afraid of intimacy with a man . . . with you. I am a grown woman, with passion and desire filling me every time you touch me. He could not take that from me, and I will not let you or anyone else deny me what is rightfully mine. I may not be experienced with a man, but I know you will not hurt me, physically or emotionally." She hesitated a moment. "But if you are having second thoughts and do not want me as much as I want you, then I will understand—"

He snorted. "Not want you?" He flexed his hips, grinding his manhood against her core. "Does this feel like I don't want you, Princess? Does this feel like I don't find you desirable? I like you very much, sweetheart, and I care for you just as much. Trust me when I say I would be honored to have you in my bed. But that's your decision. I won't push you in any way. If and when you would like to take things further, then just let me know. But under no circumstances do you come to me because you feel obligated because of the wedding or that you owe me for helping you out, understand? That is not what I want at all."

She smiled and blinked away a few tears that tried to escape her watery eyes. "Yes, I understand." She caressed his cheek, loving the feel of his evening stubble rasping against her palm. "You are a very noble man, Darius. And do not roll your eyes at me when I compliment you like that. I know Doms will not allow that, and I am making it a rule between us too. I will not roll my eyes at you if you do not roll your eyes at me." He grinned at her demand. "I want you very much, Darius. I will always be grateful for what you are doing for me, but that is not part of my attraction to you. You make me feel more like a woman than anyone else has in my entire life. I feel the heat of your gaze from across a room. My heart speeds up and the rest of my body reacts just because it knows you are near. No man has ever done that to me before."

From just inside the door to the main club, Harper appeared, cutting off anything Darius may have said. The woman grinned, knowingly, when she saw them. "Are you ready to go back? I'm getting hungry."

Placing one last kiss on Darius's lips, Tahira climbed off his lap, stood, and held out her hand. As he took it, hope and love filled her heart. She'd discovered several things in the past few minutes. The most important one was she'd found her soulmate. Now she just had to wait until he realized it too.

CHAPTER THIRTY-ONE

"Would you stop fidgeting, Barrie?"

Darius's sister glared at him from across the opulent, private elevator in the Knoxville hotel where King Rajeemh and Queen Azhar were staying for the night. It was an hour away from Brookford. While the royal couple had wanted to make their visit longer, it hadn't been possible—they were heading to New York for a session at the UN tomorrow. But maybe that was a good thing, since Barrie looked like she was going to faint at any moment.

Levi and Barrie had arrived a short time ago, and Darius and Amar had taken the elevator down to meet them and escort them back upstairs to the thirty-sixth-floor penthouses. There was a full dining room in the suite where Tahira's parents would host supper for them, as well as Prince Raj and Princess Kainda who were sharing the second three-bedroom penthouse with Darius and Tahira. The king and queen were keeping the dinner low-key, with family members only, so members of their loyal entourage would not be attending. They'd wanted Darius's siblings to feel relaxed and not overwhelmed. Only a few staff members would be on hand to assist with the meal and anything else that was needed.

Of course, there were bodyguards strategically placed all over the hotel and the buildings around it. Tahira's royal guards had accompanied her and Darius on the private jet they'd taken from Tampa to Knoxville, while Amar led the others protecting the rest of her family. An advance security team had arrived earlier in the week to ensure their safety, going over the floor plans of the building and noting any possible issues that could arise. Until the royal entourage had walked into the lobby this morning, no one at the hotel, with the exception of the manager and the security staff, had been aware of who'd reserved the two penthouses and the entire floor below them. And those people had only found out when the team had arrived to fill them in. The Knoxville police department and local FBI, however, had been aware of the royal family's visit for several days and had worked with the security team. As far as Darius could tell, Amar's men had everything under control.

The press had swarmed in not long after word of the king and queen's visit had been leaked—that had been expected—but by then the couple had been safely ensconced in their suite. An underground parking garage would ensure their departure tomorrow would go just as smoothly.

"I'm nervous, all right?" Barrie responded with a growl, as she fiddled with the neckline of her black and ivory dress for the hundredth time in the past five minutes. "Do I look okay? Maybe I should have worn the blue dress. Are these shoes too high? I don't want to be taller than anyone. It would be offensive if I looked down on them, right?"

"You look great, and they put their pants on the same way we all do, sis. Just remember to address them as 'Your Highness,' unless they say otherwise. And I'm sure your height will not be a problem." Hell, she was only five-foot-four without her three-inch heels.

"I forget—do I curtsey? What if I do something wrong? Oh my God, I'll be mortified. My palms are sweating, and I forgot to bring tissues." Instead of wiping them on her dress, she used the back of Levi's suit jacket.

Darius and Amar chuckled as Levi rolled his eyes and said, "You read the protocols more times than I did, and you don't remember any of this? No, you don't need to curtsey in the private setting, but you do bow when you're first introduced. And don't hold out your hand until they do. Now chill. You'll be fine."

When the doors opened, an amused Amar led them out to the small foyer that served both penthouses. Four heavily-armed guards had been expecting them, and one of them opened the door to the left of the elevator. The siblings followed the head of security into the spacious living room of the suite, before he disappeared into one of the extra rooms. The royal family stood to greet them, and Darius did the honors. "Your Royal Majesties, may I introduce my brother and sister, Levi and Barbara Knight." Gesturing to the patriarch first, he continued. "Levi, Barrie, this is His Royal Highness King Rajeemh, Her Royal Highness Queen Azhar, His Royal Highness, Prince Raj, Her Royal Highness Princess Kainda, and this . . . this is my fiancée, Her Royal Highness, Princess Tahira."

Without hesitation, a smiling King Rajeemh stepped forward and held his hand out to Levi, who shook it and bowed slightly at the waist. "It is a pleasure to meet you both." Barrie was flustered and blushing when the man turned to her, but she didn't make any of the faux pas she'd been afraid of. "It is an honor to welcome Darius's family into our own."

As if on cue, the rest of the royal family welcomed them,

with Tahira giving Levi and then Barrie a hug. "I am so happy to finally meet you, Levi. Barbara."

"Thank you, Princess Tahira," Barrie responded, clearly still trying to get her bearings. "Please call me Barrie. I haven't gone by Barbara since I was an infant and Levi couldn't pronounce my name."

"Barrie it is then. And please call me Tahira. I prefer it in a private setting."

"That goes for my wife and I as well," Raj said, gesturing for them all to take a seat. "Please feel free to call us by our given names. It can get quite stuffy with all the protocols. May I offer you something to drink?"

Darius had to hand it to the royals. Within no time, his brother and sister were relaxed and enjoying the evening. As always, Barrie was in her element when the casual talk began to flow easily. She was a brilliant conversationalist, and it never ceased to amaze him how she communicated with others—making certain there was never a shortage of topics, nor did she monopolize the discussion. She listened to what others had to say and contributed her own opinions without putting anyone on the defensive.

Like Darius, Levi was a little quieter, but he was constantly aware of his surroundings. Between his stint in the Marines and then his training and experience in law enforcement, it came with the territory. But he also contributed to the conversation in an easy manner. However, also like Darius, he probably couldn't wait to shed the suit he wore. Levi had grumbled about it when told he had to wear one since the royals would be formally dressed.

Taking a sip of the Tennessee whiskey he'd been served, Darius side-eyed Tahira sitting beside him on the couch. She looked stunning in her violet-colored, one-shoulder dress which stopped just below her knees and accentuated her bronze skin. It was made of a light material that swayed freely when she walked. He'd almost swallowed his tongue when she'd come out of her bedroom earlier. Her hair was up in some complicated twist, and her makeup and jewelry were understated. He was having a difficult time taking his eyes off her.

Something had happened between them the other day in the club—well, beyond the obvious. There was a change in Tahira—she seemed stronger and more confident than he'd ever seen her. She seemed more at ease and was flirting with him again, and not in the way she'd done with him and her other American bodyguards before her abduction. No, this was the kind of flirting a woman did with a man she really wanted. A man she was falling in love with. And, damn it, instead of scaring the crap out of Darius, it was doing the opposite. Somewhere along the line, he'd stopped thinking of her as a friend in need. Now, she was a woman he could imagine himself spending the rest of his life with. But there were several problems with that line of thinking—one of them being she was royalty and he was a Navy frog who'd killed people in defense of his country and while protecting the innocent. He wished he could be the man for her—for a lifetime—but that was impossible. Her home was on the other side of the freaking world, and he couldn't leave his *own* home to follow her there. His family and team needed him. Even if she wanted to live in Florida, it was highly doubtful things would work out for them long-term.

But the longer they were together, the harder he knew it would be to leave her when the time came. She deserved someone better than him. Someone sophisticated and well-bred. Someone who was more comfortable in suits and tuxedos than cargo pants and boots. Someone who could maintain the lifestyle she'd grown up in. While Darius had quite a bit of money saved, there was no way he could afford to give her a mansion like the one they were currently sharing. It would be her money that supported them in anything beyond a middle-class status. He couldn't bring her down to his financial level. However, he could give her what she needed right now.

Darius had spoken to Ian and Devon alone after returning to the barbecue. They'd agreed to start the engaged couple's BDSM training starting this weekend, in private sessions at the club when it was closed. While Ian and Darius would remain the only ones aware of Tahira's rape, Kristen and Angie would also be involved in the couple's training.

He was nervous about the whole thing, but Darius was now convinced the experience would help Tahira. He just hoped he would be a good Dom for her. Ian had given him a packet of papers to look over, and complete as needed, with Tahira. There was a long list of protocols—something Tahira was used to—and a three-page limit list. Through an embarrassing-at-times conversation the other day, they'd gone through the list of all types of BDSM play. Darius had been happy to see they were on the same page with practically every activity. While Tahira didn't have personal experience with any of the items on the list, she'd been able to tell him what she was interested in trying and what were hard limits for her. Most of those matched Darius's own. Suffice to say they would probably be the least kinky couple in The Covenant, and that was fine with both of them.

Tahira had read and signed the non-disclosure agreement the club's owners insisted on for every member or guest. The couple was also given a three-month, free membership to make certain this was something they wanted to continue to explore. Darius suspected their D/s relationship would exist mostly behind closed doors, and he was perfectly fine with that.

The rest of the evening went well, and when Barrie and Levi bid the royal family goodbye, there had been lots of hugging and friendly handshakes. After Darius's siblings confirmed he and Tahira would be visiting Brookford tomorrow, they took their leave to drive home. Tahira had wanted to see where they'd all grown up, and Darius couldn't say no to her. As for stopping in to see his father, they would have to play that by ear. If Phillip Knight was having a bad day, Darius didn't want Tahira anywhere near the man—no offense intended to either of them. It was just safer and less embarrassing for everyone.

As Darius prepared to return to the other suite with Tahira, Raj, and Kainda, Amar exited the security room. "Darius, my friend. May I have a word with you."

The man's eyes were cold. *This can't be good.*

Darius turned to Tahira. "Do you mind going with your brother and Kainda? I'll be there in a few minutes."

He could tell she'd picked up on Amar's mood, but she nodded and did as he'd asked. The king and queen had disappeared into their bedroom a few moments ago, so Darius and Amar were alone. The other man gestured for Darius to join him in the meeting room, where Jabari Bastide, the head of Tahira's guards, and two members of Amar's special-ops team were sitting at the long, oval-shaped table. Numerous monitors and computers had been set up around the room, with at least one of them hooked into the hotel's surveillance camera feeds.

Once they were behind the closed door, Darius sat down across the table from Amar, and undid his tie, letting it hang loosely from his neck—he hated the damn things.

The head of security leaned back in his chair. "I'm afraid I have some news about the investigation into Princess Tahira's abduction, and it's not good."

Darius tensed. "Tell me."

This was the first break they'd gotten since Tahira and her cousins had been rescued. He knew the investigation had stalled, but neither the royal guard nor Trident Security had been willing to let things go. Someone had been behind the kidnappings, and Darius, Ian, and Amar were afraid it was someone Tahira knew—not that they'd told her that yet. In fact, the men had decided to keep their suspicions from Rajeemh until they had some evidence that pointed to a suspect. The king had plenty to worry about and deal with, and this is what he paid Amar and his team for. He trusted his head of security to handle things and fill him in when needed.

Amar slid a stack of a dozen or so papers across the table toward Darius. "We went back to the phone records again. This time, I had Kadar and Damis call all the numbers."

As Darius scanned the printouts of calls made by Tahira and the group she'd gone on the cruise with, Amar gestured for one of his two men to fill Darius in. Kadar was the one who spoke with his thick French accent. "We didn't find anything on Princess Tahira's phone. The same for Nala's and Lahana's and those belonging to our security team."

Darius's eyes narrowed. "Farid's?"

"No, Farid's phone was clean as well. But I cannot same the same for Diallo's."

Clenching his fist, Darius tried to recall what he could about Tahira's cousin's best friend. Nothing had stood out other than he was a pompous fucktard, just like his buddy, Farid. The two men loved to flaunt their wealth and privilege in the faces of those they deemed unworthy to even kiss their asses. They traveled around the globe, staying in the swankiest hotels and attending elite parties that required its guests to have an ungodly amount of money. Diallo came from money—his father being a businessman whose family would never have to work a day in their lives thanks to his billionaire status.

Kadar continued. "As you can see, the ones I've circled

were made to a number allegedly belonging to Georgette Chapuisa, a former Miss France contestant he'd briefly dated two years ago."

"Allegedly?"

"Yes. We don't believe Miss Chapuisa is in possession of the phone, but we have someone contacting her to confirm that. It seems to be a dummy cell—a red herring, as you might say. The calls were all forwarded from that number and through several others around the world until they reached their destination—a phone we've traced to Felix Secada."

Darius saw red at the mere mention of the man who'd raped Tahira, but none of these men knew how their beloved princess had been brutalized. He barely managed to keep a leash on his fury. "Where's the fucking bastard now?"

"Partying with Farid in Miami Beach," Amar responded, dryly. "I've already called Ian and asked him to send some men to bring both the little shits to the embassy in D.C. I want Diallo on Timasurian soil for the interrogation, where I can rip his fucking head off and shove it up his ass if I need to, without getting arrested when he bawls like a baby."

Despite his rage, a snort escaped Darius. Being around his employers all the time and needing to follow protocols, it was very rare for one to hear Amar curse. In a way, it made him sound even deadlier than Darius knew he could be. The man had been trained among numerous black-ops forces from around the world, including Israel's Mossad, China's MSS, and Britain's MI6.

"Good. I'll be joining you."

Amar's intense gaze met his. "What about Her Highness and the trip to your hometown?"

"We'll still go but just cut it short." He glanced at Bastide, who acknowledged the change in plans with a nod of his head. "We'll be in D.C. by late afternoon. Do me a favor and let Diallo sweat it out until then."

"That can be arranged," Amar said with a smirk before pausing. "What are you going to tell Her Highness?"

"As little as I can until we find out what the fuck is going on." Darius sighed and stood. He was exhausted and needed sleep if he was going to deal with both his father and Diallo tomorrow. "When are you going to let the king know?"

"First thing in the morning before I leave for D.C. My men will accompany him and Queen Azhar to New York." That said a lot about how much Amar trusted his team when he handed over the detail of guarding the most important man in his country to them.

Nodding, Darius headed for the door. "Keep me posted."

CHAPTER THIRTY-TWO

When Darius returned to the suite, he found Tahira sitting alone on the living room sofa, with worry in her eyes. She'd changed out of her dress and heels into pajamas with a robe and slippers. Her gaze met his. "Is everything okay?"

"Of course," he replied with a fake smile painted on his face, as he unbuttoned his dress shirt to reveal a white T-shirt underneath.

She frowned at him. "Darius, please do not lie to me. I know when something is wrong, and we should not have any secrets between us. After all, we share the biggest secret of my life."

After removing his suit jacket, shirt, and tie and draping them over the back of one of the chairs, he sat down on the couch next to her and took her hand. He didn't want to do this, but when she put it that way, he couldn't deny her. "We may have discovered who was involved in your kidnapping."

Her eyes widened. "Who?"

"There were phone calls we've connected from your cousin's friend, Diallo, to Felix Secada."

She blanched, and Darius figured it was more from her rapist's name than the man's connection to someone she knew. Her face turned red, and outrage flared in her eyes. "I never liked him, but—but why would he have done this to me? Why would he have done this to any of us? He likes Lahana—I know it. He has always flirted with her and staring at her. Why would he put her, Nala, and me through that?"

Shrugging, Darius shook his head. "I have no idea, sweetheart. But we're going to find out instead of returning home to Clearwater after visiting my brother and sister and father. Amar is having Diallo and Farid brought to the embassy in D.C. for questioning."

An incredulous gasp escaped her. "You think Farid is involved?"

"No. Well, we don't know, honestly, but we'll find out tomorrow. Since they're best friends, even if Farid is not involved, he may know something he doesn't realize he knows."

Sagging back into the couch, Tahira shook her head. "I cannot believe . . . I mean, why?

Darius's heart broke when he saw her eyes overflowing with tears. He knew she was reliving the horror of her captivity and rape again. Reaching over, he pulled her onto his lap. He cupped her face in his hands and gently kissed her cheeks, sipping the salty tears from her skin.

"Don't cry, Princess," he whispered. "God, please don't—it kills me when you cry."

He lowered his mouth to hers, and she parted her lips immediately, allowing his tongue to pass between them and taste her. Her tongue tentatively danced with his. He should let her go, but her arms went around his neck and kept him close.

A cough, a giggle, and some murmurs came from her brother's bedroom, and Tahira pulled away, but not far. Her heavy-lidded gaze made him hard as a rock, but he restrained himself. He would follow her lead, not giving her anything more than what she asked for. Hell, probably less than she asked for. Tahira wanted to be a virgin on her wedding night, and Darius was determined for that to happen, despite her torn barrier of womanhood. His aching cock would just have to deal with it. He'd been taking cold showers almost daily. If he had to take them throughout their short-term marriage, then so be it. But at least he could show her she was desirable and not every man was a bastard who liked to hurt women. He'd show her how she deserved to be treated and not to accept anything less from whoever her future husband was.

"Would you come lie down with me for a little while?" Her husky whisper nearly drove him crazy.

"Is that a good idea? If your brother—"

"If our doors are shut, he will not suspect a thing. Besides, I am certain he has other things on his mind at the moment. He and Kainda wish to have a baby."

Her knowing wink caused him to chuckle. Tahira might be innocent, but she wasn't naïve about what was going on in the other bedroom.

"Please, Darius. Just for a little while. I do not want to be alone."

Before she could stand up, Darius tucked his arm under her legs and got to his feet. Her eyes widened in surprise, but then she cuddled against his broad chest. How could something so wrong feel so right? Had Tahira not been raped, Darius would never have gotten this close to her. He wished it had never happened and felt like a fucking ass for being grateful that it did.

He was falling for her—a woman he had no right to be

holding in his arms, but he couldn't stop himself from wanting her.

Striding toward her bedroom on the other side of the suite from where the married couple were getting things on, Darius stopped and shut the door to his own room. He carried Tahira into her bedroom and quietly used his foot to shut the door behind them. When they reached her bed, he set her down on her feet. Tahira took a step backward, her gaze never leaving his face, and her hands went to the belt of her silk robe.

He grasped her wrist. "Don't, sweetheart. I'm hanging on by a thread here. You're tempting enough fully clothed —I don't need any more distractions. I'll lay down beside you and kiss you if you want, but neither of us will be taking off anything—well, other than the slippers and shoes."

Her radiant smile warmed him from the inside out. "If you insist."

"I do, sweetheart."

Pivoting, she pulled the bedspread and sheet down, kicked off her slippers, and crawled under the covers. Darius rounded the bed and laid down beside her on top of the covers, just like he had at the hospital. He may have himself under control, but he wasn't a saint. He hadn't lied—she was very tempting.

Tahira flipped onto her side, facing him. Reaching up, she stroked his jawline, which was rough with stubble. "I have not decided which look is more handsome on you—clean shaven or like this. Just please do not let it grow long again."

"Yeah, I hate the overly scruffy look too, so you don't have to worry about that." He turned his head and kissed her palm. But when his gaze met hers again, he was surprised to see her lip tremble and her eyes water. "Hey, hey, what's this? I told you not to cry over Diallo, and—"

She shook her head. "It is not him. Did—did I deserve what—what happened to me?"

"What?" He pushed her hair back from her face. "What are you talking about, sweetheart? You didn't—"

"I mean all the flirting I did with you and my other body-guards, knowing I-I was teasing you but none of you would do anything wrong. Was—was it karma for me doing that?"

When she started sobbing into his chest, he held her close. He didn't know where this was coming from. He thought she'd been handling it so well—guess not. "Shit, sweetheart. Don't ever think that. You didn't do anything, and I mean anything, to deserve being assaulted."

He stroked her back in silence until she seemed to calm down, her tears drying. She mumbled something into his chest that he couldn't understand. "What was that?"

Lifting her head, she stared at him. There was no uncertainty in her expression, only pleading. "Kiss me, please? Remind me that I am alive and still a whole woman."

He couldn't resist her request. Capturing her lips in his own, he tried to erase every negative thought from her mind. No rape victim deserved to think they were the reason for it happening, especially his woman.

No, she's not yours! This is only temporary.

Tahira took Darius's hand and brought it to her breast. All rational thought fled from his mind. He squeezed her flesh through the material covering it, and she moaned into his mouth. Kissing along her jaw, he rolled onto his back and pulled her with him. "Straddle me, baby. I can make you feel good without having sex, without even taking your clothes off. You only need to tell me what you want. The power is yours alone. That is your body—you accept only what you choose to allow. If you get scared or just want to stop, tell me and I'll hold you until you go to sleep. Now, tell me what you want—you're in control."

When she hesitated, he thought he had his answer, but then she swung her leg over his torso. He settled her on his hips, just above his erection. This wasn't about him—this was about showing Tahira her rape didn't define who she was now.

She stared down at him, her pupils dilated. "What . . . um . . . what should I do? I do not know where to start."

"Do you trust me?"

"Of course I do, Darius."

He grinned at her matter-of-fact tone. "Then all you have to do is feel. If you want me to stop, just say the word red, like they do in the club. If you say it, I'll stop immediately. Okay?"

"O-okay."

"Good girl."

Skimming his hands up her sides, he cupped the underside of her breasts, while watching her face for any signs of her being scared. She was beautiful, and it wasn't just her outward features. The more he got to know her, the more his attraction grew. Tahira was the type of woman who walked into a room and lit it up from within. Women wanted to be her, and men just plain wanted her—and not because of her title. If she were a waitress in a low-income neighborhood, she would still have the same personality and outlook on life —of that he was certain.

Darius pushed aside the lapels of her robe and brushed his thumbs over her distended, silk-covered nipples. She gasped, and her knees tightened against his hips. The corners of his mouth pulled upward. "Like that?"

"Yes, very much."

She hadn't hesitated, and he knew she wasn't just saying what she thought he wanted to hear. He thumbed her stiff buds slowly, teasingly. Her hands gripped the material of his T-shirt covering his upper abdomen before flattening again and sliding up to his chest. She found his nipples and ran her fingers over them. When he inhaled sharply, she asked, "Are they as sensitive as mine?"

God, he was going to need at least a thirty-minute cold shower after this. "They're sensitive, but probably not as much as yours." Proving his point, he rolled her hard peaks between his thumbs and forefingers. He grinned when her head fell back on her shoulders, thrusting her breasts out further for him. She was so responsive—he could probably make her come if she let him.

Sitting up, he cupped her ass cheeks and held her in place. His mouth closed around one of her nipples. Using his tongue, he moistened the silky material, then exhaled, long and hot.

"Oh! Darius! That—that feels so good!"

"Shh, sweetheart. Not too loud." Her brother and sister-in-law were probably too busy getting it on to notice what was happening in the other side of the suite, but the last thing Darius wanted was a confrontation or Tahira being embarrassed.

She nodded and lowered her voice. "Again, please."

Turning to her other breast, he gave it the same attention, until she moaned and gripped his hair to the point of pain— something he didn't mind at all. In fact, it turned him on even more. There was something about a woman pulling his hair or scratching his back that just did it for him. But tonight wasn't about him. He wanted to bring her pleasure so she could hopefully put Diallo, Secada, and everybody and everything else out of her mind for a little while. He was starting to understand what his Dom friends had been talking about all this time. He couldn't make her forget, but he could give her something else to think about—something else to feel.

He kissed his way up to her neck and nuzzled the soft

skin just below her ear. "Have you ever played with yourself, Princess? I mean, touched your body in private to bring yourself pleasure."

When she froze, he pulled back to look at her face. Her red cheeks and gaze that wouldn't meet his didn't give him an answer. She could be embarrassed either way—if she had or if she hadn't. "Talk to me, Tahira. There's no right or wrong response here."

She sucked her bottom lip into her mouth for a moment. "No, I have not. You must think it is odd in this day and age for a twenty-five-year-old woman to be so inexperienced."

"Look at me." Grabbing a handful of her hair, he tugged on it until her gaze met his. "No, I don't think it's weird at all. In fact, I think virginity and celibacy are making a comeback in the US, if you watch any of those cable shows some of the women I know are into. Nowadays, young women and men are signing purity pacts, or whatever they call them, where they vow to not have sex until their wedding nights. If it's something that's important to you, then it's not weird, and don't let me or anyone else ever tell you differently."

"Thank you for that, Darius." She swallowed hard, then licked her lips. Her eyes were filled with desire, fueling his own. "Can you show me a little bit of . . . of how it can be, without . . . I mean, having read so many romance books, I know a man and woman can give each other pleasure without . . ."

"We can do that, sweetheart, if that's what you want. But I want you to be one-hundred-percent sure." He wouldn't be taking anything from her in return, but as responsive as she'd been, he could probably get her off easily.

"I am. I have been daydreaming about you."

His eyebrows shot up, and he gave her a devilish grin. Damn, her blush was adorable. "You have, huh? Want to tell me about them?"

Her cheeks grew even redder, and her gaze dropped to his chest. "I do not think I am brave enough for that yet."

"That's okay. Maybe some other time. What's the safe-word I gave you? In case you get scared or I do something you don't like."

"Red, like they say in the club."

"Look at me, sweetheart." When her gaze met his again, he continued. "Don't be afraid to say it, all right? I don't want to hurt you."

Her expression softened. "I know. I will say it if I need to."

Darius inhaled deeply and then let it out slowly. "Take off your robe for me—nothing else."

As he'd expected, she hesitated a moment. But then she untied the belt and shrugged the material off her shoulders. Once it had been discarded onto the floor, Darius reached up and skimmed the backs of his fingers over her pert breasts. As much as he was dying to see them, and the rest of her, it had suddenly become important to him to wait for that big reveal until after they were wed. His mind was waging a war with his heart and body. He wanted to claim her as his—to be the only man to know what it felt like to be inside her from this day forward—but he had to remember the marriage would only be temporary. For now, he could make her feel like a woman again—to bring her pleasure she'd never known.

Tahira's eyes were dilated and heavy-lidded. Sliding one of his hands downward, he paused just above her mound. Searching her face, he made sure there was no fear showing. While the hand at her breasts teased them, he swiped his thumb over her silk covered clit.

She gasped and almost leaped off him but settled down quickly again. He raised an eyebrow at her. "Again?"

"Yes, please."

A soft snort erupted from him. She was so adorable in her

refinement, but he wanted a different reaction from her. He wanted her to throw her primness out the window and scream as she shattered for him. Of course, he'd have to cover her mouth with his own, so she didn't alert her brother or the guards out in the hallway that she was having her first orgasm.

Damn. That thought had him growing impossibly hard. It had been a long time since he'd given a woman her first big-O.

His thumb caressed her clit again, this time keeping the contact as he applied some pressure and made small circles.

"Oh! Oh, Darius! That feels so—so . . ."

He smiled as her words trailed off. Her hands gripped and twisted his T-shirt, as her eyelids fell to half-mast and her hips began to move. Through her thin pajama top, he rolled and played with one nipple, giving it a tug. Her pelvis bucked, as if trying to get closer to the thumb that was bringing her to a peak she'd never reached before. All the while, Darius watched her face. He wanted to make certain the memories of her rape weren't interfering in the intimate moment.

"Darius, I feel . . ."

"Tell me what you feel, Princess."

She shook her head, but he could tell she was lost in the sensations bombarding her. "Like . . . I do not know . . . like I want to fly."

That was exactly how he wanted her to feel. Keeping the same rhythm and intensity, he strung her along until she began to beg him to send her out into an abyss.

"Please, Darius! Oh my God, please!"

At the same time, he pinched her nipple and pressed hard on her clit. When he saw she was going over, his hand left her breast and clasped the back of her neck. He quickly sat up, keeping his thumb moving, and pulled her to him, his mouth sealing over hers as she screamed her release. Her thigh muscles tightened as she rocked against his thumb. Through the silk, he felt the wetness flow from her core and soak the material.

As her climax faded, her body began to sag. Ending their kiss with a sweet peck on her lips, Darius laid back down and pulled her with him until she was draped over his torso. Her gasps for air eased as he stroked her back from her neck to her ass and up again.

Darius reveled in the fact his woman was thoroughly satisfied—it meant more to him than finding his own release, which she hadn't realized he'd found. That had never happened to him before—ejaculating without his cock being stimulated in some fashion.

He didn't want to leave her, but an hour later, he forced himself from her bed. After covering her with the sheets, he leaned down and kissed her forehead, then quietly left the room.

CHAPTER THIRTY-THREE

Not long after having breakfast with Levi and Barrie, Darius pulled their rented SUV in behind an occupied patrol car parked in front of a small plot of land. Two of Tahira's ever-present royal guards, Jabari and Zareb, were in a third vehicle behind them.

As Darius turned off the engine, Tahira glanced around. There were a few sheds, a dirty pickup truck that had to be at least fifteen years old, and a double wide trailer. The property had numerous overgrown trees and bushes and had more dirt and rocks than grass covering the lawn. It was about two miles from the quaint town of Brookford where Darius and his siblings had grown up.

"This is it?"

Darius glanced at her. "Yes, Princess. Some people actually do live like this—not everyone lives in a mansion." His sharp tone was not one he'd ever used when speaking to her before.

Reaching over, she set her hand on his arm. "I am sorry, Darius, my question was not meant in a condescending manner. I know I am one of the privileged people in this world who will never have to live in a small home like this. And I know that you have done everything you can to help your father, but he does not want the help. Please do not think that I am passing judgment on you, your father, or your siblings. I would never do that."

He placed his hand over hers and closed his fingers around it. "I know. It's just that sometimes I get defensive about the way my father is now versus the way he used to be. He might not have been the greatest father or the greatest husband in the world, but I'd give anything to have him back the way he was before the accident." He gave her hand a squeeze, then let go and opened his door. "Come on. Hopefully he's having a good day and I can introduce you without any problems. But don't be alarmed if he thinks I'm too young to be married. He kind of thinks I'm fifteen years younger than I am now, and unfortunately, I'll always be that age according to him."

"I am not worried," she reassured him with a smile. "I really am looking forward to meeting him."

"Wait here a minute."

Darius got out and approached the police officer who had also exited his vehicle. Jabari and Zareb joined them, but Tahira only had eyes for one man. She studied Darius's physique. Angie had been right the other day—it was very hard for Tahira not to ogle the man she was engaged to. Today, he was wearing snug, faded jeans, a navy-blue T-shirt that molded to his torso in a delicious manner, and a pair of black cowboy boots. If he had a cowboy hat on, he could have graced the cover of one of the modern, western romance books on her e-reader.

The men shook hands and spoke for a moment before the officer and the sentries returned to their vehicles. Meanwhile, Tahira waited for Darius to open her door. While that was something valets and her bodyguards did for her quite frequently, with Darius it was different. It seemed gallant and made her feel special and cared for in a way she never had before.

When he opened her door, she took his hand, climbed down, and walked beside him toward the trailer, loving how he intertwined their fingers and stayed connected to her. It was rare she'd held another man's hand, and even then, it was usually for only a few seconds as they'd helped her or shaken her hand. Some men tried to hold on longer than Tahira had been comfortable with. She could tell they were only fascinated by her money, her looks, or her royal standing. But she preferred a man who was interested in her as a person. One who was interested in what she had to say and challenged her intellectually. Darius was that man.

He never came across as a social climber, nor did he seem eager to get his hands on her family's money. In fact, there were times he appeared uncomfortable with her wealth. Tahira knew he was attracted to her, but she also knew she would not be another notch on his bed post, as the Americans would say. Her royal title meant little to him in terms of his own status. Some people might think that, but their friends and family would know the truth—or the truth as it was told to them.

Before they reached the door, Darius called out, "Hey, Dad! It's me! You awake?"

The door swung open and a gray-haired version of Levi Knight appeared. Darius and Barrie must take after their mother. Mr. Knight was slender, dressed in a pair of jeans and a plaid shirt with the sleeves rolled up. His face had been weathered by the sun until it appeared leathery, but he was still handsome.

"Of course I'm awake," the older man rasped. His eyes narrowed as he studied Darius and then the patrol car. "What are you doing home? You're not AWOL, are you? I'm not going to have the MPs showing up here, am I? It's bad enough the cops are running radar in front of my house. They've been sitting there for weeks and haven't written a single ticket yet."

The corners of Darius's mouth ticked upward as he shook his head. It was obvious this wasn't the first time his father had asked that. "No, Dad, I'm not AWOL. I got some time off and wanted you to meet someone."

Mr. Knight's gaze finally settled on Tahira, and Darius introduced them. "Tahira, this is my dad, Phillip Knight. Dad, this is Tahira . . . my . . . um . . . fiancée."

She smiled and raised her hand in a small wave. "Hello, Mr. Knight. It is a pleasure to meet you."

The older man raised an eyebrow. "Fiancée? She's not pregnant, is she, kid?"

Darius choked and coughed, but Tahira just giggled. "No, Mr. Knight. I am not pregnant." A test at Dr. Moreau's office a few days ago had confirmed what they'd already suspected —Tahira hadn't gotten pregnant by her rapist. Her relief had been mirrored by Darius's. "Your son and I have been . . . well, dating for a while."

"Uh-huh. Well, then, come on in and let's get acquainted."

An hour later, it appeared Tahira had passed some sort of test with Darius's father and won him over. As they sat in the trailer's small living area, sipping sweet tea, the man had grilled her about her family, her occupation, and her education. Tahira had taken her cues from Darius and downplayed her life and social status quite a bit. Mr. Knight seemed to accept her "upper-class" family, her charity work, and her private schooling without any complaints or concerns. So, they'd stretched the truth a little bit, but if that made the man happy and didn't stress him out, then Tahira didn't see anything wrong with it.

Despite his memory issues, Tahira found herself charmed

by the man. He made her laugh, regaling her with stories about Darius when he was much younger, much to his obvious embarrassment. A few times she had to look at Darius for clarification on something Mr. Knight said, such as what a "crick" or a "Titan" were. Apparently, that was a stream and a local sports team, respectively.

"So, when are you fixin' to get married?"

Before Tahira could respond, Darius beat her to it. "Actually, we're eloping, Dad. In a few weeks."

"Good. No sense in wasting money on a party for everyone else to get drunk at. You sure she ain't pregnant?"

"We're sure." Darius stood and held out his hand to Tahira. "I wish we could stay longer, Dad, but we have a plane to catch."

"That's fine. Get back to base before you're AWOL. I don't want those MPs showing up."

Tahira got to her feet. "It was a pleasure to meet you, Mr. Knight." She smiled at him. "Would it be all right if I gave you a hug goodbye?"

A broad grin spread across the man's face, and he winked at Darius. "I like her. Of course, you can, darlin'. Just don't go running off on my son like my good-for-nothing wife did."

It was sad Mr. Knight wasn't able to remember his wife had died and hadn't abandoned him. Darius had told Tahira their marriage hadn't been a match made in heaven, but she believed it would still be better for one to feel grief instead of misplaced anger and resentment.

"I won't, I promise." Especially since Darius was her soulmate.

Tahira gave his father a brief embrace, then sweetly kissed his cheek. Surprisingly, the man blushed, and then he politely shooed them out the door.

Minutes later, they were back in the SUV, with their protective tail behind them, heading through the heart of

Brookford on their way to a small airport where their jet was waiting for them. Darius's arm was resting on the padded compartment between the two seats, and it felt natural for Tahira to set her hand on top of his. He glanced at her, then turned his hand until their palms met. When their fingers intertwined like they had earlier, she smiled. For the first time since they'd agreed to be married to save her from public humiliation from those who would unfairly judge her, Tahira felt like they were a real couple. Was Darius feeling it too?

CHAPTER THIRTY-FOUR

Ian blocked the door to the interrogation room in the security office of Timasur's embassy in Washington D.C. With his arms crossed, he glared at Darius. "You either chill out before you go in there, twatopotomus, or you don't go in there at all. Trust me when I say I would love to torture the bastard and bury him where he'd never be found, but he knows too many people to just make him disappear, and Farid, the little shit that he is, knows we have him. Amar also promised the king we wouldn't kill him. If he is behind this, he'll go to prison in Timasur. Apparently, the inmates there adore Tahira and would love to get their hands on anyone who hurts her. You might want to remember that for future reference by the way."

Darius ignored that last part. "Oh, I won't kill him, Boss-man. That would put him out of the pain and misery I'm going to inflict on his ass."

A door opened down the hallway, and Amar strode out, carrying a manila folder, and headed toward them with Cain and Romeo behind him. Darius's two teammates and Ian were the ones who'd accompanied Diallo and Farid from

Miami after snatching them from their hotel suite in the middle of the night. Ian was eager to catch the next flight back to Tampa, not wanting to be away from Angie too long as her due date approached.

Amar stopped between Ian and Darius. "Farid swears he has no clue Diallo was in contact with Secada or anyone else in Diaz's organization. He's a weasel and would turn on a friend in a heartbeat if he thought it would get himself out of trouble. I led him to believe we had hard evidence and were looking to pin this all on both of them. He cried like a baby but couldn't give us anything. I'm inclined to believe he's telling the truth. He doesn't know anything." He turned his attention to Ian but nodded his head to the side toward Darius. "Is he going to be any trouble?"

Grinding his molars, Darius growled, but he understood their concerns. Ian eyed him for a few moments, then shook his head. "Nope, he's not. Batman, don't make me fire your ass again. Shades, Romeo, let's go." Pivoting, Ian strode toward the door that would lead them to the embassy's rear exit where a car was waiting to take the three men to the airport. "Keep me posted."

"How do you want to do this?" Darius asked Amar. While he *really would love* to torture Diallo into confessing, he knew it was in everyone's best interest for him to refrain from doing so. He'd also promised Tahira on the flight from Tennessee that he wouldn't kill or crucify the man. She was currently in the embassy's residence wing, talking to her charity staff on Skype. He was glad she was keeping busy, instead of stressing out and waiting to hear if Diallo was the one who'd betrayed her and her cousins.

The head of security gave him an evil grin. "It's been a long time since I've played the 'good cop.' I'll start while you stand in the corner, looking like you want to rip his head off." He nodded for the guard to unlock the door to the interrogation room, then grabbed the back of a nearby rolling desk chair. "We'll play it by ear from there."

That was fine with Darius. Taking a deep breath and putting on his resting-prick face, he followed Amar, with his chair, inside and slammed the door shut, causing Diallo to nearly jump out of his skin. The twenty-nine-year-old man glanced between them, annoyance written all over his face, as he sat on a chair that was purposely uncomfortable. While Darius took a position to the right of the door, glaring at Diallo, Amar pasted on a friendly smile and sat across the table from their suspect. There were several unwritten rules about conducting an interrogation—tricks of the trade—and Darius knew them well.

1) Isolate the suspect and leave him alone to sweat it out for an hour or more.

2) Make sure the room is either too hot or too cold.

The thermostat for this one was set at seventy-eight degrees.

3) Give him or her an uncomfortable chair to sit on.

The wobbly, wooden one Diallo was sitting on was perfect.

4) Give the suspect plenty of water or soda but limit his bath-room breaks.

5) Play "good cop" and "bad cop."

6) Lie through your teeth whenever necessary.

There were others, of course, but Darius knew with Amar's background and training, the man wasn't concerned with what would be admissible in court—certain liberties would be taken today, if need be. With the evidence backed up by a confession, if Diallo was guilty of arranging to have the women kidnapped, for whatever reason, it was a sure bet that any and all Timasurian judges would throw the book at him.

Clearly seeing the silent fury on Darius's face, Diallo went with whom he thought was the friendlier and more coopera-tive of the two men. "What the hell is going on, Amar? Where's Farid? Those goons woke us up and dragged us to D.C. without any explanation. I've been sitting here for hours, and no one will tell me why. They even took away my phone. I want it back, and I demand you let me go!"

Amar set the folder on the table. It was a typical interro-gation room that could be found at any police station in the states. Aside from the heavy metal table, the only other decor in the room was a large two-way mirror that allowed others to observe from the next room.

"I'm sorry I was delayed, Diallo," Amar said with faked sincerity. "And please forgive me for needing to interrupt your trip to Miami, but we've had some developments in the investigation of Princess Tahira's, Nala's, and Lahana's abductions and needed Farid's and your input."

Diallo's eyes widened. "Seriously? Well, why didn't those fucking idiots just tell us that?"

A snort erupted from Amar as he nodded his head in agreement. "Yes, well, Ian Sawyer tends to be a bit brash and uncouth at times, but he and his men are good at what they do, so His Royal Highness insists on keeping them on retain-er." He opened the folder—the first page was blank—and took a pen from his shirt pocket. "Before we start, did you remember anything that happened before or during the cruise that maybe you forgot to tell us about? I mean, some-times people recall things a few days or weeks later that they hadn't thought of at first."

The weasel relaxed back in the chair but frowned when it tilted to the side with a thump. Darius took note that Diallo's eyes shifted to the left as he thought for a moment. Experts often say that when someone looks to the left, they are trying to recall the truth—when they look to the right, they're trying to make something up.

"I can't think of anything I haven't already told you. The cruise was going great—we were all having a good time—and we were supposed to meet the girls after they went to the waterfalls."

"And nothing out of the ordinary happened before the cruise?" Amar asked.

"Like what?"

"Anything."

Diallo shrugged. "Nothing I can think of. Why?"

Avoiding the question, Amar pulled out one of the papers from under the blank one, turned it around, and placed it in front of the other man. He used his pen to point at the phone number that was highlighted numerous times. "Recognize this number?"

Leaning forward, Diallo scanned the page. "No, should I?"

"Considering you called it repeatedly in the weeks before the cruise, I would think so."

His brow furrowed. "Why would I call someone I don't know?"

"Oh, you know her, all right," Darius spat. Diallo's gaze shot to his face. "It's registered to your ex-girlfriend, Georgette Chapuisa."

"Georgette? That's not her number." His hand went to his hip. "Shit. Where's my phone? I'll show you Georgette's number—I still have it. And what's this got to do with anything anyway? I haven't seen her since before New Year's."

Amar pulled Diallo's phone from his back pocket. "Your phone is right here." Instead of handing it to the other man, he set it on top of the folder. "But you're correct—it's not Georgette's phone. I've already had someone contact her, and she never opened an account with this number. But I'd already suspected that. You see, that number," he pointed to the highlighted one on the paper again, "was forwarded to several other phone numbers before it reached the person you called."

"What are you talking about? I didn't call that number."

Diallo was getting agitated. Good, Darius thought. Suspects tended to screw up when they were out of sorts.

"Well, apparently you did, Diallo, because that's the list of all the calls made from this very phone. You may have deleted the calls from the history on your phone, but that doesn't remove them from the history your provider was able to give us."

"I. Did. Not. Make. Those. Calls! I've never seen that number before in my life. Now, what's this all about anyway?"

It was time for Darius to step in and be a bad-ass. Good thing he had no trouble getting into character when it came to this asshole. Striding over to the table, he grabbed the front of Diallo's shirt, hauled him out of the chair, and shoved him against the wall. Of course, Amar made a feeble "good-guy" remark, telling him to calm down, but Darius ignored him, as expected. Instead, he got right in Diallo's face. The man had paled and was struggling to get free, but that wasn't happening. Darius growled. "You little shit, I'll tell you what it's all about. You know where that call ended up? Who picked up on the other end of the line?" They were rhetorical questions, and he didn't wait for any answers. "It was one of the men who kidnapped Tahira, Nala, and Lahana —your buddy, Felix Secada."

Diallo's eyes bulged, and his mouth gaped. "Wh-what are you talking about? I don't know who—who kidnapped them! I-I don't know anyone by that name! Why would . . . crap! Why would you think I had anything to do with that? I would never do anything to hurt them!"

"Bullshit!" Darius yanked on the man's shirt and pushed

him back against the wall again, hard enough to rattle his head. "How much money did you get for them?"

Grasping Darius's wrists, Diallo tried to get away from him, but his efforts were futile. "You're fucking crazy! Let me go, damn it! I had nothing to do with any of that! Amar, get him off me! I'll have you both fucking fired for this!"

Amar tapped Darius on the shoulder. "Easy. I told you to stay calm. Let him go and get out." Darius hesitated a moment then released the bastard, stepping aside so Amar could move in. "I'm sorry, Diallo. This is not how I wanted this interview to go. Please, sit down. Can I get you something to drink? This won't take much longer."

That was the last Darius heard as he left the room and banged the door shut. Without acknowledging the guard, Darius entered the room next to the interrogation room. From there, he'd watch the rest of the show through the two-way mirror. Not bothering to take a seat, he leaned against the window frame.

In the other room, Amar employed several tactics, including trying to convince Diallo that he was involved, that they could show he'd been coerced in some way. But Diallo's story never changed. Either he was really good at deception or the asshole was telling the truth.

A half hour later, Amar left Diallo alone and met Darius out in the hallway. He shook his head. "I'm sorry, my friend, but I think he's telling the truth."

Despite his earlier desire to beat the living daylights out of Diallo, Darius had to admit he agreed with Amar. "So do I." He ran a hand down his face. "Which means we're back to square one."

"Actually, I think it's square two."

Darius frowned. "What do you mean?"

"If it wasn't Diallo, it's someone he knows. Someone who had access to his phone or was able to hack into it and forward a call. And, someone who knew to use Georgette's name to open a cell account. If we hadn't called the numbers, we would have never figured out it wasn't her phone."

"But we still don't have a motive. It could have been anyone he knows. Hell, it could have been someone who got close to him, specifically to use him. He's too dumb and conceited to think anyone would want to hang out with him for any other reason than he's a cool guy—which he isn't. So, now what?"

Amar shrugged. "We keep digging, my friend."

"Shit."

CHAPTER THIRTY-FIVE

Tahira twisted her hands together as she stared into the mirror. The bruises on her face had finally disappeared completely. The ones on the rest of her body were gone as well, and she was grateful she no longer had to see the reminders of her assault. The tight, black miniskirt and skimpy, gold camisole she was wearing were at the suggestion of Angie and Kristen, and she hoped Darius approved of them. While she had panties on—Darius thought she'd be more comfortable that way—she'd forgone a bra. She wasn't well blessed in that department and could easily get away with not wearing one.

Today was the first day they were training in the club, and she was grateful it was during the daytime when it was closed and only the two women, Ian, Devon, and maybe Mitch would be there. She was nervous enough as it was and didn't need more attention focused on her and Darius, although, one would think being constantly in the public eye would've made a difference. But it didn't.

She was more worried about Darius. Even though they'd discussed trying a D/s relationship, and Trudy had agreed with them giving it a shot when they'd spoken to the thera-pist together last week, Tahira was still concerned about it. Was Darius just doing this for her, like he'd done for their impending nuptials, or would he be getting something he needed out of it too? He was a dominant man who took charge when he needed to without hesitation in any given situation. But would he fit into the lifestyle like his friends and teammates did? She didn't want him to feel like a fish out of water. If he wasn't comfortable with her submitting to him, even in a non-sexual manner, then she would tell him the lifestyle wasn't for her either. But she was afraid she'd be lying to him if she did that.

After talking in private with Trudy, and then with Angie and Kristen one evening, during a girl's night in Angie and Ian's apartment, Tahira was certain she was a submissive. She'd done some research on several websites the women had recommended, and while many of the types of play did not appeal to her, the thought of handing control over to Darius, even for a few hours, sounded like heaven. She wouldn't have to be "on" and smiling like she had to be all the time in public. She could just relax and let him take over. He would honor her limits, and she would be safe with him. She could even cry if she needed to—something she avoided at all costs if anyone but Darius was around. In his arms, Tahira didn't need to be anyone but herself—a woman who'd fallen in love with the man who'd saved her in more ways than one. And yes, she was in love with him.

The door to the locker room opened, and Angie waddled in, her hand at her lower back. She smiled when she saw Tahira. "You look like you're about to be thrown to the wolves. Relax. After a few minutes, you'll be more comfort-able than me. I can't wait for Little Bit to come out into the world. I feel like a beached whale with back pain, and don't tell Ian I said that. I've already racked up a bunch of punishments for when we can play again. Actually, I'm looking forward to them. Now I know what Kristen had been talking about when she was nearing her due date with JD. Devon was driving her nuts with his hovering, and Ian is the same way. I was glad I had some time to myself when he had to go to Miami and then D.C. for Amar. What was that all about, anyway? He didn't tell me."

Tahira was grateful for Angie's babbling. It helped take her mind off the fact she was in a sex club and calmed her down a bit. She also trusted the women to keep her confidence. "It is not public knowledge, but Amar, Ian, and Darius thought my cousin's friend might have had something to do with my abduction."

The other woman's jaw dropped. "Seriously?"

"But he did not," she quickly added. "They questioned him and believed him when he said he did not know what they were talking about." Tahira had been sort of relieved it hadn't been Diallo. She hated to think someone who had been around her so much had been involved in something so heinous as arranging for the women to be kidnapped and sold as sex slaves. Unfortunately, they still didn't know who'd done it. But she didn't want to think about any of that now, so she changed the subject. "Do I look all right?"

"Seriously?" Angie repeated. "Girl, you'd look stunning dressed in a garbage bag. Trust me, Darius will be drooling. In fact, he told me to tell you he's waiting outside for you, since I was coming in here to use the bathroom. Take a deep breath and go—I'll be back out in a few minutes."

After taking one last look in the mirror, Tahira did as Angie suggested and took a deep breath before walking on shaky knees and bare feet to the door. Darius was standing a short distance away when she entered the downstairs portion of the club. As she approached him, his gaze roamed her body from head to toe and back again, and his nostrils flared, causing her to blush. His tongue peeked out and wet his full lips, as he held his hand out to her. "You look beautiful, Princess. Come here." She placed her hand in his and was surprised when he lifted it to his mouth and kissed her knuckles. "You're shaking." He pulled her into his embrace and stroked her hair. "You're safe, sweetheart, but say the word and we'll go home. If this isn't what you want . . ."

She pulled back just enough that she could see his handsome face. "No, please, I want to stay. I am just a little nervous."

Smiling, he bent down and placed a brief, sweet kiss on her lips. "I'd be worried if you weren't." Still holding her hand, he stepped back. "Shall we?"

"Lead the way, Sir."

"Hmm. I kind of like that coming from you." He started walking toward the center of the pit, where the others were waiting for them. "I just can't get used to your staff calling me sir all the time."

"Now you know why I asked you and several other people here to call me by my first name. 'Princess' and 'Your Royal Highness' get tiresome after a while."

He gave her a sideways glance. "Do you want me to stop calling you princess?"

"No. It sounds different coming from you—it is like a term of endearment."

Stopping short, he turned her toward him and stared into her eyes. "It is, Tahira. Just like when I call you sweetheart. You know, sometimes I feel like I'm Cinderella and you're Princess Charming, but when we're alone or with close friends, it's just Darius and Tahira—I like it that way."

"So do I." She giggled. "And you would be Cinderfella, not Cinderella."

"Huh?"

She laughed harder at his confused expression. "It is an

old movie with Jerry Lewis and very funny. I watched it many times when I was younger. One of my au pairs loved old American movies and introduced me to many of them. We will have to watch it sometime when we are not in the mood for horror films."

"Sounds like a plan."

As they approached Ian, Devon, and Kristen, Tahira noticed something right away—besides the fact the two men were sitting in comfortable armchairs, and Kristen was relaxing on a large pillow on the floor next to her husband with her eyes closed and her head resting on his thigh. No, what Tahira noticed out of the ordinary was that neither man stood to greet her. That had never happened before.

"I can see those wheels turning in your head, Tahira," Ian said with an amused smile. "You're in my territory now. In this club, you're a submissive, and the Doms here will treat you as such. You hung your tiara at the door—you'll get it back on your way out."

Tahira's eyes narrowed as she cocked her head to the side. "Hung my tiara? I did not wear a tiara. Is that one of your Americanisms? What does it mean?"

"The real saying is 'hung your hat.' It means . . ." Darius responded as he took one of the empty, leather seats across from the other two men. ". . . in here, you're just like everyone else. No special treatment; no being called princess by anyone other than me; and no one bowing to you because of the crown you wear outside of The Covenant. It also means, when I want, you'll be at my feet, like Kristen is at Devon's."

He gestured to an oversized, burgundy pillow on the other side of his chair. Thankfully, Kristen and Angie had told her to expect this. Skirting around Darius's legs, Tahira lowered herself to her knees on the pillow and found a comfortable position.

"You learn fast, Batman," Devon said with a chuckle.

Grinning, Darius shrugged. "I picked Shades's and Duracell's brains earlier."

The other women had told Tahira that Cain had been practicing the lifestyle for years, while Tristan had started his training not long after he'd started working for Trident. She might be seeing them in the club at some point and would have to remember they would be there as Doms, not her bodyguards.

"Relax, Tahira." Ian held out his hand to Angie as she joined them and pulled her onto his lap, resting his hand on her large belly in a possessive manner. "We're just going to talk today and get you used to the D/s atmosphere. I looked over your limit list with Master Darius . . ." His gaze flickered to Darius for a moment. "By the way, I won a hundred dollar bet with Boomer that you'd get that title someday. And I know that, as a couple, you'll never be hard-core. You have very few green and yellow limits, which is not uncommon for those new to the lifestyle, and you both can renegotiate as your D/s relationship grows. Both Trudy and your Dom think dipping your toes into BDSM will help you deal with your abduction, Tahira." And her unmentioned rape, of course. "And I agree with them. So, I'm going to ask you one last time—are you here under your own free will? Are you willing to hand over control to your Dom as you've negotiated already? And are you willing to follow the protocols of this club while you are here? That includes calling the Doms Sir or Mistress or their preferred address."

She got the obvious hint. "Yes, Sir, I am here under my own free will and agree to everything you said."

"Good girl."

If she wasn't mistaken, there was a proud tone in the man's voice, and it made her feel more confident. She could do this.

Darius placed his fingers under her chin and turned her face until she was looking in his eyes. They were filled with warmth and adoration. "Are you comfortable?"

She shifted onto her hip and nodded. "Yes, thank you for asking." He raised his eyebrows at her, and she added, "Sir."

Beaming, he said, "You're welcome."

Ian had told her the truth—the six of them just talked for the next hour and a half. A few times, the Sawyer brothers had demonstrated something on their subs, to make sure Darius and Tahira understood the different types of play—with none of them involving sexual intercourse. Ian had managed to steer the conversation away from the topic anytime Tahira started getting uneasy—the man could read body language and expressions better than anyone she knew with the exception of Amar. As if he'd also sensed her bouts of apprehension, Darius had taken the opportunity to touch her and ground her to him each time. She was amazed at how in tune he was with her, even without her vocalizing her fears or concerns. She'd heard and read about the kind of connection many couples had, but this was the first time she'd experienced it, and she loved finding out it was real and possible.

They'd told Darius how to check her extremities if he used any of the restraints she'd agreed to try—if they were too tight, they would cut off her circulation. With Kristen draped over his lap, Devon had shown Darius how to administer a non-punishment spanking—only striking his wife's rear end and upper thighs lightly and never in the same spot twice. Tahira was grateful they'd all stayed clothed—Kristen had been dressed similarly to Tahira, while Angie wore a cute, maternity sundress.

She got the impression the other two couples had given them a very vanilla introduction into the lifestyle. They'd gone over all the protocols and ways that Darius could help

Tahira relax and relinquish control to him during a scene. By the time they parted, Tahira had felt more confident she and Darius were doing the right thing and couldn't wait to get home to discuss things with him in private. Maybe they'd practice a few of the new things she'd learned.

CHAPTER THIRTY-SIX

D arius stared at the ass with a combination of amusement and sense of being creeped out. He'd thought Ian was kidding when he'd handed him the "Butt-in-a-Box," as the head Dom had called it. It was a silicone covered "ass" that reminded Darius of the same stuff that CPR dummies were made of. He was supposed to use it to practice spanking his sub. If he hit it too softly, a digital female voice would say "harder," while a red light lit up on the attached control box. If he hit it too hard, he'd get an "ouch" and the red light again. Just right, and the damn thing would moan while giving him a green light. *Seriously? Who thinks up shit like this? Someone with too much time on their hands, probably.*

"Are you going to take it out of the box or just stare at it all evening?"

Tahira had joined him in a sitting room attached to his bedroom after they'd shared a nice dinner while discussing what they'd learned at the club. She seemed much more comfortable talking about it when it was just the two of them. While they would need to continue to train at the club,

Darius knew most of their D/s relationship would take place at home. Neither of them was an exhibitionist, although they were both, apparently, a bit voyeuristic. He'd been surprised when Tahira had confessed to getting turned on when Devon had spanked Kristen, which he'd admitted he'd found arousing as well.

He glanced at her to see a cheeky grin on her face. She loved this. "Keep it up, Princess. Soon this thing will be replaced with your backside."

"I am willing to try that after you practice a bit. Are you going to name 'her'?"

He snorted loudly. "Not."

Sighing, he took the life-sized ass out of the box. "You're going to watch me do this?"

Her giggling warmed his heart. She was putting the rape further and further from her mind as time passed and was laughing more lately. While he knew she was still having some nightmares and some waking flashbacks—she was coming to him for comfort now when they occurred—she was getting back to her old self.

Well, not really. Her old self had been cute and nice. This newer version of Tahira was someone who stirred Darius's heart and soul. He was falling in love with her—hell, he was already there. Did she feel the same? In another place and time, could they have made a marriage work? It would be difficult to let her go when the time came, but it would be even worse to see her fall in love with some jackass who Darius would want to kill for just breathing the same air as Tahira.

"Of course. As you said, it is my ass that will be replacing it soon, so I think watching will help me prepare for it."

She'd been tittering her way through her words, and Darius couldn't suppress his own laughter. Taking a seat next to her on the small sofa, he set the contraption on his thighs.

Tahira grabbed the control box from where it had been hanging down the side of his leg by its cord, stood, and plugged it into the wall next to the couch. As she sat beside him again, she flipped the "On" switch. "She is ready when you are."

He glared at her. "You're having way too much fun with this."

Her smile dropped, and sadness filled her eyes. Darius wanted to kick his own ass when she said, "Before my abduction and rape, I enjoyed all the fun in my life. I want that back, Darius. You make me smile and laugh. You make me remember the joys in life. I will not let those bastards win. I am taking back everything they tried to strip from me. You have helped me with some of it, but I must take control of my life in order for me to live it like I wanted to before everything had changed. I am grateful I only remember bits and pieces of what was done to me. I wish Lahana was the same—she said she remembers everything."

"You spoke to her again?"

She shook her head, sadly. "No. She is still refusing to answer my calls or texts. Nala told me. She said Lahana is still angry that you rescued me in time and no one stopped him from raping her."

"But I wasn't in time." He moved the artificial ass from his lap to the floor, then shifted his hips to face her. He cupped her cheek. "I'm sorry I—"

"No, Darius. Do not apologize again. None of what happened was your fault. In fact, you saved me from a worse fate. Lahana had been with him for hours and look how she was returned to us—bruises all over her. I only had a few. He was probably going to rape me again, and you stopped him from doing so."

No matter how many times she told him it wasn't his fault, he would forever carry the guilt of not reaching her before that fucking bastard defiled her. While he would never be able to make it up to her, he could at least try. Lowering his head to hers, he kissed and licked her mouth, encouraging her to open for him. As their tongues dueled, he pulled her onto his lap. To hell with the fake ass—he wanted the real thing.

Positioning her until she was straddling him, he molded his hands to her butt cheeks and squeezed. Over the years, he'd played some light "slap and tickle" with many women, but he'd never made any of them cry. After his conversations with his Dom buddies and Dr. Dunbar and some research, he now knew making Tahira cry, during BDSM play, could be very cathartic for her. She didn't need to be "on" with him—pasting a false smile on her face and pretending everything was fine. Behind closed doors, she was free to be just Tahira—woman, friend, lover. Her royal title wasn't necessary in this setting, and he honestly believed she preferred it that way. While he wouldn't lay a sharp hand on her ass just yet, not without practice, getting her used to him touching her so intimately was a good place to start.

Damn, he was going to need his second or third—he'd lost count—cold shower of the day after this.

TIMASUR: FORTY-EIGHT HOURS BEFORE THE ROYAL WEDDING . . .
"There you are!"
Tahira glanced over her shoulder at Darius's exasperated tone and grinned. He'd been getting lost in the palace over the past two days, complaining about needing breadcrumbs to find his way—after all there were five floors, eighty rooms, about half as many corridors, multiple staircases, and two elevators in the place. Add in a few secret passageways

she'd loved to play in as a child, and still did on occasion, it was the ultimate place to play hide and seek, if one desired.

The palace sat on twenty-five acres of manicured lawns and maze-like gardens. It was gorgeous, but Tahira had always preferred the vacation home nestled in the mountains two hours north of Diado, Timasur's capital city. It was there she'd felt more like the average person—there'd been a lot less bowing and catering to the royal family there. Her parents were more relaxed there too. Tahira could recall having campouts and climbing trees with her brother and cousins.

Darius stopped next to her and threw up his hands in frustration. "I seriously need a map for this place. I'm military, Tahira. Maps and GPSs are standard equipment for me. Who do I see to get the floor plans of this place? I'm not averse to bribery at this point."

Laughing, she linked their arms together and led him toward the nearest staircase. "I was just on my way to see my bridesmaids getting their last fittings, but that can wait a few minutes. So, come with me. Amar keeps copies in the security office. I am certain you will qualify as a person who can be trusted not to publicize them."

"Cross my heart. Your secrets are safe with me."

Despite his joking manner, it was true. Her secrets would always be safe with Darius. He was an honorable man, and she trusted him with all her heart.

The palace staff was busier than it had been in a long time. Last minute preparations were being made for the weekend's festivities. Friday would be the traditional, ethnic wedding, held in the gardens behind the palace, while Saturday's nuptials would take place at the city's main cathedral. The public and press would be lining the streets to catch a glimpse of Tahira on her way to be married and then again when the couple left the cathedral to attend the reception, at a nearby venue. Many of the over four hundred guests were royal family members and politicians from European and African countries. If this had been the full-scale celebration Tahira had fought against, the number of attendees would've crested the one thousand mark.

Even though the guest list had been carefully culled, Tahira's and Darius's friends and family would all be in attendance. Some had flown in from the United States yesterday and this morning, while a few more were scheduled to arrive tomorrow. Although, Ian had insisted Angie get her obstetrician's permission to fly across the Atlantic Ocean in Trident's private jet, five weeks before her due date. Tahira had assured the couple the best doctors in the city would be on call in case, God forbid, the woman went into premature labor. Ian had been showing signs of stress until Brody had pointed out that if "Little Bit" was born in Timasur, he or she would have dual citizenship. For some reason, the expectant father had gotten a kick out of that and seemed more at ease ever since.

After leaving Darius in good hands with the security staff, Tahira returned to the second floor and located the sitting room where her bridesmaids were being fitted in their dresses for both ceremonies. She found the staff of seamstresses making sure each woman would look beautiful on her special day. Lahana, who didn't look happy to be there, Nala, Barrie, and two of Tahira's other cousins, Shani and Abena, were all in one of their two custom-made dresses, as the designer and seamstresses checked their fittings and prepared to make any needed adjustments. Meanwhile, the Trident Security women, Kristen, Angie, Kat, Harper, Fancy, Lindsey, Jenn, Ian's goddaughter, and Dakota, who was engaged to Darius's teammate Logan Reese, sat on the comfortable couches and chairs around the room. They were relaxing and enjoying the fruit, finger sandwiches, and sparkling water the kitchen staff had prepared for them.

Laughter and chatter filled the room, but Tahira noticed one person was not having a good time. Lahana was frowning at her, her face taut with anger and envy. Tahira wished her cousin wouldn't blame her. It hadn't been their fault that Lahana, Tahira, and the other women had been sexually assaulted, but since Tahira had kept her own rape from her family, friends, and the rest of the world, Lahana didn't know she'd suffered as well. Maybe it was time to change that. Only a handful of trusted people knew Lahana had been raped. They'd kept that out of the press, and she didn't talk about it to anyone except Nala and a therapist her mother had insisted on. Tahira's secret would be safe with her cousin.

Making her decision, Tahira would find some time to get Lahana alone later today and talk to her. They could support each other, and hopefully become friends again. Tahira didn't want the huge elephant in the room to come between them.

"Princess Tahira! It's about time you joined us. Come sit." Jenn patted an empty spot on the sofa next to her. While she'd asked the Trident women to call her by her first name in private, with the staff present, they were using her title.

Tahira took the proffered seat and thanked a staff member when the young woman handed her a glass of sparkling water with a lime wedge. She glanced around the group. In various stages of pregnancy, Angie, Fancy, and Harper, who'd recently announced she and Marco were expecting their second child, had been given rocking recliners for comfort. "Are you all having a good time? Do you need anything?"

There were a chorus of yeses to the first question, and then a round of nos to the second.

"Everything is perfect," Fancy gushed. "And the palace and

grounds are gorgeous. The landscaping is stunning. We'll have to join the men out in the gardens later."

"Is that where they have gathered?" Tahira had been with her own staff going over the last-minute details, so she was wondering where they'd disappeared to. Raj had told her he'd take care of the TS men while the women were busy with whatever they would be doing.

"Yup, in the gaming area," responded Kristen. "Devon and Marco are taking advantage of the nannies you arranged for JD and Mara, so they're all out there playing Cornhole and taking bets on who is the best archer. Our men and bows and arrows—it wouldn't surprise me if one of them ended up being shot in the butt."

Everyone laughed—except Lahana. Without saying a word, she stormed into the attached powder room and slammed the door. An uncomfortable silence filled the room for a moment, but then the women tried to act like nothing had happened. Two minutes later, Lahana came back out, threw her dress at one of the seamstresses, then stalked out of the room.

Tahira's gaze met Nala's, and the younger woman shrugged and shook her head. Sighing, Tahira turned back to her guests. "I apologize for my cousin's behavior. She has not been herself since . . . since . . ." While she trusted the TS women, there were staff members around. Discussing the kidnapping in their presence was not an option.

Angie held up her hand. "Say no more. We understand, and it's fine."

"Thank you." Pasting on a smile she didn't completely feel, Tahira answered the women's questions about the wedding ceremonies. But after fifteen minutes or so, she couldn't stand it any longer. The guilt she felt for lying to Lahana was eating a hole in her gut. Tahira had to find her and tell her she knew what the other woman was going through and that they would find a way to heal—together. "I am sorry, but if you will excuse me, I need to go speak to my cousin."

She hurried out to the hallway and glanced in both directions. She hadn't seen which way Lahana had gone. Thinking she'd returned to the guest suite she always stayed in on the third floor, Tahira headed for the stairs.

One flight up, two maids were finishing their duties, cleaning the guest bedrooms and bathrooms, and bowed as she walked by. "Good day, Your Highness."

Giving them a quick, distracted smile and wishing them a pleasant day as well, Tahira continued down the hall and stopped in front of Lahana's door. She knocked, then waited. Seconds ticked by with no response. She was about to give up, thinking she'd been wrong in her assumption, when the door swung open. Lahana frowned at her from behind sunglasses. "What do you want?"

Surprised at the venom in Lahana's voice, Tahira stuttered. "I-I wanted to talk to you, cousin."

"We have nothing to talk about."

When the door began to close, Tahira used a hand and foot to stop it. "I think we do. May I come in? Please?"

A few moments passed before Lahana sighed and stepped back. Tahira followed her inside and shut the door behind them. Taking a deep breath, she let it out slowly, then gestured to a small sitting area. "Can we sit down? There's something I need to tell you."

CHAPTER THIRTY-SEVEN

With a map of the palace and grounds tucked into the back pocket of his Dockers, Darius managed to find his way out to the gaming area of the gardens. A small bar had been set up, and his brother and friends were enjoying a few pints of Guinness with Prince Raj and some of his male cousins. Several of them were shooting arrows at targets with hay bales behind them, while others tossed bean bags at the slanted Cornhole boards, trying to sink them in the small, round opening to score the most points. So far, neither Farid nor Diallo had shown their face, although they were both supposed to be attending the ceremonies, and that was fine with Darius—as long as they stayed out of his way. Unfortunately, the king's weasel of a chief of staff, Sebak, had been driving him nuts about this or that protocol, all the while making his disdain for the princess's fiancée clear with subtle digs. Darius didn't give a crap though, and assumed nothing he could ever do would win the man over.

Both TS teams had flown over for the celebration, leaving Doug Henderson and Tiny Daultry in charge. Nathan was manning the computer systems, while the office manager,

Colleen, was taking care of everything else. Ian had even passed a mission or two over to Chase Dixon's Blackhawk Security so everyone on the Alpha and Omega teams could be in Timasur.

Levi was the first one to spot Darius as he approached. "Hey, the groom's here! It's about time you joined us, bro. Grab yourself a pint. This place is awesome!"

After getting a glass of Guinness from the bartender, Darius watched the activities in amusement for a few minutes. The betting between Marco and Brody was getting interesting as usual. They finally settled on what the loser of an archery challenge would have to do—dress up in drag— heels, wig, and all—on the first day back to work next week, when members of Tampa PD's SWAT would be at the compound for a joint training session. Darius would have to have someone take lots of photos for him, since he'd be on his honeymoon. Oddly enough, that word didn't scare him as much as it used to.

While the two men geared up with their bows and arrows, the other men took monetary bets on who would win. Darius joined them, and when all was said and done, he was a few hundred dollars richer when Brody was declared the winner, which didn't happen often in these contests. Now Darius definitely needed someone to take photos— Marco in drag? That was going to be hysterical, without a doubt.

"Walk with me, twatopotomus."

Rolling his eyes, Darius swallowed a mouthful of Guinness and fell into step beside Ian, who strolled toward the entrance of a maze created by tall shrubs. "What's up, Boss-man?"

Ian took a sip of his dark drink and waited until they were within the elaborate labyrinth before speaking again. "Last chance to back out of this."

That was not what he'd expected to hear from his employer, teammate, and friend, even though Ian knew the reasoning behind Darius's upcoming marriage. "You still think I'm making a mistake?"

"Don't put words in my mouth." He took a right turn as if he knew exactly where he was going. Darius followed, mentally calculating how to get back out of the maze when he needed to. "It doesn't matter if I think you're making a mistake, the question is do *you*? Is this going to backfire on both of you?"

"No, it's not."

"See, that's where I think you're wrong."

Darius stopped short. "You just said it doesn't matter what you think."

Turning around to face him, Ian shrugged. "I lied—sue me." He crossed his arms and spread his legs. Darius knew the man was settling in for one of his "you're being a dipshit" talks. Darius had been on the opposite side of several of them during his time in the SEALs and, again, while working for Trident. There was nothing he could do but stand there and listen. "You know, the only way this will work between you two is if you admit to yourself and her that you're in love with her."

"What the hell are you talking about?"

"I'm not blind, Batman. Neither is my wife, and she's looking forward to you and Tahira having many beautiful babies, as the princess would say. She loves kids, by the way, if you haven't figured that out yet."

Pivoting, Darius paced up and down the aisle the shrubs made, running a hand down his face. "I'm not good enough for her. We're from two different lifestyles—hell, we're from two different worlds. I can't give her a place like this." He lifted his hands and gestured to their surroundings.

"Did she ask you for a place like this?" Ian mimicked

Darius's hand motions, but with an obnoxious flare. "I'll bet she never asked you for anything, because you've already been providing her with everything she wants and needs. Don't you know that a marriage means joining your lives and finances and all that other shit together. It's no longer yours and mine—it's ours. They even made a movie or two out of that saying. You deserve an ass kicking if you can't see what's right in front of you, Batman—some superhero you are. This thing between you two may have started because of your sense of honor and duty—because your suppressed Dom-ness decided to finally come out of hiding. But somewhere along the line, it turned into the real thing . . . for both of you. Don't you see the way she looks at you? Like you're her whole world and nothing else matters?"

"She's got a case of hero-worship. That's all."

Ian glared at him. "If I didn't know it would ruin the wedding pictures and put me on my wife's, the queen's, and Tahira's shit lists, I'd deck you right now. That woman does not have a case of hero-worship. She's in love . . . with you, you jackass." He threw his hands in the air. "God, why are men such idiots when *the one* shows up in their life? And, yes, that's a rhetorical question because I was an idiot with my Angel in the beginning. Thankfully, I wised up fast, and now we're procreating. Scary thing, yes, but there it is."

Ignoring his boss's sarcasm, Darius zeroed in on the one thing that'd made a small kernel of hope spring to life deep within him. Was it true? Tahira loved him? And if she did, would it be enough to bind them together forever? He wasn't sure. "So, what if Tahira decides living in Tampa isn't what she wants? Visiting this place I can deal with, but living here full time? That's not me, Boss-man. What if she decides she wants this grand lifestyle she's known all her life that I can't give her?"

"Then tie her ass up and show her the lifestyle you *can*

give her—the one that includes you being her Dom and just fucking loving her. You know, there are two types of women —the ones who are social climbers and marry for money, and the others who marry for love. I honestly believe if Tahira hadn't fallen in love with you, we wouldn't be here today. She would have set you free and come up with a different way to deal with the aftermath of what happened to her. So, the question is, are you going to continue to be an idiot, or are you going to grab hold of her with both hands and never let her go?"

Tilting his head back and thinking about his answer, Darius spun on the ball of his foot toward the rear façade of the palace. Over the tops of the shrubs, movement on one of the balconies caught his eye and had his heart stopping in his chest. "Shit!" Throwing his glass of ale to the ground, he took off at a dead run, praying he was going the right way.

WITH A SIGH, TAHIRA FOLLOWED LAHANA AS SHE PASSED THE suite's sitting area and strode out to the balcony where a half-filled pitcher of lemonade and several glasses waited on a small table. An umbrella provided some pleasant shade. Her cousin sat down on one of the two available chairs, picked up her drink, and took a long sip. Staring out over the gardens, she asked, "So, what do you want, Tahira?"

Again, that venomous tone bothered Tahira—her cousin and she had always gotten along, but since the rescue, they seemed worlds apart. Taking the other seat, she poured herself a glass of the pink refreshment. "I was hoping we could talk about . . . about Argentina."

"What about it? It's a god-forsaken country with too many insects."

"You know what I mean, cousin." Tahira brought the glass

to her lips, but the moment the cool liquid hit her tongue, she coughed and sputtered. "Wh-what is in this?"

Lahana sniffled and rubbed her nose, her movements jerky. "Haven't you ever had gin and lemonade before? It's quite delicious."

As Tahira studied the other woman, she could see her current drink wasn't the first one of the day. "I-I know you're having a hard time dealing with what that bastard did to you." Lahana snorted, and Tahira dropped her gaze to her lap. "He—he raped a lot of those girls. He—"

"Ha! Oh, Tahira, Tahira, Tahira—the naïve little princess. He didn't rape me."

She shook her head in confusion. "What do you mean? Of course—"

"Oh, please. I like it rough, and Felix knew that."

Felix? Darius had told her Secada's first name at some point, but until now, Tahira had forgotten it. How did Lahana know it? Had Amar told her? And what did she mean when she said he hadn't raped her?

Standing, Lahana sashayed over to the balcony's railing and looked down. "As usual, there'll be plenty of pomp and circumstance for the little princess. Whatever she wants, she gets. Although, I'm surprised a man as virile as Darius Knight is willing to marry a virgin, when a woman like me has so much more to give him. Maybe I'll offer him some action tonight before he gets tied down to you."

More confused than ever, Tahira got to her feet and approached Lahana. "Cousin, what are you talking about?"

"Seriously, Tahira, you really should get out more. I can't believe you're still a freaking virgin."

Lahana pulled a small vial from the front pocket of her capris. Opening it, she dipped the fingernail of her pinkie into a white powder, then brought it to her nose and sniffed. Tahira's eyes widened when she realized her cousin was using cocaine. Hobnobbing with the rich and famous for years had exposed Tahira to drugs and alcohol, although she'd never partaken in the former and only imbibed on the latter in moderation.

"What are you doing? Stop!" She grabbed Lahana's arm, causing her to drop the vial, spilling the white powder onto the concrete balcony.

Her eyes filled with fury, Lahana lunged at Tahira, her hands grasping her neck and squeezing. "You bitch!"

Stunned, Tahira stumbled backward, grabbed her cousin's wrists, and tried to break free. Fueled by the drugs and rage though, Lahana had the upper hand. She pushed Tahira against the hard, wrought-iron railing, and it dug into her back. "I should have had him rape you first. Then your hero wouldn't have had time to save you. You would've been disgraced. But, no, the precious princess wins again." Her face was red and sweaty as spittle shot from her mouth, hitting Tahira in the face. "Do you know how long I've had to live in your shadow? Everyone bowing to you, calling you 'Your Royal Highness' like you were something special? Well, you're not. You're just a naïve little prude. But you're always first in line for everything and the rest of us are second best, right? Everywhere we go, men give you all the attention because they want to marry a princess. That's why I planned Jamaica. You and Nala would've been out of my hair, and after my alleged escape, I would have been in the spotlight, getting all the attention I deserved!"

Gasping for air, Tahira clawed at Lahana's hands, arms, and face. She twisted and struggled against the hold. She swung her fists, but they landed harmlessly. Her lungs burned for oxygen. Lifting her leg, she brought her heel down hard, hoping to hit Lahana's toes that were exposed by her sandals. The other woman merely grunted in pain, but it had done the trick to distract her and loosen her hold just enough for Tahira to rotate her body. Bringing her arm up, she was able to elbow her cousin in the face, knocking her back a few steps.

Panting, she glanced toward the open French doors, wondering if she could make it inside before she was attacked again. She'd no idea Lahana hated her so much she would hatch a scheme to have her and Nala raped and sold as sex slaves. They'd grown up together. Traveled together. Shared secrets with each other. Sure, Lahana could be bitchy at times, but so could half the women Tahira knew.

One of the chairs was in her way, but she could toss it aside and run past. However, it was too late. With a roar, Lahana rushed her, but Tahira sidestepped toward the door and shoved the other woman away. Too her horror, Lahana's momentum flipped her over the railing. She flailed her hands, trying to grab something . . . anything to stop her descent. Her screams were deafening as she fell thirty feet to the ground below.

Shouts and screeches came from the garden area, but nothing could drown out the sound of Lahana's body landing on the stone terrace below with a heavy *thud*. In shock, Tahira stood there, staring at where she'd seen her cousin last, shaking and unable to go to the railing and look down. The blood had drained from her face, leaving her light-headed, and she wavered on her feet.

Behind her, the bedroom door flew open, banging against the wall, and suddenly Darius was there. "Tahira!"

His strong arms scooped her up and carried her inside, as she slammed her eyes shut, trying to erase the image of Lahana falling. Several people entered the room, but the only other voices she recognized were Ian's and Amar's. From their hushed tones, it was obvious her cousin was dead.

Darius sat down on something, settling her on his lap and holding her trembling body. She clutched his shirt and buried her face into his neck as tears poured down her cheeks. His heart was pounding in his chest as fast as hers was. He rubbed her back and kissed her forehead. "Shh . . . it's over, sweetheart. I've got you. Shh . . . I've got you and I'm never letting you go. I love you."

CHAPTER THIRTY-EIGHT

Three Weeks Later - Florida . . .

I n the penthouse of the Opal Sands Resort in Clearwater Beach, Tahira's nerves had butterflies taking flight in her stomach. She stared at her reflection in the mirror in the master bath, as her wedding dress hung from a hook on the closed door. She'd pulled her hair down from its fancy updo and put on the elegant, white peignoir set her mother had given her for this special evening. Tonight was when Tahira would give herself to her new husband in every way. Their wedding had been postponed several weeks, due to Lahana's death. Not willing to bring shame to the family of the king's brother, the palace had released a statement saying the young woman had fallen to her death in a horrible accident. As a result, the wedding would be rescheduled so the engaged couple could mourn their loss with the rest of the royal family.

The only witnesses to what'd really happened had been Darius, Ian, and a few other men from Trident Security. By the time those in the gaming area had realized what was happening, most had only seen Lahana's fall, not what had preceded it. When questioned by Amar and Darius, Diallo had admitted Lahana had often borrowed his phone when they were out together, saying she'd either forgotten hers or its battery was dead. He'd never thought anything of it, and they'd believed him.

They were still trying to track down how Lahana and Secada had met each other. The woman had often traveled to various cities around the world, partying with Diallo and Farid or several girlfriends, so there were many possibilities. Darius had said he suspected it was during one of the several trips to Dubai Lahana had taken during the past two years. As one of the biggest party cities in the world, it catered to anyone with money—whether it was legally obtained or not.

Tahira still couldn't believe how Lahana had turned on her. The woman had obviously been good at hiding her jealousy and hatred. Who knew how long she'd harbored them? Tahira and her family would be dealing with their grief and hurt from the betrayal for a long time. Lahana had not been the sweet, fun girl Tahira had grown up with, but that was how she wished to remember her.

Instead of having the grand wedding that'd been originally planned, Tahira had convinced her parents to allow her and Darius to have a much smaller church wedding here in Clearwater Beach, with just family and friends—including Darius's father. Everyone had understood their need for a more understated celebration.

She'd still been in shock the first time Darius had said he loved her, but he'd repeated many times since then, and so had she. Tahira wasn't certain what exactly had made him realize what she'd already known was true, but she would be forever grateful. The last thing in the world she'd wanted was for them to start their marriage with that still unsaid between them. As soon as the words had first registered in her mind, she'd studied him for a moment and had known he wasn't just saying the words to comfort her. While most of the time, his aura had been muted, that was no longer the case since that fateful day. Now, whenever Darius was filled with passion and desire—which was quite often when they were together—the reds, pinks, and purples swirled around him. There were times he'd camouflaged his body's wants and needs from his expression, body language, and words, when others were present, but he wasn't able to turn off his aura during those moments. She'd known exactly what he was experiencing since she'd been feeling the same things.

Taking a deep breath, Tahira put her hands on her stomach, willing the butterflies to settle down. Darius would never do anything to hurt her—that wasn't the problem. Tahira was just afraid she wouldn't live up to his expectations. They'd taken more classes at The Covenant and had even been cleared for certain types of BDSM activities. She'd found she was quite fond of spankings and sensation play. While Darius had given her many orgasms over the past six weeks, he hadn't allowed her to give him any in return. She'd even suggested one night, that under all the circumstances, and that they'd professed their love for each other, that she'd be willing to not wait for their wedding night. However, Darius had adamantly refused, stating that it had been important to her all her life to wait, and he wasn't going to be the one to screw that up for her. Unfortunately, for him, that had meant lots and lots of cold showers.

Turning, she opened the door, stepped out into the bedroom, and froze in her tracks. The lights were off, but dozens of votive candles were lit and glimmering around the room. Several vases of flowers had also been added while she'd been taking the bubble bath Darius had insisted on. Now she knew why—he was so darn romantic it made her heart swell.

Darius stood barefoot next to the bed, still wearing his tuxedo pants and nothing else. Her eyes roamed his muscular chest, shoulders, and arms, taking in each of his colorful tattoos, as her pulse increased and her clit throbbed. She'd study the beautiful ink later, but for now, beneath the silk material, her nipples hardened and begged for his touch. He was the most handsome man she'd ever known, and he was all hers—forever.

A few days after Lahana's funeral, on the night before they returned to Florida, he'd arranged a special dinner at a secluded restaurant in Diado. After dismissing the wait staff from their private dining room, Darius had gotten down on one knee and proposed to her, the way she'd always dreamed her soulmate would ask her to marry him. Instead of replacing her grandmother's engagement ring that she'd been wearing, he'd given her a simple, but stunning diamond and emerald choker. In a few days, they'd be having a ceremony at The Covenant, when she would formally accept the collar which would announce to the BDSM world that Darius was her Dom. While they wouldn't be playing at the club often, they would still be joining their friends there on occasion.

Holding his hand out, Darius crooked his finger. "Come here, Princess, and let me look at my beautiful wife."

She glided across the room, her bare feet sinking into the luxurious carpet. Taking his hand, she waited while he looked his fill. "You're the most beautiful woman I've ever seen. You know, that's what I thought the first night I saw you at the estate, when the Omega Team was on your security detail for that AIDS fundraiser. You were coming down the stairs in an emerald-green gown, and everyone stopped and stared. You were stunning, and I think my heart and lungs seized for a moment before starting up again. Then I remembered that there was no way in hell I'd ever have a chance with you, because we were from two different worlds."

Taking a step closer, she shook her head. "We are not from two different worlds, Darius—we are from the same one. We may have been raised an ocean apart, but we have the same values, the same ethics, the same needs, and the same desires. We are soulmates. I figured that out long before you did."

He put his arms around her waist, and the last bit of distance between them disappeared. His cock grew thick and heavy against her lower abdomen. "Yeah? How did you know that?"

"Hmm. Maybe someday I will tell you. We have other things to do tonight. Kiss me, please." She ran her palms up his chest, enjoying how the coarse hairs tickled her. Going up on her tiptoes, she wrapped her arms around his neck.

"Your wish is my command, Princess. But don't get used to topping from the bottom." They both chuckled at his attempt to sound stern. He was still a work in progress when it came to disciplining her like the other Doms did with their subs, but neither of them minded. Each couple had to figure out what best suited them.

Lowering his head, he brushed his lips against hers, and she immediately melted in his arms. Her mouth opened, allowing his tongue to tangle with hers. He grasped a handful of her hair and used it to angle her head the way he wanted. Leaving her lips, he kissed and suckled his way down her neck. She felt him slide the satin and lace robe from her shoulders and down her arms until it fell into a pool at her feet. Seconds later, her nightgown followed until she was standing completely naked before him for the first time, despite their playtimes the past few weeks.

Darius took a step back and his gaze raked her body from head to toe and back again. "I didn't think you could ever be more beautiful than you already were to me, but I was wrong. Are you nervous, sweetheart?"

There was no need to lie to him. "Honestly, I was before I came out here. But, now, seeing the love in your eyes, there is no reason for me to worry. I know you will be gentle yet passionate, and I trust you implicitly. Playing with you these past weeks has also helped. Now, I want to know what it is like to make love with you. To belong to you in every way."

He held his arms out to his sides. "Then undress me."

Her eyes lit up like she'd just been given the best birthday present she could ever wish for. Stepping forward, she somehow managed to undo the button of his pants as her hands shook—not in fear or trepidation, but in anticipation. While she'd felt him through his clothing, she'd never seen him completely naked. Her mouth watered as she lowered the zipper, then pushed his pants down to the floor. The boxer briefs he wore bulged with his manhood, and she tucked her hands underneath the waistband at his hips, sliding the material down until his erect cock sprung free. It was long and thick and magnificent.

"Touch me, Tahira." His voice was suddenly gravelly, and it sent chills down her spine.

Reaching out, she tentatively wrapped her hands around him, feeling the veins, sinew, and his pulse against her palms. A liquid pearl appeared at the tip, as he grew even harder. A strangled groan escaped him, and he covered her hands with his own. "Tighter, sweetheart. God, I've waited for this moment for so long."

So had she. But before she'd realized he'd moved, she was scooped up in his arms and laid out on the bed like a feast. And that's exactly how he was looking at her.

"Sorry, but if I let those innocent hands touch me like that for too long, I'll go off like a rocket. I'll let you explore to your heart's content later, baby, just let me get us past this first time."

He lay down beside her, and his mouth immediately latched on to one of her nipples as his fingers played with the other one. Tahira's back arched of its own accord as sparks coursed through her body from her breasts to her clit. "Oh, Darius!"

His five-o'clock shadow rasped against her skin, as he licked and sucked on the rigid peak. His hand left her breast and trailed down her torso, leaving goosebumps in its wake. When his fingers slid over the trim strip of curls, just above her clit, and into her wetness, he froze a moment before his head shot upward. His eyes were wide as he stared at her. "You're bare there?"

She nodded and giggled at his stunned expression. "Yes. I hope you like it. I have been told it makes a woman more sensitive and that men like it too. Angie and Kristen assured me the spa we went to the other day was discreet and sanitary. Apparently, the owner is a member of The Covenant."

"Remind me to send them flowers or something tomorrow. And I don't just like it, I love it."

He sat up and moved until he was lying down between her legs. Placing his hands on her thighs, he spread them wide. She felt a few seconds of embarrassment, her cheeks heating, as he just stared at her, but that fled the moment his fingers teased her smooth labia. "Beautiful," he said, almost reverently.

Leaning forward, he licked the length of her slit, and Tahira nearly came on the spot. "Easy, sweetheart. I can see it won't take much to send you flying. I want to taste you and have you come in my mouth before I make love to my wife."

When his tongue did something wicked to her, she bucked her hips. "Yes! Please! Again!"

With his experience, he worked her into a frenzy with

just his lips and tongue, alternating his attention between her core and her clit. Tahira grabbed handfuls of the sheets as she squirmed beneath him. Panting, she begged for release. Since the first orgasm he'd given her, Tahira had become addicted to them, but this one threatened to leave all those others in the dust.

When one of Darius's fingers delved inside her, she detonated. Fireworks went off behind her closed eyelids, and she screamed as the climax took hold of her and shook her relentlessly. But Darius didn't let up. Using two and then three fingers, he stretched her, preparing her to take his cock deep within her. When he sucked on her clit, it sent her over the edge again, this orgasm stronger than the last.

Her chest heaved as she floated back down. Darius crawled up her body and kissed her. Tasting herself for the first time on his tongue and lips was intoxicating. Pushing up on his arms, he held himself over her and stared down. "Are you ready, sweetheart? I'll try to go slow and be as gentle as possible. It shouldn't hurt but tell me if it does."

She knew what he was saying—with her hymen already broken, there wouldn't be any sharp pain or blood when he thrust inside her. She reached up and caressed his jaw. "I am ready, Darius. Make love to me."

"Bend your legs and put your feet on the bed." After she followed his instructions, he held his cock in his hand and rubbed it against her slit. His gaze returned to hers before he pushed inside. Her body yielded to him as he stroked in and out, going a little further with each pass. Her walls stretched to accommodate the invasion. Each time she felt a little twinge of resistance or she gasped, Darius pulled out then slid back in again. It felt incredible, and she thanked God she couldn't remember the moment her rapist had penetrated her. But even if she had, Darius would be erasing it from her mind. His love had healed her, and she would forever remember their first time together as husband and wife. Nothing would ever take that away from her. She was his and he was hers—forever.

Sweat beaded his forehead and chest, and she knew he was holding back. Once he was fully inside her, she pulled on his neck, bringing him down so they could kiss. Gradually, his thrusts grew faster, harder, and together they found a rhythm. Tahira felt herself climbing again. Pushing up on his arms again, Darius watched her face through half-closed lids. Pleasure and need were etched on his face, and she wanted to watch him as he came, but her own orgasm was pulling her under again. This time when it hit her, she took him with her.

He collapsed on top of her, then rolled onto his back, drawing her close until she was tucked into his side. Her head rested on his shoulder, and she swung her leg over his. For several minutes, they lay there, replenishing the oxygen they'd briefly denied their lungs and reveling in the afterglow of their lovemaking. It had been everything she'd dreamed it would be.

"Are you okay, sweetheart?"

"I have never been better in my life."

Darius chuckled. "Hmm. I guess that leaves little room for improvement for next time."

Grinning, she turned her head, kissed his muscular chest, then snuggled closer, satiated and content in the arms of her lover, husband, friend, and soulmate.

EPILOGUE

"Well, well, well, if it isn't the Duke of Gotham. Didn't think you were ever going to leave the honeymoon suite, Batman."

Groaning, Darius strode into the Trident Security conference room where most of the operatives and supervisors had gathered for a morning briefing. Boss-man hadn't been the only one teasing him about his new title—Duke of Kasala—that King Rajeemh had bestowed upon him following the wedding. Thankfully, it was one he wouldn't have to use often, just at formal functions in Timasur, however, the press had been referring to him that way. Hopefully, all the hubbub would soon die down, and he and Tahira could find a new, comfortable, normal life together. For now, they were living in the Clearwater Beach estate—it had been the easiest thing to do, and Darius preferred to know Tahira was protected there when he wasn't around. He still had his job to do—it was something they both agreed he wouldn't give up for now.

"If you think we're going to be bowing and kissing your ass, think again," Devon added with a smirk.

Darius took an empty seat between McCabe and Foster. "You have permission to shoot me if I ever demand that. I finally got most of the staff at the mansion to stop bowing. Thank God I didn't get a "Royal Highness" title. I'd go fucking nuts."

"Where's Tahira?" Lindsey asked from across the table.

"Visiting with Angie and Kristen. She's nervous about tonight and wanted to talk to them." When Darius had told Tahira he wanted to attend the meeting, even though they were leaving for Tahiti tomorrow for their honeymoon, she'd decided to take the ride with him. This evening was their collaring ceremony, and he had to admit, he was really anticipating it. Telling everyone he was her first and last Dom meant a lot to him. Tahira had told him she felt the same.

They'd barely been off the estate grounds since leaving the hotel they'd spent the first two nights in as husband and wife, and he knew she'd been looking forward to some time with people who treated her like everyone else. The club members didn't bow to her or gush over her, and as a result, Tahira was able to relax and just be herself. No crown. No protocols, other than D/s. No media hounding her. In the club and in their bedroom, she was just Tahira, Darius's sub, wife, and lover. And according to her, that's all she'd ever wanted. "So, what's on the agenda?"

Ian glanced at his watch. "Just waiting on—"

"I'm here!" Logan Reese rushed in and took a seat. "Sorry, I'm late—hit traffic."

"All right, let's get going. As of right now, I'm on labor alert until my kid decides to finally join this fucked-up world we live in. That means you're calling Dev for everything that's not a dire emergency. If he thinks I need to know about it, he'll pass it on."

Picking up a folder, Ian proceeded to run through a long

list of assignments, doling out new ones and getting updates on cases in progress. For the first in a very long time, Darius was looking forward to going on vacation, but knowing he'd be spending most of it in bed making love to his new bride was probably the reason behind it. He was still getting used to the fact he was married and a ring proving it was on his left hand.

Before Darius knew it, the meeting was breaking up. As they all filed out of the conference room to start their days, his teammates and friends slapped him on the back, telling him to have fun and not to do anything they wouldn't do. Since that wasn't much, it left him with a lot of leeway.

"Come on, Batman—I'll walk over to the studio with you. I want to check on Angie."

When they entered the little cottage that housed Kristen's and Angie's workspaces—perfectly set up for the famous author and creative artist—the three women looked up and smiled. Little JD was swinging back and forth in some cradle contraption, kicking his legs and giggling. Between him and Tahira, sitting on a nearby sofa, was Beau. The black and white dog was enjoying the ear scratching Darius's wife was giving him.

For a moment, Darius had an image of Tahira with their child. He or she would have his green eyes and her dark hair. Maybe they'd even get a dog for the kid to grow up with. But no matter what they did, they'd do it together. Somehow, some way, Darius had found his soulmate. The woman who took his breath away from across the room. The woman he would love, cherish, and respect until his dying day.

If you're following the best reading order of the Trident

Security series and its spin-off series, up next is *Torn in Half: Trident Security Book 12* - now available.

If you've started the best reading order somewhere in the middle, go back to the beginning and read *Leather & Lace: Trident Security Book 1.*

If you or someone you know has been the victim of a sexual assault, please contact the National Resources for Sexual Assault Survivors and their Loved Ones for assistance. No one should have to suffer in silence for something that was not their fault.
Hotline: 800.656.HOPE

OTHER BOOKS BY

Samantha A. Cole

USA TODAY BESTSELLING AUTHOR

***Denotes titles/series that are available on select digital sites only. Paperbacks and audiobooks are available on most book sites.

***THE TRIDENT SECURITY SERIES

Leather & Lace

His Angel

Waiting For Him

Not Negotiable: A Novella

Topping The Alpha

Watching From the Shadows

Whiskey Tribute: A Novella

Tickle His Fancy

No Way in Hell: A Steel Corp/Trident Security Crossover (co-authored with J.B. Havens)

Absolving His Sins

Option Number Three: A Novella

Salvaging His Soul

Trident Security Field Manual

Torn In Half: A Novella

***HEELS, RHYMES, & NURSERY CRIMES SERIES
(WITH 13 OTHER AUTHORS)

Jack Be Nimble: A Trident Security-Related Short Story

***ANTELOPE ROCK SERIES

(CO-AUTHORED WITH J.B. HAVENS)

Wannabe in Wyoming

Wistful in Wyoming

AWARD-WINNING STANDALONE BOOKS

The Road to Solace

Scattered Moments in Time: A Collection of Short Stories & More

***THE BID ON LOVE SERIES

(WITH 7 OTHER AUTHORS!)

Going , Going, Gone: Book 2

***THE COLLECTIVE: SEASON TWO

(WITH 7 OTHER AUTHORS!)

Angst: Book 7

SPECIAL PROJECTS

First Chapters: Foreplay Volume One

First Chapters: Foreplay Volume Two

First Chapters: Foreplay Volume Three

Trident Security Coloring Book

Shaded with Love Volume 5: Coloring Book for a Cause

Cooking with Love: Shaded with Love Volume 6

***SPECIAL COLLECTIONS

Trident Security Series: Volume I

Trident Security Series: Volume II

Trident Security Series: Volume III

Trident Security Series: Volume IV

Trident Security Series: Volume V

Samantha A. Cole
USA TODAY BESTSELLING AUTHOR

USA Today Bestselling Author and Award-Winning Author Samantha A. Cole is a retired policewoman and former paramedic. Using her life experiences and training, she strives to find the perfect mix of suspense and romance for her readers to enjoy.

Awards:

Scattered Moments in Time - gold medal in the 2020 Readers' Favorite Awards in the Fiction Anthology genre

The Road to Solace - silver medal in the 2017 Readers' Favorite Awards in the Contemporary Romance genre

Wannabe in Wyoming - bronze medal in the 2021 Readers' Favorite Awards in the General Romance genre

Samantha has over thirty books published throughout different series as well as several standalone novels. A full list can be found on her website listed below.

Sexy Six-Pack's Sirens Group on Facebook
Website: www.samanthacoleauthor.com
Newsletter: www.smarturl.it/SSPNL

facebook.com/SamanthaColeAuthor

twitter.com/SamanthaCole222

instagram.com/samanthacoleauthor

amazon.com/Samantha-A-Cole/e/B00X53K3X8

bookbub.com/profile/samantha-a-cole

goodreads.com/SamanthaCole

pinterest.com/samanthacoleaut

tiktok.com/@samanthacoleauthor

Printed in Great Britain
by Amazon

25766155R00176